*She knew he b...
closer now.*

The raspy snap of a cigarette lighter startled
her. The light of the flame was barely enough
to illuminate the face of the man holding the
lighter. But it was more than enough, Gabrielle
thought, as she locked gazes with a man she
hadn't seen in nearly two years and would have
preferred never to set eyes on again.

"You." The word was an accusation. "I should
have known."

"Yeah, you probably should have," he agreed,
smiling that smile that every woman in the
world except her seemed to find so damn
irresistible. "I mean, how many other men do
you know crazy enough to steal you from the
church steps on your wedding day?"

"Why, Connor? Why did you do it?"

His smile slowly gave way to a bold, insolent
grin she remembered all too well. "Well,
because I'm as impatient as ever, I suppose. I
just couldn't stand to sit around the church
waiting for the minister to get to the part about
speak now or forever hold your peace."

Dear Reader,

It's summertime, and the livin' may or may not be easy—but the reading is great. Just check out Naomi Horton's *Wild Blood,* the first in her new WILD HEARTS miniseries. In Jett Kendrick you'll find a hero to take to heart and never let go, and you'll understand why memories of their brief, long-ago loving have stayed with Kathy Patterson for sixteen years. Now she's back in Burnt River, back in Jett's life—and about to discover a secret that will change *three* lives forever.

We feature two more great miniseries this month, too. Cathryn Clare's ASSIGNMENT: ROMANCE brings you *The Baby Assignment,* the exciting conclusion to the Cotter brothers' search for love, while Alicia Scott's THE GUINESS GANG continues with *The One Who Almost Got Away,* featuring brother Jake Guiness. And there's still more great reading you won't want to miss. Patricia Coughlin's *Borrowed Bride* features a bride who's kidnapped—right out from under the groom's nose. Of course, it's her kidnapper who turns out to be Mr. Right. And by the way, both Alicia and Patricia had earlier books that were made into CBS TV movies last year. In *Unbroken Vows,* Frances Williams sends her hero and heroine on a search for the heroine's ex-fiancé, a man hero David Reid is increasingly uninterested in finding. Finally, check out Kay David's *Hero in Hiding,* featuring aptly named Mercy Hamilton and enigmatic Rio Barrigan, a man who is far more than he seems.

Then join us again next month and every month, as we bring you more of the best romantic reading around—only in Silhouette Intimate Moments.

Yours,

Leslie Wainger

Leslie Wainger,
Senior Editor and Editorial Coordinator

Please address questions and book requests to:
Silhouette Reader Service
U.S.: 3010 Walden Ave., P.O. Box 1325, Buffalo, NY 14269
Canadian: P.O. Box 609, Fort Erie, Ont. L2A 5X3

BORROWED BRIDE

PATRICIA COUGHLIN

INTIMATE™ MOMENTS®

Published by Silhouette Books

America's Publisher of Contemporary Romance

If you purchased this book without a cover you should be aware
that this book is stolen property. It was reported as "unsold and
destroyed" to the publisher, and neither the author nor the
publisher has received any payment for this "stripped book."

 SILHOUETTE BOOKS

ISBN 0-373-07722-X

BORROWED BRIDE

Copyright © 1996 by Patricia Madden Coughlin

All rights reserved. Except for use in any review, the reproduction
or utilization of this work in whole or in part in any form by any
electronic, mechanical or other means, now known or hereafter
invented, including xerography, photocopying and recording, or in
any information storage or retrieval system, is forbidden without
the written permission of the editorial office, Silhouette Books,
300 East 42nd Street, New York, NY 10017 U.S.A.

All characters in this book have no existence outside the imagination of
the author and have no relation whatsoever to anyone bearing the same
name or names. They are not even distantly inspired by any individual
known or unknown to the author, and all incidents are pure invention.

This edition published by arrangement with Harlequin Books S.A.

® and TM are trademarks of Harlequin Books S.A., used under license.
Trademarks indicated with ® are registered in the United States Patent
and Trademark Office, the Canadian Trade Marks Office and in other
countries.

Printed in U.S.A.

PATRICIA COUGHLIN

is also known to romance fans as Liz Grady and lives in Rhode Island with her husband and two sons. A former schoolteacher, she says she started writing to fill her hours at home, after her second son was born. Having always read romance novels, she decided to try penning her own. Though she was duly astounded by the difficulty of her new hobby, her hard work paid off, and she accomplished the rare feat of having her very first manuscript published. For now, writing has replaced quilting, embroidery and other pastimes, and with more than a dozen published titles under her belt, the author hopes to be happily writing romance novels for a long time to come.

To my aunt Alice Francis and her daughters, Shirley,
Alice and Irene

Chapter 1

It was a perfect day for a wedding.

Outside the church on Providence's east side, the sun was shining, birds were singing and puffy white clouds sailed across a watercolor blue sky. Gabrielle Flanders adjusted the comb securing her headpiece and brushed back a tendril of her shoulder-length dark brown hair, which had been painstakingly arranged in an upswept cascade of curls for the occasion.

The short veil on her headpiece matched the delicate ivory lace of her knee-length dress. The dress, according to Lena of Lena's Bridal Shoppe, was the perfect choice for the second-time bride. The roses in her bridal bouquet had been dyed to match the pale apricot trim on her dress. So had her satin shoes and the icing on the wedding cake and even the ribbon tied around the crystal sun-catchers to be given as favors to each of the three hundred guests attending the country-club reception to follow the ceremony. Everything about the wedding was as perfect as this gorgeous June day she and Adam had been given to begin their life together.

Everything, that is, except the odd way she was feeling.

Gabrielle sighed, grateful for this unexpected moment alone. Her five-year-old son, Toby, who had been thrilled at the prospect of being her ring bearer, had suddenly turned shy at the last second and decided he would prefer not to walk down the aisle in front of all those people. Fortunately her younger sister, Lisa, her only attendant, had been on hand to hustle him inside to sit with his grandmother, leaving Gabrielle alone on the church steps.

Maybe, she told herself, she had simply been too preoccupied with last-minute details these past few days to know what she was feeling, never mind what she ought to be feeling. Perhaps this private moment was all she needed to gather her thoughts and let the proper mood of anticipation kick in.

Gabrielle closed her eyes, drew a deep breath and waited for it to happen. A buzzing sound broke her concentration, drawing her attention to her bouquet and the bee that was circling it menacingly. She jerked the flowers aside and swatted at the plump yellow jacket with her free hand until it flew away. Keeping her eyes open this time, she tried taking another deep breath and willed her emotions to take over. Nothing. Strange. It would seem she definitely ought to be feeling something about now. Jittery or excited, perhaps even with an old-fashioned qualm or two thrown in for good measure.

Anything would be an improvement over the way she was feeling, which could only be described as resolved. In fact, she felt pretty much as she had the day she'd gone to the bank to refinance her mortgage at a lower interest rate, confident that she had made the right decision and braced to get through the tedious paperwork required to complete the process. The trouble was that she wasn't embarking on a banking transaction now, but her own wedding.

The bee returned just as the organist started playing what sounded alarmingly like the processional hymn, her signal to start down the aisle. What on earth was taking her sister so long? Sidestepping the persistent bee, Gabrielle strained to identify the music coming from inside the church, but what sounded like the loud roar of a motorcycle drowned out the notes.

Frowning, she instinctively turned her head to look in the direction of the noise coming from the street behind her. It was a motorcycle, all right, and her eyes opened wide with shock as she saw it jump the curb, cross the sidewalk and head straight for the church steps. For a fraction of a second it seemed to hesitate at the bottom step, its powerful engine throbbing. Then the motor revved even louder, and Gabrielle reeled backward as the bike shot forward, bouncing up three broad, low steps to reach the platform where she now stood with her back pressed against the church door.

She froze, not sure in which direction she ought to run . . . if she even could run wearing these darn high heels. A second later it became a moot issue. The rider edged the massive bike closer until there was no way for her to move, much less escape. She was trapped between the motorcycle and the solid wooden door at her back. Her heart pounded as she felt a sudden rush of all those emotions she'd been willing herself to feel only a moment ago . . . jittery, anxious, excited. She felt them now, all right, but for the wrong reasons.

Clutching her bouquet as if it were a lifeline, she sensed more than saw the biker's gaze through the tinted windshield covering his face. His helmet—like his boots, jeans, leather jacket and gloves—was solid black. Aside from projecting a certain lack of imagination, the outfit lent the man a decidedly sinister air. Gabrielle couldn't imagine what kind of stupid game he was playing and she wasn't in any mood to find out.

Keeping her eyes on him, she fumbled behind her for the door handle. Her only chance for escape was to maneuver the church door open enough to slip inside. She leaned forward, straining to give herself a few inches more room. A big mistake. The movement put her off balance at the same time it brought her within arm's reach of the biker, and before she knew what he intended he had snared her around the waist and hauled her onto the motorcycle in front of him.

Once again the engine revved and the bike lurched forward, causing him to tighten his grip on her midsection so suddenly it knocked the wind from her. They were back down the church steps and crossing the sidewalk before Gabrielle recovered enough to scream. A violent jolt as the bike took the curb turned her cry for help into a pitiful, fractured yelp that was carried away by the wind hitting her full force in the face.

"Ohmigod, ohmigod, ohmigod," she moaned, hanging on to the biker's leather sleeve as the motorcycle continued to pick up speed, taking sharp corners and weaving a path through the slow-moving Saturday-afternoon traffic.

She wanted to squeeze her eyes shut so she couldn't see how close they came to the cars they streaked past, but unfortunately panic seemed to have frozen them in a wide-open position. Never before in her life had she been so frightened. Not when Joel was killed, not when Toby was sick. The fear at those times had been strong, but different, more personal and contained. This was like something coming at her from outside, a frantic, gut-twisting, in-your-face terror like she had never before experienced.

Who was the madman seated behind her? Where was he taking her? And why? And how long before anyone back at the church realized she was missing and figured out what had happened? Dozens of questions flashed through Gabrielle's mind without focus, much less answers. Only one thought took hold. Toby. Her little boy. What on earth would he think when he realized his mommy was gone?

"Ohmigod, ohmigod, ohmigod."

They were on Smith Street, headed north across the city and drawing startled smiles and impromptu cheers from people they passed. The smiles and cheers confused her until she remembered that she was wearing a wedding dress and a veil and carrying a damn bouquet of roses. Of course, she thought with dismay, anyone seeing the two of them might easily assume this was some sort of wildly romantic honeymoon escape.

"Help!" she shouted as they ran a red light and missed the back of a minivan by inches. "Help, please, I'm being kidnapped."

She had a feeling that her effort was in vain and her words were being swallowed by the wind even before the arm around her waist silenced her with a tight warning squeeze. Frustration flared inside her. She couldn't scream for help and she couldn't give in to the impulse to struggle to get free because she was afraid any rash movement would upset their precarious balance and send them crashing. Hitting the ground at this speed was not something she would want to experience even if she'd been the one wearing the helmet.

They continued north on Route 44, approaching the small town of Centredale, where, she recalled, the road they were on would soon become one way in the opposite direction. He would have to slow down for the turnoff, Gabrielle told herself with satisfaction, and when he did she would make her move. At the very least she would be able to signal or shout for help. There were lots of people around. Perhaps she could even toss her bouquet to a passerby. It wasn't quite as time-honored as dropping bread crumbs to mark her path, but it would help point in the right direction anyone who came looking for her.

To her amazement and disgust, however, he sped past the turnoff and continued straight into the oncoming traffic, hugging the side of the road so tightly Gabrielle swore her toes brushed against the cars parked along the curb. At one point he avoided a head-on collision with a garbage truck by swerving onto the sidewalk and sending pedestrians scattering for the next block or so.

He really was a maniac, she decided, a madman with no regard for his own safety, much less hers. Her anger grew along with her panic. She no longer wanted to close her eyes. She wanted to pay attention to every detail so that she could give a full accounting of every law he had broken when she was called on to testify against him at his trial for kidnapping and driving to endanger and ... and ...

She gulped and stopped. She didn't want to think about what other crimes he might be guilty of committing before this was over. Instead, she concentrated on her surroundings. Even more than she wanted details for her testimony, she wanted to know exactly where she was at all times. Sooner or later she would have a chance to escape and she planned to make the most of it. Maybe, if she was lucky, she could get back in time to salvage her wedding and spare Toby from having to wonder if his mother was going to go away forever the same way his daddy had.

Her hopes dimmed as they left Centredale and headed into the rural part of Rhode Island. This was farm and apple-orchard country, where cars and witnesses, as she had already begun to think of the people they passed, were scarce. Her captor was still driving at a speed that felt about eighty miles per hour, but either she was getting accustomed to flirting with death or the wide-open road fooled her senses into thinking it was less dangerous.

She was just beginning to relax her shoulder muscles, which ached from the tension, when the bike veered sharply to the right, putting them directly on course to hit a moving van stopped up ahead.

He was purposely trying to scare her, Gabrielle thought, furious that kidnapping her, ruining her wedding day and traumatizing her son weren't enough to satisfy him. He also had to go out of his way to scare her. There was no other explanation for this little game of chicken he seemed to be playing as he continued to accelerate even as they drew within a block of the parked van.

Gabrielle tightened her grip on his sleeve and bit down on her lip. She was on to him now, and she'd be damned if she'd give him the satisfaction of screaming.

Not until they were only half a block away did she notice the ramp extending from the open rear of the van to the street—and it dawned on her that his reason for heading straight for the van wasn't anything as innocuous as scaring her.

The front tire of the bike hit the edge of the metal ramp with a small bounce, and for an instant she had the sensation of walking a tightrope…at a very fast pace. A whimper later they were inside the van. She might have shut her eyes, or it might just have been that there were no lights in there, but mercifully she didn't see the front wall of the van coming at her until the motorcycle's tire hit it and sent them bouncing backward.

At last they had stopped moving, but before Gabrielle could relish the thought she sensed the bike tipping onto its side and knew she was going with it. She flailed to break her fall and felt herself being turned by strong arms as she went down so that she landed on her side on top of the biker.

"You okay?" he asked, his deep voice sounding distant as it came from inside his helmet.

Gabrielle cut short her relieved sigh and levered away from him as best she could. Something, her veil maybe, seemed to be caught on the strap of his helmet.

"No," she said. "No, I most certainly am not okay. I am dizzy and nauseous and my head aches, not to mention—"

"Yeah, you're okay," he muttered, not waiting for her to finish her litany of righteous complaints as he slid her body away from him.

He got up quickly, jerking free of her veil, which in turn yanked the comb that anchored it to her head, pulling her hair so hard it brought tears to her eyes.

"Ouch," she cried.

It wasn't fair, she thought. After all she'd been through in the past half hour or so—being abducted and carried off on a terrifying ride through the streets of Rhode Island and crashing into the back of a dark van—she had managed fairly well not to succumb to the hysteria that was crouched inside her, waiting to pounce. After all that, it wasn't fair that all it should take was having her hair pulled to push her to the very edge of her control.

She rubbed her scalp, doing her best to straighten the veil, which had slipped to one side. All the while tears spilled from her eyes in a silent stream that she couldn't stop. Her captor had his back to her as he worked the rope to raise the ramp and slide it back into the van before reaching overhead to lower the door.

Damn him, damn him, she thought, fear and anger twisting into one giant knot inside her. It was seeing the daylight disappear as he lowered the door, however, that propelled her forward in a panic.

"No," she cried just as the heavy metal door hit bottom with a thud, throwing them into complete darkness and making it hard for her to get her bearings. Two loud thumps followed, as if he was pounding on the van wall. It must have been some sort of preplanned signal, Gabrielle realized, as the van immediately began to move.

She wasn't expecting it, and the sudden motion landed her on her hands and knees.

She heard his footsteps on the other side of the van.

"Where are you?" he asked, his voice sounding clearer suddenly, as if he'd removed his helmet.

His hand found her shoulder.

Gabrielle twisted away from him and skittered backward. "Don't touch me, you bastard."

"For God's sake, Gabrielle . . ."

He knew her name. She had been toying with the idea that this was some sort of impulsive joke on his part, that he had simply seen her on the church steps and given in to some innate impulse to act like a colossal jerk. However, the waiting van and now the fact that he knew who she was seemed to dispel that possibility and suggest something more ominous.

"Where did you go?" he asked, moving again.

She backed up until she was sitting against the wall. "I mean it, stay away from me."

He stumbled and cursed.

Gabrielle smiled in the darkness. Good. She hoped he broke his rotten neck. She'd rather take her chances with the driver of the van, even if he was also in on the whole thing. Whoever it was couldn't be any worse than the mad biker. Her ribs still hurt where he had crushed her to him during the ride there.

"I want to know where you are," he said, sounding as frustrated as she felt. "Quit playing games."

"Ha! That's a laugh."

"What is?"

"You, accusing me of playing games."

"Aren't you? Playing hide-and-seek with the lights out."

He sounded much closer, and she cursed silently, realizing too late that she had been a fool to speak and let her voice lead him to her.

"Who was the one who put out the lights?" she muttered, deciding that since he already knew where she was, there was no sense biting her tongue now. "Who started this little game in the first place?"

"This isn't a game, Gaby."

"Oh, really?" she said, alarmed by his suddenly soft tone and his use of the nickname reserved for close friends and family. She knew he had moved even closer now. She could smell him, his scent a blend of soap and leather, and she thought she might have even felt his breath on her skin. She stiffened, trying not to sound as scared as she felt. "You could have fooled me."

"I did," he said.

The raspy snap of a cigarette lighter being lit startled her. She blinked as her eyes adjusted to the light of the flame that was barely enough to illuminate the face of the man holding the lighter. It was more than enough, Gabrielle thought as she locked gazes with Connor DeWolfe, a man she hadn't seen in nearly two years and would have preferred to never set eyes on again.

"You," she uttered, the word alone an accusation. "God, I should have known."

"Yeah, you probably should have," he agreed, smiling that smile that every woman in the world except her seemed to find so damn irresistible. "I mean, how many other men do you know crazy enough to steal you from the church steps on your wedding day?"

"Why?" she demanded. "Why did you do it?"

"Why?" The smile slowly gave way to a bold, insolent grin she remembered all too well. "Well, because I'm as impatient as ever, I suppose. I just couldn't stand to sit around the church waiting for the minister to get to the part about speak now or forever hold your peace."

Chapter 2

Connor DeWolfe, more commonly known to friend and foe alike as simply "Wolf," lifted his thumb away from the lighter. The flame disappeared, leaving them in darkness once again. He preferred darkness to confronting the look in Gaby's blue eyes. Hatred—that's what he saw when she looked at him. The kind of hatred that he knew cut right to the bone.

What did you expect? jeered a voice inside him. As far as Gabrielle Flanders was concerned, he'd been making her life hell in one way or another for years, had personally destroyed her first marriage and now had topped it all off this morning by busting up her wedding. Under the circumstances hatred seemed a pretty appropriate response. Unfortunately, knowing that didn't make it any easier for him to take, especially not when it was coming from this woman.

"Put that lighter back on," she ordered.

"No. Burning it continuously uses up too much fuel, and we might need the light later."

"For what?"

He scowled, impatiently shoving the lighter into his jacket pocket. "I can't think of anything offhand, but it never hurts to play it safe."

"Ha. Come off it, DeWolfe, you've never played it safe in your life." Her tone was riddled with contempt. "Why don't you just admit that you don't want any light because you're afraid to look me in the eye?"

Connor had the lighter back out of his pocket and lit in less than two seconds. He held it between them, meeting her gaze with steady defiance, until the metal grew hot enough to scorch his thumb.

"I'm not afraid of anything," he said as he finally extinguished the flame.

"Of course not," she said. "My mistake. After all, it takes brains, or at least a modicum of common sense, to feel fear at the appropriate times."

"Ah, flattery. Is that your little way of saying 'Welcome home'?"

"Actually it's more my way of saying 'Go to hell.'"

He sighed audibly. "It sure is nice to know that you're the same honey-tongued angel as always."

"And you're the same impulsive, ill-mannered, self-centered jerk."

"Now that we've caught up on old times," he began, grateful that she couldn't see the raw nerve struck by her assessment of him, accurate though it may be, "why don't you try and relax? We'll be riding back here for about an hour."

"An hour?" she echoed. The frantic note he'd detected a little earlier was back in her voice. "No, I can't stay locked up in here for an hour. I have to get back to the church. I mean it, Connor, please. I don't know what kind of stunt you think you're pulling or whether you expect Adam to get a big laugh out of having you stealing the woman he's about to marry right out from under his nose, but this time you've gone too far."

"It's not a joke."

Her small laugh was strained. "What else could it be? What other possible reason could you have for kidnapping me?"

"I didn't kidnap you," he said, irked by the very idea.

"Then what would you call it?"

Good question. Connor dragged his fingers through the dark hair he hadn't bothered to have cut in months and rubbed his palm across his jaw as he thought it over. The contact with two days' worth of black stubble made a rasping sound in the quiet van.

"Borrowing," he said finally. "I'd call it borrowing you for a while."

"Why?" she demanded, first feebly and then with a white-hot fury he really was in no mood to deal with. "Why, damn it?"

Connor gritted his teeth in the darkness. Even if he had been ready to discuss it, her tone left no doubt that she wasn't ready to listen.

"I have my reasons," he said simply.

"Oh, what a relief. In that case I guess I will just take your advice and sit back and relax. Silly me, all this time I'd been laboring under the misapprehension that you didn't have a good reason for ruining my wedding, risking my life and probably scaring my family, including my five-year-old son, half to death. But as long as you have your reasons, then everything is just hunky-dory." Silence. "You ass."

Connor lowered himself to the floor without replying and sat a short distance from her with his back against the wall, his long legs stretched in front of him. For a few minutes the only sounds were the hum of the big truck's tires on the road and the persistent hiss of air where there was evidently a leak in the rubber seal around the door. He was beginning to think he might get real lucky and receive the silent treatment from her for the entire ride when Gaby spoke.

"Will you at least tell me where you're taking me?" she asked him.

"No," he replied.

"Why on earth not? I think I have a right to know that much."

She sounded indignant and he didn't blame her.

"I can't argue with that, Gaby. The fact is you have a right to a lot of things you can't have. That's just the way it has to be sometimes."

"No, it doesn't have to be that way... it just seems to turn out that way whenever you're involved."

She paused. Holding back, thought Connor, not saying what was really on her mind. Just as he was holding back, not saying a word about what was right there between them, what would always be there.

When it became clear he wasn't going to offer whatever she was waiting for—a reply, explanation, apology—she spoke again, her tone clipped and angry.

"All right, then at least explain to me why you won't tell me where we're going."

He scowled. "Can't you just wait and—"

"No. I can't."

"Fine. I'll tell you on one condition."

"What?" she replied, suspicion in her voice.

"That after I tell you, you shut up for the rest of the way there."

"I'm not making any deals with you."

"Suit yourself."

A minute passed. Connor couldn't suppress an ironic smile. He could almost hear the wheels in her head spinning. How long did he have, he wondered, until she figured out that refusing his offer gained her nothing more than the satisfaction of refusing him?

"All right," she said at last. "Tell me."

"And if I do, then you'll be quiet until—"

"Yes, yes, I'll be quiet," she interrupted. "Tell me."

"The reason I won't tell you where we're headed is because I know you aren't going to like it any more than you liked being snatched away from your wedding or being stuck here with me. So I just figured I'd make things a little easier on both of us by saving it all up and letting you bitch at me about everything at once. Is that what you wanted to hear?"

"No, frankly. The only thing I want to hear from you is that this is all a mistake and that you're going to turn around and take me back to the church as fast as you possibly can."

"Don't hold your breath," he muttered.

"Oh, I'm not. But I just want you—"

"Remember our deal," he broke in.

"I remember," she assured him. "But I have one final thing to say to you and I'm going to say it whether you want to hear it or not. I just want you to know that I hate you for doing this to me, Connor DeWolfe."

"You hated me anyway," he reminded her quietly.

"Yes, but now I'll hate you forever."

Connor leaned his head back and closed his eyes. Forever. That sounded about right, like what he deserved. And he could deal with it. He had to. Under the circumstances what choice did he have?

The ride to an out-of-the-way drop-off point in Connecticut took a little over an hour. When the van came to a stop, Connor quickly stood and raised the rear door. Just as quickly Gabrielle was on her feet beside him.

He reached out and clasped her arm. "Hold on. I want your shoes."

She blinked at him in confusion as her eyes adjusted to the sudden infusion of sunlight. Her hair had come loose beneath her veil, making her look like a figure in a Renaissance painting. He had almost forgotten how beautiful she was and for a few seconds he just stared at her.

"My shoes?" she said, drawing his full attention back to the moment at hand. "What on earth for?"

"Just take them off."

"Forget it," she snapped, trying to yank free. Beautiful and willful. He'd almost forgotten that, too.

Tightening his grip on her, he bent to grab her foot with his free hand. "Suit yourself."

"Wait…what are you…? All right, I'll take them off." She clung to his back in an attempt to stay upright as he lifted her foot off the floor. "Connor, stop, I said I'll take…"

"Too late," he told her, pulling the shoe from her right foot before releasing it. "You'll learn," he continued, getting a firm grip on her left foot, "that I only give an order once."

"An order? Of all the . . ." Again she struggled to get free. There was no way he was going to let her go, however, and when she inevitably lost her balance he went down with her rather than give in.

They both ended up on their butts with their legs entangled and her dress hiked up high enough to expose the lacy garter belt holding up her stockings, as well as lots of bare thigh in between the two. Connor was transfixed. He knew he shouldn't stare, but he couldn't look away any more than he could have given in and let her win a few seconds ago. Self-denial just wasn't his forte.

"Now are you satisfied?" she demanded, glaring at him.

"Not quite," he replied, his tone dry as he slipped the shoe off her left foot and shoved it into his jacket pocket along with its mate. "There. That's much better."

He lifted his leg off hers, freeing her, and she immediately scrambled to her feet, tugging her dress down as she went.

"Did you hurt yourself when you fell?" he asked, standing beside her by the open door.

"As if you care."

"Believe it or not, I do. Very much, in fact."

"Well, you sure could have fooled me. After all a few scrapes are nothing compared to what's going on inside me, worrying about what all those people back at the church are thinking, what my poor mother is thinking, not to mention Toby and how he must . . ." She broke off abruptly and bit down on her bottom lip.

Connor steeled himself to the sight of her pain. He'd known going into this what he would be up against and that there would be no turning back. Not unless he wanted to risk letting her be hurt even worse, and that he wouldn't do. Not if it killed him. He'd screwed up once and Gabrielle had paid the price. Never again.

"There's a phone right over there," he told her, pointing in the direction of a phone booth by the side of the two-lane road.

It was the only thing in sight for as far as they could see. It was the reason he had arranged to be dropped off there in the first place. "I'll let you call home and tell them you're all right, but you have to say exactly what I tell you to say. Nothing else."

She spun to face him, her eyes flashing like dark sapphires. "Why?"

"Because I said so, that's why."

"Oh, I see, the same reason I had to give you my shoes."

"I took your shoes so you won't go running off the second I turn my back to get the bike out of here."

"What's the matter, Connor?" she taunted. "Afraid your hostage might escape?"

"For God's sake, Gaby, for the last time, you are not a hostage. And if you'll shut up for a second and look around, you'll see there's nowhere for you to escape to. If you take off, I'll chase you down in a few minutes. I just don't want you to go hurting yourself trying to run in those stupid pink shoes."

"Apricot."

"What?"

"They're not pink, they're apricot. Iced Apricot, to be precise."

"I see. Well, whatever color they are, the heels are still ridiculous, and you probably would have broken your ankle before you got twenty yards."

She sniffed and folded her arms tightly across her chest.

Deciding that was probably as close to concession as he could hope for, Connor went to work lowering the ramp and rolling the motorcycle out to the street. He turned to offer her a hand, which she of course refused, choosing to pick her way down the ramp in her stocking feet.

He was closing the door behind them when he noticed her bouquet tossed in the corner of the van and hoisted himself back inside to retrieve it.

He handed it to her and got a brittle "thanks" for his trouble.

"You're welcome." He took a step toward the cab of the truck to thank his buddy behind the wheel for the lift and tell him he owed him one, then hesitated and turned back to her.

"And, Gaby, for what it's worth, you looked really beautiful standing out in front of that church."

She glanced sullenly at the hole in the toe of one stocking and the black grease stains along the hem of her rumpled dress. "You got that right. Looked. Past tense."

He shrugged, turning away quickly before he lost control and smiled. He couldn't help it. The bouquet had been a kind of reality check, reminding him all over again of why she'd been at the church in the first place and the obvious fact that she had worn that garter belt to please his old friend Adam on what was to have been their wedding night. Maybe it would turn out that he was wrong about Adam, wrong about everything, and that he himself was exactly what Gaby accused him of being, an impulsive jerk.

Maybe. In the meantime Connor wasn't sure what to make of the unexpected feelings being churned up inside him by thoughts of her with Adam. He only knew that it pleased him royally that he and not Adam had been the one to see how beautiful she looked in her iced apricot garter belt and stockings.

Iced apricot. The words stuck in his head as he thanked his friend and watched the van pull away. Although he could never have come up with so poetic a description on his own, he was astute enough to see how well it suited Gaby. Her smooth skin sort of reminded him of ripe apricots. And there was no question that her manner where he was concerned was definitely icy.

Iced apricot. The thought appealed so much, he supposed it was only natural for a man to wonder what hot apricot would be like.

Along with the Harley, he had pulled from the van a couple of large knapsacks so tightly packed they were straining at the seams. Gabrielle stood by and watched as he struggled to strap them to the bike in a spot where they would be as much out of the way as possible. He'd figured that she wouldn't take up much space, being only about five foot five and slender, but the ride ahead was straight uphill. That fact, plus the added cargo they'd be hauling, would make it even more of a challenge than the getaway from the church had been. He had to make sure that both the bags and Gaby would be safe. It wasn't easy, and Connor didn't have to look up to know that she was relishing every moment of his frustration.

By the time he finished, he'd bitten back every curse he knew, and sweat was running between his shoulder blades. The only thing stopping him from stripping off his leather jacket was the knowledge that if he did he'd have to find someplace on the already overloaded bike to stow that, as well. He'd rather sweat.

After double-checking the kickstand to make sure it was secure, he turned to her. "Let's go make that call."

Gabrielle felt a combined rush of excitement and relief. She quickly rejected the impulse to thank him, reminding herself he deserved to be flogged for what he was doing to her, not thanked for merely having enough decency to allow her to call and let her family know she was still alive. Evidently it didn't take long for the Stockholm syndrome to kick in, she thought disgustedly as they walked the short distance to the phone booth. She picked her path carefully, grimacing each time her bare feet landed on a sharp stone.

"I can carry you if you like," Connor offered when they were about halfway there.

Gabrielle slanted him a look of disdain. "I'd rather crawl."

He shrugged. "That's another option, I suppose."

In spite of her bare feet she increased her pace so that she was out in front of him, where she didn't have to see his mocking smile. Reaching the phone booth first, she stepped inside, slammed the folding door shut and reached for the receiver, her heart pounding with excitement. Only then did she remember she didn't have a purse or money on her.

Gritting her teeth, she slid the door open. Connor smiled as he dropped the quarter he was holding into her hand, but when she went to shut the door again, he stopped it with his foot.

"Here's the deal," he told her, his smile gone. "You've got two minutes. You tell whoever answers that you're fine, that you simply got cold feet at the last minute and—"

"I will do no such thing. I won't lie for you or—"

"You'll do exactly as you're told, Gaby, or no call."

She exhaled, struggling to control her fury. "Fine. I'll tell them I got cold feet."

"And that you need some time alone to think things through."

"All right."

"A week."

"A week?" she echoed, stricken.

He nodded. "A week. You can tell them not to worry, that you'll be in touch."

"They'll never believe me," she told him. "My mother and my sister know I would never do anything as thoughtless and irresponsible as taking off from my own wedding . . . and even if I did something as silly as get cold feet, I would never, ever leave Toby without—"

"It doesn't matter what they believe," he interjected harshly. "They'll at least hear your voice and know you're all right, and you'll have the satisfaction of getting a message to Toby."

Toby. Everything inside her yearned to see and hold her little boy.

"I have to talk to Toby myself," she said.

"Not unless he answers."

"For heaven's sake, Connor, he's only five years—"

"It will take too long."

"I have to, Connor." She swallowed her pride. "Please. He's just a little boy . . . a little boy whose daddy . . ."

"All right, all right," he said giving in exactly as she had suspected he would.

For future reference she tucked away the knowledge that underneath all that reckless macho bluster, even Connor DeWolfe had a conscience that could be pricked if you used the right needle.

She reached for the phone. His hand closed over hers, stopping her.

"Remember," he warned, "nothing about me or where you are."

"I don't know where I am," she reminded him, her smile tart.

"Good, then you won't try to drop any hints. I mean it, Gaby. Anything cute and I'll rip the phone right out of the wall. That will only alarm them more."

He was right, of course, and her smug little plan to do exactly what he was warning against fizzled inside her. Glumly she realized that she had no choice but to do as he'd instructed. She couldn't risk having him break the connection and upset her mother or Toby any more than they must be already. Especially not when she had no idea when she might be able to contact them again.

She lifted the receiver, dropped the quarter into the slot and punched in her mother's number. When a recorded voice instructed her to deposit additional coins to complete the long-distance call, she turned to find Connor had them ready for her. He was well prepared; she had to give him that much. Unfortunately. Under the circumstances she wished with all her heart he was behaving more like the irresponsible, undependable hotshot she remembered so well.

Just as she heard the first ring, he startled her by moving inside the booth. He had to lean against her in order to slide the door shut behind him, crowding her against the back wall, filling the small space with the scent of leather and man.

"What are you doing?" she challenged, as disturbingly aware of every inch of him as she had been of his heated gaze a few minutes ago, when thanks to him they'd fallen on top of each other in the back of the van.

"Making sure there aren't any road noises they might be able to identify and trace later."

"Of all the stupid... Hello," she said, straining to sound normal as she heard her mother's voice on the other end of the line. "Mom? Is that you?"

"Gabrielle? Oh, thank goodness. It's her," Gabrielle heard her mother say to someone else. Her sister maybe, or Adam. Probably both. "It's Gabrielle. Where on earth are you, Gabrielle? We're all worried sick."

"I'm fine, Mom. Please don't worry. I just...I just got a last-minute case of nerves and I had to... to get away." She glared at Connor as she spoke the lies he'd ordered. "I need some time to think things over. Alone."

"Well, goodness, Gaby, I don't know what to say. I was so sure you knew what you were doing."

"So was I, Mom, but things changed. I'll explain everything as soon as I get back."

"All right, sweetheart, you just come on home and..."

"I can't, Mom," she said, her voice cracking as a longing to be back home where she belonged erupted inside. "Not right away."

"But, Gaby..."

"Please, Mom. I...I need some time to myself. To think. Will you please take care of Toby for me until I get back?"

"Well, of course I will. But...oh, dear. Gaby, Adam is right here and he'd like to say a word to you."

"No."

"Gaby, really, I think you owe it..."

"Not now, Mom," she said firmly. "I don't have time. Please put Toby on."

"Toby? But Adam..."

"Mom, get Toby for me, and hurry. My time is running out, and I don't have any more change on me."

"All right." She turned away from the phone, and Gaby heard her calling for Toby and trying to explain to Adam that Gabrielle insisted on speaking with her son. Gabrielle heard Adam's voice, loud and indignant. She winced. I'm so sorry, Adam, she thought. Sorry for the pain and the humiliation you must be feeling. She would make it up to him somehow, but right then her overriding concern was Toby.

"Mommy?"

"Toby? Oh, Toby, hello, sweetie. It's Mommy."

"Where are you, Mommy?" he asked, the familiar sound of his voice bringing tears to her eyes. "I waited and waited, but you never came down the aisle like you were supposed to."

"No, I know I didn't, sweetie. Something came up, and Mommy had to go away in a hurry. I'll tell you all about it when I get home."

"I thought you were mad at me because I was afraid to carry the pillow with the rings."

"Oh, no, Toby. I wasn't mad at you."

"Were you afraid, too?"

"Maybe a little. Listen to me, Toby. I want you to stay with Nana for a while, and be very good for her, all right?"

"But where will you be?"

"I'll be home soon," she told him, aware of Connor tapping his watch impatiently. "And when I do, we'll..." She struggled to think of something to give him to look forward to. "We'll go ride the horses again. You and Adam and me, all right?"

"That's it," Connor mouthed, lifting his hand to the connection lever on the phone.

"I have to go, Toby. I love you, sweetie. Tell Nana goodbye for me and that I love her, too."

"Okay, Mommy. I—"

Connor lowered the lever, cutting off the connection.

"Damn you," she shouted. "He was still talking to me."

"I told you two minutes," he said. "I let you go over as it is."

Gabrielle tilted her head to meet his determined gaze. He was a big man, bigger than her late husband, Joel, had been, bigger than Adam. Six foot two and powerful. The muscles she knew were beneath that leather jacket, the muscles that allowed him to grab her and toss her around as if she were of no more substance than a bag of feathers, were a matter of function rather than fashion. They'd resulted from years of reckless physical activity, not membership at some expensive health club. Strong and impulsive and undependable—that was Connor DeWolfe, and at the moment she was totally at his mercy. Crowded into the small, hot phone booth, he seemed bigger than ever to Gaby, and still she would have fought him tooth and nail if she'd thought there was even a slight chance that doing so would get her back home to Toby faster.

It wouldn't.

"Let me out of here," she ordered.

He'd been watching her with an odd, almost assessing expression. Ridiculous, thought Gaby, since she and Connor had sized each other up long ago. He also started to say something in reply to her demand, then snapped his jaw shut and reached behind him to shove open the door.

"Yes, ma'am."

He led the way back to the bike, walking faster than she could have even if she'd been wearing shoes. Halfway there he glanced back at her and frowned.

"Hurry up. We've got a long ride ahead of us."

Gaby made a face at his back, but she did try to move a little faster. For all she knew, he might decide to drag her along if she fell too far behind. In spite of her efforts to keep up, he reached the bike before her. As she approached he was standing with his back to her, rummaging in a small leather pouch strapped beneath the handlebars.

For the first time it occurred to Gabrielle that the long ride he warned of was going to have to be made on this motorcycle. She already felt battered and weary, and every bone in her body rebelled at the thought of climbing back on the black-and-chrome monster. She was eyeing it warily, wondering where she was going to sit and how, when Connor turned.

The sunlight glinted off the knife in his hand, and Gaby screamed.

"For God's sake," he said, grasping her by the shoulder as she tried to back away. "What's wrong with you?"

Her gaze slid from the six-inch blade to his grim expression. It was a toss-up as to which was more menacing.

"Me?" she managed to say. "What's wrong with me? What's wrong with you? Why are you doing this, Connor? Why do you want to hurt me?"

He looked stunned, as if she had taken the knife and turned it on him, planting it deep in his belly. His eyes narrowed as he stared at her as blankly as if he was looking at a total stranger. It was not, Gaby decided, a reassuring moment.

"Hurt you?" he asked. "Why on earth would you think I want to hurt you?"

"Damn it, Connor, you're holding a knife on me. What should I think?"

He glanced at the knife as if he'd forgotten he had it and quickly dropped his arm to his side. "How could you think . . . hell, Gaby, hurting you is the last thing I want to do. You have to believe me. I never want to hurt you again." He lifted his hand as if to touch her face. "I only want to take care of you."

Gabrielle flinched and his hand froze in midair. Take care of her? Her mind reeled at the absurdity of it. She'd always said he was crazy, but she'd meant it in the reckless, daredevil sense of a man who had never really grown up. Maybe she'd been more on target than even she had known. Maybe he was truly insane.

"The same way you took care of Joel?" she whispered.

Instantly his gray eyes became shuttered, his expression hard. Gabrielle held her breath, her heart thundering in her chest, as he took a step closer and grabbed the hem of her dress in the front. He pulled the sheer fabric taut.

"What are you—?"

"Quiet," he ordered, hunching down.

She watched in horror as with one efficient slash of the knife he slit her skirt from the top of her thighs to the hem.

"Turn around."

Gabrielle did as he said, not sure if she was trembling more from her anger at being manhandled or relief that he evidently didn't have even more sinister plans for the knife. The thoughts that had flashed through her mind when he suddenly turned with it in his hand still made her feel queasy. And a little silly. As crazy as he was acting, this was Connor after all. A man she had known for years. Her son's godfather. A friend. Sort of. She tossed her head defiantly. All right. So maybe she had overreacted a bit. It was damn hard to know how to react to any of this.

Connor quickly slit the back of her dress in the same way he had butchered the front.

As she whirled back to face him, he flipped the knife shut with a quick, unmistakably practiced motion and dropped it into the pouch.

"My beautiful dress," she cried, glancing at the tatters fluttering around her legs in the soft breeze. "It's ruined."

"Instead of whining, you ought to be thanking me. You'll be a lot more comfortable riding behind me than you were up front." He shot her a taunting grin. "Or are you bitching because you'd really rather be back in my arms again? Is that it, Gaby?"

"Not in this lifetime," she snapped.

"Good. Because I was getting real tired of having that damn veil blowing in my face." He lifted his gaze to the top of her head. "In fact . . ."

Before she could stop him, he had yanked the veil off and tossed it into a ravine by the side of the road. He stepped back to look at her. "Much better," he declared. "Now you have another reason to thank me."

"For throwing away a handmade, imported lace headpiece that cost a small fortune?"

"No. For making you look more like yourself and less like Adam Ressler's bride."

Chapter 3

The long ride provided Gabrielle with plenty of time to brood about how much she hated Connor DeWolfe and how she was going to make him pay for what he was doing to her. It was easier to think clearly now that they weren't hurtling through traffic, with her in fear for her life every second. Also, as much as it galled her to admit that Connor was right about anything, she did feel safer and marginally more comfortable riding behind him than she had sprawled across the front of his seat.

Apart from the bumps in the narrow road, which seemed to wind endlessly up the side of a small mountain, the worst part of the ride was having to sit with her chest pressed against his back and her arms wrapped around his waist. It wasn't a matter of choice, since there was simply no other way to hold on. At least his leather jacket made for a reasonably sturdy barrier between her chest and his broad back. True, it wasn't the solid granite wall she would have preferred between them, but it was far preferable to the situation in front.

He'd unzipped his jacket before they started out, letting it fly open in the breeze so that her palms were separated from his midsection by only the wash-softened cotton T-shirt he wore underneath. Each time he leaned into a curve or shifted his weight, she was aware of his hard muscles clenching and rippling beneath her fingertips. She swore she could even feel him breathing and several times she found her own breath unconsciously coming in unison with his. When that happened she purposely held her breath for as long as she could and then took great pains to make sure she exhaled when he inhaled and vice versa.

She didn't care if it was childish. She hated Connor De-Wolfe with every fiber of her being.

He was also right about one other thing, however. She had always hated him, or at least disliked and distrusted him immensely. All that, Gabrielle thought grimly, in spite of the fact that he'd been her late husband's best friend and that he, Adam and Joel had been business partners in one of the most successful restaurants in the state. She'd married Joel right after college, for better or worse, and ever since then, as far as she was concerned, Connor was the worst.

From the start she'd been convinced he brought out the worst in Joel, as well. When he was around Connor, it had been as if the sweet, dependable man she loved was suddenly plummeted back to adolescence, with no scheme too outrageous to undertake, no feat too dangerous to attempt if Connor put forth a challenge. Oh, she'd tried to hide her feelings of disapproval for Joel's sake, but inside she had always been afraid that sooner or later Connor would get Joel into real trouble, that he would wind up fired or arrested or bankrupt.

Gaby closed her eyes against the familiar threat of tears. If only it had all ended that innocuously.

She stiffened behind him, resenting Connor even more for bringing back these particular tears, and on this of all days. Today was supposed to have been a new beginning, for her and for Toby, not the resurrection of the worst heartache of her life. The only bright spot in the whole ordeal was the knowledge that Connor was suffering, as well. She'd seen the subtle signs that he, too, still endured very raw emotions where Joel was concerned. Good, she thought with an icy stab of satisfaction, he deserved to suffer.

Connor and Joel had been friends long before she'd met Joel in college. They had gone to the same elementary school and high school, playing football together and double-dating on weekends. She had heard all the stories of their wild exploits dozens of times. Stories about Joel, the studious, dependable doctor's son, and Connor, the kid from the wrong side of everything with the massive chip on his shoulder. In college Joel had persuaded Connor to join the same fraternity as him, and it was there they met Adam. The three became close friends, but even within that friendship there was always a special bond between Joel and Connor.

After she and Joel married, Gaby had done her best to tolerate Connor, and in turn, Joel had been patient with her less-than-enthusiastic feelings for the man he thought of as a brother. She had even harbored a secret hope that Connor was an adolescent habit Joel would eventually outgrow. That didn't happen. He'd been a frequent visitor at their home, and occasionally they all vacationed together. Vacation. Ha, Gaby thought, shuddering at the memory of some of the most frustrating, tension-filled weeks of her life. Eventually the three friends, Joel, Connor and Adam, became business partners, as well, pooling their savings to buy a struggling restaurant on the waterfront in Providence, renaming it the Black Wolf Tavern—the name taken from Connor's nickname—and surprising everyone by turning it into a thriving operation.

It was generally agreed that Adam deserved most of the credit for the success of the Black Wolf. He managed the restaurant full-time, while Joel had continued with the accounting firm where he'd been a fast-rising star and handled the restaurant's books on the side. And Connor...well, Connor just went along for the ride as usual. Technically he was a cop, a highly respected explosives expert assigned to the state police SWAT team, but even that hadn't been high risk enough to satisfy the man's insatiable craving for danger, Gaby recalled contemptuously. Motorcycles, mountain climbing, flying lessons, he incessantly sought out ways to risk his neck, and too often for her peace of mind—and Joel's, as well.

Joel and Connor. Connor and Joel. They were together as kids, together in business and they were together the day of the explosion inside the Black Wolf. Except that day Connor was the only one who made it out alive.

Gaby pushed the thought away. During the past two years she'd relived that nightmare more times than she could count. Even on days when she was feeling her most resilient and in control, as if she might actually succeed at picking up the pieces and going on with her life, the memory of that awful day could bring her to her knees emotionally. And at the moment she was far from feeling either resilient or in control.

Desperate for a distraction from her own thoughts, she turned her attention to the landscape around her. She'd completely forgotten her resolve to pay attention to details in case a chance to escape should present itself. Of course that possibility was appearing more remote with each passing mile. They seemed to be in the middle of nowhere, with nothing but woods all around them. But at least they were no longer riding uphill, she thought, grateful for the chance to relax her grip for a while.

They rounded a bend, and suddenly the woods on her left ended, revealing a clear lake dappled with late-afternoon shadows. Gaby felt a flicker of familiarity, almost a sense of déjà vu, before recognition hit her full force. She didn't just feel as if she'd been there before, she realized. She *had* been there. They had spent a week here the summer before she became pregnant with Toby. There was a cabin across the lake that belonged to one of Connor's pals on the force. She and Joel, along with Adam and the woman he was dating at the time... Laura... Lauren... Lenore, that was it. The four of them had come up together, and although his date had bailed out at the last minute, Connor had joined them for the last four days of their stay. Alone.

Gaby felt her face heat at the memory of those long-ago days and then came a rush of anger.

"You bastard," she shouted in his ear, wanting to make sure he heard her over the noise of the engine and the wind.

Connor jerked his head away, telling her she had been heard, all right. He slowed as the road narrowed and bent sharply, following it around to where she could now see the corner of the cabin. The only dwelling for miles around, it was exactly as she remembered it, built of dark, rough-hewn logs and shielded by trees, with a large wraparound deck designed to take full advantage of the view of the lake.

Connor turned his head just enough to talk to her. "I take it you finally recognized where we're going," he shouted over the noise.

"I recognize it, all right," she replied stiffly. "Why on earth did you bring me here?"

She felt him shrug, and he let up on the throttle enough to make shouting unnecessary. "I needed someplace to bring you. This was available . . . and out of the way. And safe."

They came to a stop on the crushed-stone driveway next to the cabin, and she wasted no time climbing off and putting some distance between them.

"Safe?" she asked, unconsciously rubbing her legs. They felt numb from the long ride. "What do you mean, safe?"

He hesitated. "I mean that I needed a place where no one would think to look for you, and where, if anyone does come looking, I can see them before they get here."

"You make it sound like we're hiding out, for heaven's sake."

He shrugged. "I guess that about sums it up."

"From whom?" she demanded.

He unfastened the canvas knapsacks and carried one, along with his helmet and other gear, up the steps to the deck without replying.

Gabrielle followed, stopping at the bottom of the steps. "From whom?" she asked again. "Answer me, damn you."

He turned, his expression one of grim resignation. "I'm not absolutely sure. Yet. But I'd say Adam is as good a bet as anyone."

"Adam? Are you joking? Or have you completely lost your mind?" She laughed shortly. "What am I saying? Of course you have. If you were sane, none of this would be happening."

Connor continued toward the door of the cabin. "Want to grab that other knapsack and bring it inside with you?" he called back to her.

"No." She folded her arms across her chest and glared at his back as he walked away. "No, I do not want to carry the other knapsack inside. I don't even want to go inside. I don't want to be here, especially not with you, and I refuse to do one more thing to cooperate or make your life easier. I plan to fight you every step of the way and make things miserable for you until you let me go. Do you hear me?" she asked, her voice reaching a crescendo.

He had disappeared inside. Now he returned, crossing the deck with a familiar long-legged amble that suggested he was a man who didn't hurry for anyone or anything. Even his walk was annoying, thought Gaby. His expression, as he reached for the final knapsack, had become blasé.

"What were you saying?" he asked.

"I said," she replied through gritted teeth, "that I have no intention of sharing that cabin with you for one night, much less a week."

Connor sighed and reached to carefully place the canvas bag on the top step. "I see. I suppose I could just go along with that stupid idea . . . after pointing out, of course, that most women would consider spending a night out here alone a whole lot less appealing than sleeping under a roof with me."

She smiled sarcastically. "Bragging, Connor?"

"I said under the same roof, not in the same bed," he reminded her, unleashing a slow grin of his own. "But if you're interested in something more . . ."

"I'm not. Believe me."

"In that case, as I was saying, I could mention the fact that you never know what might crawl out of those woods after dark, or how cold and damp the nights can get this close to the lake, even in June."

Gaby shivered in spite of knowing that was exactly how he wanted her to react. "I happen to enjoy the night air," she said defiantly.

"Do you also enjoy cuddling up next to a raccoon?"

"More than some creatures I can think of."

"Touché."

"Then it's settled," she said, already wondering what she had gotten herself into.

"Not quite. I said I could mention all those things to you and then sit back and wait for you to put on your little rebellious-pioneer-woman act until you got tired or hungry or scared enough to admit you were wrong and come inside. But we've both already been through a lot today, and I'm not going to let you put us through that little charade, too. So for your sake as much as mine, I'm only going to say this once." He took a step toward her, his indulgent smile vanishing. "You walk into that cabin on your own right now, or I swear I'll haul you in there."

She met his gaze without blinking, and for one long, torturous moment Connor was convinced she was going to call his bluff and that he was going to have to grab her, toss her over his shoulder and carry her kicking and screaming into the cabin. Thoughts of how he would keep her there were even more troublesome. He'd included rope with the supplies he brought up earlier and he was prepared to use it if he had to. But God knew he didn't want it to come to that.

What he wanted was to sit down and calmly explain everything to Gabrielle and have her understand and tell him he had done the right thing in snatching her off those church steps. Hell, he wanted her to tell him he'd done the only thing he could have done, given what he knew. Maybe she would even be grateful to him for stopping her from making what might be a huge mistake and maybe, for just a second, she might even look at him with something other than contempt.

He didn't expect any of that, of course. Or deserve it, he reminded himself. That was just the way he wanted it to happen. Realistically speaking, he would be grateful if Gaby simply went into the house as he'd requested.

It was a major relief when, after making him sweat for what seemed hours, she did precisely that. Lifting her chin and sweeping him with a look of silent indignation, she strode past him and up the stairs, going out of her way to kick the knapsack as she passed.

Connor smiled ruefully and bent to catch it as it tumbled down the steps. Hopefully that would be the extent of her retaliation. Gaby had never struck him as a vengeful woman, and Lord knew she had cause to be. As he recalled, she was stubborn as hell, however. If he couldn't get her to listen to reason and persuade her that what he was doing was in her and her son's best interest, it was going to be a very long week.

He watched as she walked to the back door of the cabin, taking note of the fact that she didn't so much as glance toward the corner of the deck where there were a couple of lounge chairs and a barbecue grill, the old-fashioned kind that used charcoal instead of propane gas. Maybe she didn't remember the last time they were here, he thought. Then again maybe she just didn't want to remember. Connor didn't glance in that direction, either, but he still remembered every second, every heartbeat of that long-ago afternoon.

He followed Gaby inside, turning on the light in the kitchen. Off the kitchen was a bay-windowed alcove for dining and a large living room, all decorated in sturdy neutral-tone fabrics and furniture just battle scarred enough that you felt comfortable putting your feet up. The wall of the living room that faced the lake was almost entirely glass. Still, the towering fir and cedar trees surrounding the cabin shielded it from most of the sun and kept the interior always cool and restful.

A spiral staircase led upstairs, where there were two loft bedrooms and the sort of opulently decadent bathroom one didn't normally find in a log cabin. Besides being generous with its use, the cabin's owner, his friend Charlie, was a man of exquisite taste and great imagination. An ice-cold beer, barbecued T-bone steak and sunken tub big enough for two were Charlie's idea of heaven. Connor had to hand it to the man; if it wasn't heaven, it was damn close.

He picked up one of the knapsacks and tossed it to Gaby, who was standing stiffly beside the kitchen table. He tried hard not to notice how much of her legs were exposed as a result of his handiwork with her dress.

She caught the knapsack and held it away from her, eyeing it suspiciously.

"What's this?" she asked.

"Take a look."

She slowly unzipped it and looked inside. Glancing up at him with a frown, she asked, "Clothes?"

He nodded. "I thought that sooner or later you might get tired of wearing your wedding dress and want something a little more practical. It's just a couple of T-shirts and pairs of shorts, a sweatshirt, jeans. Oh, and underwear, of course."

She stared at him in what looked like disbelief. "How—?"

"How did I know your size?" he broke in. "I used my imagination."

"No. How long have you been planning this?"

"About twenty-four hours," Connor replied, shrugging. "Ever since I got back home and found out you were planning to marry Adam."

She looked pale suddenly, and Connor thought he saw her hand shake as she lifted it to push her hair back from her face.

"What is it?" he asked. "What's the matter?"

She laughed weakly. "What isn't? I just can't believe that you actually planned all this... right down to packing for me." She made an impatient gesture with one hand. "Oh, I knew you had to have arranged for the van to be waiting there for us, but this—" she grimaced at the knapsack of clothes "—seems so...calculated. So..." She paused and swallowed hard. "So definite." Looking back at Connor with a wistfulness that tore at something deep inside him, she asked, "This really isn't a joke, is it?"

He shook his head. "No. It isn't."

As he watched, she seemed to sag with... What? he wondered. Defeat? Acceptance? Too soon to tell.

"Listen," he said, gentling his tone, "why don't you go upstairs and change and I'll fix us something."

''No.'' She shook her head emphatically. ''I don't want to change or eat or do anything else until you tell me what this is all about.''

''I think maybe—''

''Now, Connor.''

''I'd forgotten how impatient and demanding you could be,'' he muttered. ''And do you have to keep calling me that?''

''What?''

''Connor.''

''It's still your name, isn't it?'' she asked sarcastically.

It was his name, all right, but for as long as he could remember he hadn't liked being called it, especially not by a woman.

''I prefer Wolf,'' he reminded her.

Her lips curved in a satisfied smile. ''Then yes, I do have to keep calling you Connor. Now, are you going to keep your promise or not?''

''What promise are you talking about?'' he asked, regarding her cautiously.

''You promised when we got where we were going you'd explain everything. Well, we're here, and I want to know what's going on. Why the hell did you want to stop me from marrying Adam?'' she asked, her voice rising sharply. ''Why are you so damn determined to ruin my life?''

''I'm not,'' he said, feeling cornered. He'd wanted to wait for an opportune moment to explain things to her. He could see now that even if such a moment was feasible, she wasn't going to wait for it to come around.

''Really?'' she drawled. ''Well, for a man who's not trying to ruin my life, so far you've made two very impressive attempts at it.''

''Maybe this time I'm trying to save your life—did you ever consider that possibility?''

''No. Not for a minute.''

''It's true.'' He raised his hand to ward off her exclamation of disbelief. ''At least it might be true.''

''And someday the sky might fall. That doesn't mean I have to run out and invest in a cave.''

"If my suspicions are right, the threat to your life could be a little more imminent than that. You could be in real danger, Gaby." He hesitated before deciding he had to be totally honest with her to get her to understand. "And so could Toby."

"Toby?" Her chin came up, and her eyes first widened in surprise, then narrowed with an almost feral glint. Just like a mother lioness whose cub has been threatened, Connor thought, thinking that in spite of everything Toby Flanders was a mighty lucky kid. "What are you talking about?"

"Sit down and I'll tell you everything."

She obediently sank onto one of the mismatched chairs gathered around the massive oak pedestal table in the dining alcove. He moved to join her, detouring by the refrigerator for a beer. He'd borrowed Charlie's truck and driven up with some supplies last night. He held a can aloft to offer her one, but Gaby shook her head.

"Soda?" he asked. "Juice?"

She shook her head again. "No. Thank you. I would like a glass of water, though."

He dropped a few ice cubes into a glass and filled it with water for her. This time he was certain her hand shook as she lifted it to take a sip.

"Calm down," he said quietly, sitting in the chair beside hers. "I promise you Toby isn't in any danger right now."

"But you said . . ."

"I said he could be . . . and I only said that much because I want you to understand how serious this is."

She nodded. "All right, just tell me."

"It has to do with the explosion," he began by way of warning.

"My God, not again."

She started to get up, but he stopped her by placing his hand firmly over hers on the table.

"Sit down." More gently he added, "Please. Let me finish."

"Go on."

Connor took a gulp of beer, searching for words. Except for the endless questioning immediately following the explosion, he hadn't discussed what happened that day with anyone in nearly two years and he wasn't ready to now.

"Like everyone else, I bought the results of the official investigation into the explosion at the restaurant. I accepted the conclusion that the bomb was—"

"Was intended for you," she broke in, an edge to her voice. "It was done in retaliation by some gang members you'd arrested, and Joel just happened to be in the wrong place at the wrong time. I read the report, too."

"Yeah, that's right." He kept his gaze on the table before him, where he was absently batting the metal tab from the beer can back and forth between his fingers. "You don't know how that made me feel."

"I know how it should have made you feel," she said in that same cool voice. "Responsible. Guilty. Reprehensible."

His smile was reflexive and self-mocking. "I take it back. You do know."

"You should have felt responsible," she reiterated, visibly struggling for control. She wasn't the only one. Connor felt as if a balloon full of heat were filling up in his chest. "It wasn't as if you didn't have advance knowledge," she continued. "They warned you... they sent threatening letters...hell, they'd even tried once already and screwed up.... Damn it, Connor, you knew it was going to happen."

"I didn't." He made an impatient gesture. "Oh, sure, I knew about the threats and the stuff they found wired under my car the week before, but I didn't know what they might try next or where or when they might try it. I didn't even know if they were serious. Cops get threats all the time, Gaby. It's all part of the game. Did you expect me to lock myself in a cage and stop living?"

"I don't know. I only know I didn't expect you to put my husband—your best friend—in danger, too. I didn't expect—"

Her voice broke off, the tears running down her face so profusely it was impossible for her to speak clearly. The urge to reach out and wipe them away rose up so strongly inside him that Connor shot to his feet to get away, knocking his chair over in the process. He left it where it fell, too agitated to sit.

"Maybe I didn't," he said to her.

Gaby wiped her face with her hands. He tore some paper towels from the roll on the counter and thrust them at her.

She dried her eyes before shooting him a bewildered look. "What did you just say?" she asked.

"I said maybe I didn't put Joel in danger that day. Maybe it was the other way around."

She frowned, her tone incredulous. "What are saying? That Joel caused that explosion? That he put you in danger?"

"Of course not," he said, shaking his head. "Joel couldn't have known it was going to happen any more than I did. All I'm saying is that maybe the explosion wasn't aimed at me the way you and I and everyone else assumed. Maybe we were all intended to assume that to hide the fact that the real target was Joel."

She smiled. Connor hadn't been sure exactly what her response would be when he finally told her his suspicion, but the last thing he expected was a smile.

"I see," she said. "Let me see if I've got this straight. You're saying that the explosion that killed Joel, a happily married man, a father, an accountant, for God's sake, the same explosion which you—a cop with plenty of enemies and a history of trouble—managed to survive, was intended for my husband all along? Is that it?"

"I said he might have been the target."

"That certainly would be nice for you, wouldn't it, Connor? It would get you right off the hook, ease your conscience, give you a chance to come back home from wherever it was you ran away to, an excuse to stop licking your wounds."

"Mexico."

"What?"

"Mexico. Just for the record that's where I ran away to lick my wounds."

"I don't care, do you hear me?" she shouted, standing. "I don't care where you went. I don't care why you came back. And most of all I don't care what lies you want to tell yourself to try to soothe your conscience as long as you don't try telling them to me or go trying to drag me and my son into it, do you hear me?"

"It's not a lie," he said flatly. "It may not prove to be true. That's what I came back here to find out. But it's not a lie."

"So after nearly two years, out of the clear blue, you've come up with this notion that the bomb might have been meant to kill Joel rather than you, and based on that you come charging back to Providence, ruin my wedding and tell me I have to hide out from the man I'm going to marry. What precisely is poor Adam's role in all this supposed to be? Let me guess, he planted the bomb, right?" she asked, her tone blatantly mocking.

"Maybe," he said, shocking her into silence. "That's what I intend to find out. And it's not just some idea I pulled out of thin air. I got a call a couple of weeks ago from a friend back here on the force. He told me they picked up a guy for a bombing that had a lot of the same markings as the one at the Black Wolf."

Gaby clasped her hands together, her fingers tightly knotted, and stared at him. "They caught him?" she asked, her voice small and hollow. "I didn't know."

"I asked them not to tell you . . . or anybody else, for that matter. The guy they picked up has a record going back to the Stone Age, along with half a dozen outstanding warrants. They had plenty to hold him while they leaned hard on him. It didn't take long for him to roll over to his part in the blast two years ago. The last thing any smart con wants is to take the fall for an attempt on an officer's life. He laid it all out for them, told them how it was a contract job. . . ."

"A contract job?" she asked, her arms locked tightly across her chest as if she were trying to hold herself together.

"That means the guys who planted the explosives were specialists hired to do the job."

"But the gang that threatened you . . ."

"That supposedly threatened me," he corrected. "It looks now as if that was a ruse, all part of the plan to lead us in the wrong direction. And it worked. These guys are very, very good at what they do. They're also very expensive."

"That doesn't even make sense," she exclaimed. "Joel was an accountant. He used to joke about how boring he was...even you used to make jokes about it," she reminded him, her voice strained and quaking. "Who would pay anyone to have him killed?"

He met her gaze without offering an answer.

"Adam?" she asked, clearly stunned. "Is that really what you think?"

"I already told you, I don't know." He paced across the room. "When I got that call, I had the same reaction you just did. I kept asking myself who would want to hurt Joel, and the answer kept coming up 'nobody.' Then I started thinking like a cop, and everyone became a suspect. I made a list of all the possibilities, as wild and unlikely as they seemed. You think Adam is a long shot?" he asked her. "Hell, Gaby, I had you on that list."

"Me?"

"Like I said, everyone is a suspect. Finally I eliminated all the real way-out possibilities. Like you."

"I suppose I should thank you for that at least," she muttered.

"I called my friend back and had him get in touch with that fancy accounting firm Joel was working for at the time. Higley, Bigley and—"

"Higgins, Blackwell and Clarke," she corrected.

"Right, those guys. The state police already had an investigator checking it out. There was nothing suspicious there. I knew that Joel also handled the books for the restaurant so I decided to check out that angle. I started with my own records. I get the same biannual profit-and-loss statements you must get."

She nodded.

"I don't know what you do with yours, but I toss mine, unopened, into a file marked Miscellaneous." He gave a self-deprecating grimace. "Actually it's more of a shoebox than a file, and it's not marked anything, but I dragged out all the old reports and studied them."

"And?"

He shrugged. "And when I was finished, I understood why it is I toss them in the box without opening them. I have no idea what all those columns and figures mean. My share of the profits is direct-deposited in the bank and it's more than I need to live on. That's all I care about... or rather, all I did care about until this came up. I knew I needed help, so I asked around and found a numbers nerd I could trust and asked him to look over the statements."

"What did he say?"

"He told me he needed more information to draw any meaningful conclusions. I called Adam and told him I was having some nightmare tax problems and needed to have an independent audit of the books done in order to straighten out my own mess." He saw her surprise. "I take it he didn't mention anything about it to you?"

"No. And I should think he would have since..."

"Since what?" he prodded when she hesitated.

She shook her head. "Nothing. Go on."

"I'm not sure he even bought the tax story, but what could he say? I am an equal partner. Anyway Nathan, that's my numbers guy, turned the books inside out. He did a lot of talking to me about money in and money out, expenses as related to profits and—"

"For heaven's sake, Connor, get to the point."

"Bottom line?"

She nodded anxiously.

"He says the ratios are off somewhere."

"That tells me a lot. Does he think Adam is skimming off profits?"

"No, exactly the opposite."

"Because that really doesn't make any sense. I mean, the business is flourishing, profits are better than ever since Adam expanded to include catering. Besides, for all practical purposes, once he and I are married he'll own two-thirds of the business. Why would he want to risk..." She finally halted and tipped her head to the side, her eyes narrowing in confusion. "Did you say the opposite?"

Connor nodded.

"You mean..." Her frown deepened. "What do you mean?"

"I mean there's a lot of money coming into the business, a lot of money going out in assorted expenses and a lot of money being racked up in profits...so much profit that you and I were happy to simply cash the checks and leave the rest to Adam."

"So what? I don't know about you, but I have no problem with the business making money, especially not when I have Toby's future to consider."

"I have nothing against profits, either," he told her. "As long as they're legitimate."

"You think Adam is doing something illegal?" she asked, her expression incredulous.

"Yeah," he said, hating to have to be the one to pop her fairy-tale balloon...again. "That's exactly what I think. I don't understand it the way the numbers nerd does...the way Joel must have," he added, holding her gaze. "Eventually I'll have Nathan explain it to you in detail. For now I can tell you that he's got the figures to prove that there's simply too much money everywhere on the books for the amount of business actually being conducted."

"But Adam says that the catering end of it alone..."

"Nathan took all that into consideration."

"Then where is all this extra money coming from?"

His smile was unavoidably sardonic. "Good question. Unfortunately I don't have an answer. Yet. I am willing to venture a guess that it isn't coming from anything wholesome."

"Why?"

"Because, my innocent, only dirty money needs laundering."

"Money laundering?" She looked stunned. "Is that what you think is going on at the Black Wolf?"

"It fits."

He watched her wrestling with all he'd dumped on her in the past few minutes. She bit her bottom lip, looking worried, then shook her head adamantly.

"No. I don't believe it. I won't believe it. Maybe the books are wrong...or your numbers man is. Anyone can make a mistake. You can't simply sneak around looking at the books and then jump to a conclusion like that," she told him. "It isn't fair to Adam."

"Fair to Adam?" he snarled. "Believe me, Adam is the least of my concerns. And I haven't jumped to any conclusions. Think about it, Gaby, it all fits. Joel was the one who handled the books. I think he found something that didn't smell right two years ago, and that's why he called a meeting with Adam and me at the restaurant that day. Only instead of a friendly business meeting, someone arranged for some surprise fireworks." He slammed his empty beer can onto the counter. "Joel died, for God's sake, and I came damn close, but thanks to Adam the Black Wolf somehow miraculously rose from its own ashes and went on, and now we've got money flowing through there like it's our own personal Fort Knox."

She sank back onto her chair, pressing her hands together in front of her face as if she were praying.

"Oh, no," she murmured. "I can't believe this is happening. Just when I thought everything was going...when it seemed that..." She drew herself up and glared at him. "That restaurant is all I have, it's Toby's future...all we have left of Joel."

"I know all that," he said, his voice sounding low and raspy, like something out of his control. "You don't know how I wish this wasn't happening."

"Really?" she asked, getting to her feet once more, her usually soft-looking mouth pulled into a tight, thin line. "Is that what you wish, Connor? Well, let me tell you what I wish. I wish you had just minded your own business and not gone trying to dig up more trouble for everyone. I wish you had just stayed the hell in Mexico and away from me and my son. I wish I'd never met you. I wish Joel hadn't been your best friend, but most of all," she said, her voice cracking with bitter anger, "I wish...I wish it had been—"

She halted abruptly, her chest heaving with the effort of choking off what she had been about to say.

"Yeah, I know," he said. "I wish it had been me instead of Joel, too."

Chapter 4

It had been a horrible thing to say, even if every word had come straight from her heart. Gaby stared at the ceiling above her, built from rough-hewn logs like everything else in the dratted cabin, and wondered if the fact that the words had come from her heart made them even worse.

One thing was certain; it hadn't made any difference that she'd bitten her tongue at the last second. Connor had understood exactly what she meant to say. Hearing him utter the words she'd been wanting to lash out with for so long hadn't been quite the triumph she'd imagined, however. Instead, the moment had somehow drained all the emotion from her, leaving her feeling empty and numb inside.

Even the bitterness that she'd clung to for so long had been stripped away as she looked into his eyes. Or rather, tried to. Although they'd stood there staring at each other for a long moment, his gaze had been flinty and closed to her.

I wish it had been me instead of Joel, too, he'd said to her.

Gabrielle shivered all over again as she recalled his tone, the way his words had sounded as if they'd been chiseled from a glacier, leaving her no doubt he meant every one of them. As if, she thought grimly, they had come from his heart, as well.

After Joel's death she'd been convinced that no one else could possibly feel the same depth of anguish that she felt. Oh, she'd known that Connor was suffering, too, but in the midst of her pain and anger she hadn't considered that given the shared history and close friendship between Joel and him, his loss had been almost as devastating as her own. She hadn't wanted to consider it. Last night, in that agonizingly silent moment, she'd been forced to confront his grief. What she'd seen was sorrow so deep, so overwhelming, it could make you question your own life. She knew firsthand how that kind of sorrow felt.

Her salvation had been Toby. He'd been her impetus to go on, her reason to drag herself out of bed in the morning when all she wanted to do was pull the covers up over her head and cry, a reason to smile even when she felt like screaming. In the past two years she'd thanked God a million times that she had Toby, someone who needed and loved her, someone who was a part of Joel that she could hang on to. What had Connor had to hang on to to help him through his pain?

Gabrielle sighed as she tried to sort through the feelings, old and new, churning inside her. It wasn't easy. If Connor hadn't stalked from the kitchen after their little scene last evening, she would have been forced to. As it was, she'd spent the rest of the night alone up here in the room she'd claimed as her own. When he had rapped on the door later and curtly asked if she wanted to eat dinner, she had just as abruptly replied that she would rather starve.

She nearly had. She'd awoken this morning with her stomach growling painfully. Still she'd waited until she heard him finish puttering in the kitchen and go outside before she ventured downstairs to help herself to the coffee he'd made and toast a cinnamon-raisin English muffin for breakfast.

He had left the knapsack full of clothes outside her door, and after breakfast she had reluctantly helped herself to them, as well. She'd showered and washed her hair and dressed in a pair of khaki shorts and a cream-colored T-shirt before retreating into her room once again. She wasn't sure whether to feel pleased or annoyed that everything he'd brought for her fit perfectly. Including the lingerie. The bra and panties were even a style she would choose for herself, neither too plain nor too fancy. Pale ivory, they were made of a body-hugging ribbed cotton knit and trimmed with a narrow band of crocheted lace.

She would have expected something different from Connor. Either some ugly monstrosity that was the wrong size and just happened to be the first thing he grabbed, or else something made of red satin and trimmed with black lace that would serve to both titillate his legendary libido and satisfy his adolescent need to shock. The fact that instead he'd chosen something so absolutely right for her was very unsettling.

How could he possibly know her so well, she fretted, when some of her assumptions about him had been so wrong?

Swinging herself off the bed, she paced across the room to break her thoughts. There was no way she was going to let herself get sucked into taking that path. Now more than ever, she couldn't afford to indulge in any self-doubts or second guesses where Connor DeWolfe was concerned. So he had gotten lucky with the clothing he selected. Big deal. That didn't change what he was, what he had always been. Reckless and impulsive, an adrenaline junkie always on the lookout for the next big risk, the next rush. That was the real Connor, and she of all people understood that he couldn't be trusted for a minute.

She still didn't completely grasp everything he had told her yesterday, only that he had drawn a line with him on one side and Adam on the other. Adam, who had always been there for her these past two years, who had sat with her and held her hand at the hospital when Toby was so sick, who had promised her a future when the one she'd counted on had been blasted out of existence. Adam offered her what she wanted most, she reminded herself, a safe, secure life for herself and for Toby. As opposed to Connor, who had never offered her anything but aggravation and heartache.

In a contest between Adam and Connor, she didn't even have to blink to know whose side she ought to be on.

In fact, as she'd told him yesterday, she refused to even consider the allegations he'd made against Adam. After all, the only thing she had to support any of it was Connor's word. She rolled her eyes. Hardly what she would consider irrefutable proof. For all she knew, it was a complete hoax and the state police hadn't arrested anyone for the bombing at the Black Wolf, and the investigation into it was as stalled as ever. And Connor was simply...

Simply what? she asked herself for at least the hundredth time since she'd shut herself in that room all alone. She pulled aside the white ruffled curtain to gaze without seeing at the lake as her fingertips drummed restlessly on the wooden sill. Any other time she would have enjoyed the peaceful tableau, with the sun glistening on the clear water, a light breeze ruffling the branches of the surrounding trees and dozens of birds providing soft background music. But not today. Today she was too upset to enjoy anything.

What in the world could Connor hope to gain from stopping her wedding and hauling her up here to this cabin in the middle of nowhere? Amusement? Perhaps at Adam's expense? She bit her lip, wishing she could convince herself that was it. Lord knew she'd tried. But she couldn't.

In spite of his many faults, and the myriad well-deserved accusations she'd hurled at him yesterday, there was no denying that Connor had cared deeply about Joel and that he'd been shattered by his death. Even she couldn't believe that he would treat the matter lightly or use the explosion that had killed his friend as part of some stupid joke.

Last night she had woken again and again and lay there in the dark trying to figure out what other possible reason there could be for what he was doing to her. Ransom came to mind, but was quickly dismissed. The restaurant was earning more than any of them had ever dreamed it might, and Connor shared fully in those profits. Besides, unlike Adam, the man had never had expensive tastes. Far from it. Old jeans and boots and enough money in his pocket to have fun—that had always been the extent of his material needs. Nothing Gaby saw yesterday suggested he'd changed any in that respect.

One after another she had examined each motive she could possibly conjure for his actions, and one after another they crumbled in the bright light of reason. It was her misfortune to be consummately logical, and logic told her that as farfetched and ridiculous as it seemed, the only explanation that made any sense at all was the one Connor had offered in the first place. The one she had refused to accept.

Was it possible that he was right? That Adam had involved the Black Wolf in something illegal? If so, she reasoned, it followed that he might also be somehow involved in Joel's death. Everything inside her rebelled at that thought. Why? Gaby asked herself, struggling to dissect her own response. Was her vehement gut reaction prompted by loyalty to the man she planned to marry? Or was the reason more selfish? Perhaps her feelings were due to the fact that if Connor's suspicions proved true, it would be tantamount to another explosion in her life—and Toby's—just when it seemed everything was going to work out for them at last.

Only one thing was certain. If by some chance Connor was right, sticking her head in the sand wasn't going to make it all go away. And there was still the possibility that he was wrong and that there was a very simple explanation for everything, she told herself reassuringly. An explanation she might even be able to provide now that some of her anxiety had subsided. She had been so tense and furious with him yesterday it had been hard to hear what he was saying, much less think rationally.

She turned away from the window with a resigned sigh. There was no way around it, she decided. She was going to have to find Connor and listen again to what he had to say. This time with an open mind.

Connor bent over the outboard motor he was working on and tried for at least the fifth time to position his screwdriver to grip the screw positioned just beneath the swivel bracket. He needed to loosen the screw to remove the bracket so he could get at the transom clamp. Once that was off, he would be able to lay the motor on its side, lift off the cowling and see what the hell was wrong with the clutch lever. He carefully twisted the screwdriver, and once again it slipped off the screw without moving it so much as a millimeter.

"Damn," he muttered as he used his free hand to wipe the sweat from his forehead. The red bandanna he'd tied around his head to keep the sweat from running into his eyes wasn't doing squat.

Straightening, he flexed his shoulder muscles and squinted first at the sun, which hung like a ball of fire in the cloudless sky overhead, and then at the oversize thermometer mounted on the side of the house. Eighty in the shade. No wonder he was sweating. It was too damn hot for June and too early in the day for a beer.

Especially, he thought derisively, when his brain cells were still struggling to regroup after the six-pack he'd chugged down last night. It had been a long time since he'd felt compelled to drink so much he could still feel it the next day. His fuzzy head was a reminder—not that he needed one—that dealing with Gabrielle was going to complicate his life in ways he should have been smart enough to anticipate.

He'd expected her to be furious with him for ruining her wedding, he'd expected her to fight him tooth and nail and he'd expected to feel like a louse for doing what he had to do. What he hadn't expected was that two years wouldn't have changed in the slightest the way Gabrielle made him feel.

He gripped the screwdriver and grunted with the effort of making yet another unsuccessful attempt to loosen the screw, wishing he had never promised Charlie he'd take a look at the temperamental motor while he was here.

Two long years. Two years of risking his life every way he knew how, of staying on the move, of trying to outrun a guilty conscience and the bloodred memory of the explosion that took the life of the best friend he ever had. Maybe the only friend he ever had. In all that time he'd rarely wanted a woman. Never had he wanted one badly enough to go out of his way to have her or to drink too much because he couldn't. In less than twenty-four hours Gabrielle had him drinking and wanting and hating himself for it.

He stood with the tool poised over the motor and simply stared into its grimy, rusted crevices, his thoughts trapped in a no win land between desire and guilt. The truth, something he was ashamed to admit even to himself and would never confess to anyone else, was that he had always wanted Gabrielle. He gritted his teeth and rode the wave of revulsion the acknowledgment always brought with it. From the first moment he saw her all those years ago, he had been hooked in a way he couldn't understand, much less explain.

Not that it was love at first sight. Far from it. They'd clashed right from the start, so much so that whenever they were together there always seemed to be sparks flying just beneath the surface of their mutual effort to be courteous. Besides, from day one Gabrielle had belonged to Joel, and that alone meant he was honor bound to keep his hands off her. It should also have meant that thoughts of her were off-limits, but for some reason he had never been able to quite manage that degree of nobility.

It bothered him that he couldn't. Then and now. He prided himself on his willpower. There was nothing he couldn't do, no challenge he couldn't face and conquer, if he set his mind to it. He was a man who disdained weakness in others, but most of all in himself. And Gaby's hold on him—as private and unacknowledged as it was—represented a weakness. She was like a fever he couldn't shake, a craving that simmered in the darkest corners of his soul.

His feelings for her confused and intimidated and irritated him in about equal parts. He wasn't good with feelings in general, and the only person he would ever have even attempted to discuss these particular feelings with was Joel, and of course that had always been out of the question.

The fact that Joel was dead only made the situation worse. Another man might feel that a friend's widow was not quite as forbidden as a friend's wife. Connor's lips curled into a sardonic smile. Obviously good old Adam subscribed to that philosophy. But not him. Oh, he understood that she was a young woman and life went on and all that. But as far as he was concerned, she was still Joel's and still off-limits and she always would be. Maybe if he hadn't had these feelings before, while Joel was alive, it would be different. But he had.

Of course, it had been easier to accept that she was off-limits when he was in Mexico with half a continent between them. It was clear that now that he was back home he was going to have to be vigilant and keep reminding himself of why he had come back in the first place. He had to remember that he was here because he owed it to Joel to protect Gaby and Toby from anyone who might hurt them. And that included him.

Suddenly he was aware that he was clenching the screwdriver so tightly it was cutting into his palm. Loosening his grip, he stared at the motor. Maybe, he thought, trying to overhaul it this morning hadn't been such a good idea after all. He was seriously contemplating abandoning the task in favor of the big hammock down by the water when he heard footsteps on the gravel driveway behind him. He groaned inwardly as every muscle in his body tightened in anticipation of round two with Gaby.

She was moving at a snail's pace, and not until she reached the front of the picnic table he was using as a workbench did Connor glance up. He was amazed to see her holding two glasses of what looked like iced coffee. Forcing a smile caused his head to throb, but he made the effort anyway.

"Morning," he said. "Which one has the arsenic?"

She managed a small smile. "Neither. It's meant as a peace offering."

"Really?" he asked, mock suspicion in the slight tilt of his head.

She laughed outright. "Yes, really. Take your pick if you don't believe me."

His gaze narrowed as he studied the two drinks she held out to him before reaching for the one in her right hand. The glass was cold and beaded with tiny drops of condensation, and suddenly his mouth was watering for the taste of iced coffee. He stopped with the glass only inches from his lips and eyed her over the rim. Arsenic seemed a little farfetched, but it occurred to him that there was no telling what she might have come across in Charlie's medicine cabinet.

"You first," he ordered.

"For heaven's sake." She rolled her eyes and took a big sip from the glass in her hand. "Happy?"

"I wouldn't go that far," he muttered, and chugged half of his coffee in one gulp.

Gaby regarded him with amusement. "I was going to ask if you wanted more sugar, but evidently it's okay as it is."

"It's perfect. Thank you." He took another, more restrained sip, wiping his mouth with the back of his hand. Lowering his glass, he glanced at her T-shirt and shorts and was instantly assailed by an image of her clad only in the bra and panties he knew she had to be wearing underneath. The day suddenly seemed even hotter. "I see the clothes fit," he remarked, averting his gaze to the lake behind her, as if he found something out there absolutely fascinating.

"More or less." She took another sip. "Did you really think I'd try to poison you?"

Connor shrugged. "Why not? I'm sure you think I deserve it. Or worse."

"True."

He met her gaze with a sardonic smile. "I thought you said this was supposed to be a peace offering."

"It is."

"Does that mean you've come to your senses, had a miraculous change of heart overnight and now realize that I'm right about everything, and that instead of the arrogant, hardheaded SOB you accused me of being, I'm actually a knight in shining armor?"

"I wouldn't go that far," she said, her tone dry as she mimicked his earlier words. "It does, however, mean that I'm willing to listen again to what you have to say and see if somehow together we can't come up with a reasonable explanation for whatever you think is going on."

"I know what's going on, Gaby," he said. "I'm just not sure of all the details or of exactly how Adam is involved."

"*If* Adam is involved," she amended.

His mouth tightened. "He is, trust me."

"I'm afraid I can't do that. I can't just take your word for the fact that a very dear friend of mine, a man who was only good to me and my son when I really needed someone, the man I intend to marry, is involved in some sordid money-laundering scheme and may even have been behind the death of my husband."

"Fine," he said. He fumbled in the toolbox for a smaller screwdriver, telling himself that since he really hadn't expected her to trust him, it shouldn't bother him so much that she didn't. "You don't have to take my word for it. You don't have to do anything. I only filled you in on what was going on as a courtesy and because you seemed so hell-bent on knowing. Your confidence and cooperation—or lack thereof—are really inconsequential."

"What is that supposed to mean?" she demanded. She stood with her weight on one hip, her arms crossed in front of her, her cool, haughty gaze getting to him like an itch in a place he couldn't scratch.

"Nothing diabolic, so you can stop looking at me as if I'm something you stepped in with one of your fancy iced apricot pumps."

"Speaking of which, there were no shoes in with the clothes you gave me."

He turned back to the motor. "That's right."

"So I'd like my own shoes back if you don't mind."

"I do mind."

"Why, for heaven's sake? You can hardly expect me to walk around barefoot all the time," she complained, her voice rising. "The stones killed my feet just getting out here."

He slanted her a distracted look as he moved to the other side of the table in hopes of finding a better angle for the screwdriver. "Then you won't be straying too far, will you?"

Understanding flared in her eyes, followed by a flash of anger.

"Of all the . . . do you really think you can keep me here by keeping me barefoot?"

"I think the odds are a lot better than they would be if I'd thrown in a pair of comfortable sneakers." He felt the screwdriver begin to slip. "Ah, damn."

"You're impossible," she told him, her words clipped and angry. "To think I actually came out here hoping we could have a rational conversation and maybe come up with answers to some of the questions you've raised."

"The hell you did," he retorted, not sure at that instant if he was more frustrated by her or the motor. "You came out here hoping you could chip away at what I told you yesterday."

Her silent shrug only served to spur him on.

"I'm sure you'd love to twist it and slant it to make it look like we're talking about a small bookkeeping error instead of a professional wash-and-dry operation for hundreds of thousands of dollars a year. And barring that, I'm sure you'd love to persuade me that your dear old friend Adam is just some kind of innocent bystander to whatever is going on instead of being at the center of it, involved in fraud and racketeering and maybe murder right up to his lying eyeballs."

"You have no proof of any of that."

"Yet," he snapped, leaning over the motor to glare at her.

"Yet?" she scoffed. "How do you expect to come up with any proof while you're hanging around here baby-sitting me?"

"I don't have to. Half the state police crime and undercover units are working on it right this minute, and the proof will come. Count on it, Gaby. And when it does, it's going down...and Adam Ressler is going with it."

Her head shook with bleak amazement. "You sound almost happy about it. I thought Adam was your friend."

"Yeah, I thought so, too."

"Don't you think that you at least owe him the benefit of the doubt?" she pressed. "That you should try talking to him?"

"The way Joel tried to? No, thanks."

Gaby went pale.

Connor tossed aside the rag he'd been using to wipe grease from the motor. "Look, I'm sorry. I shouldn't have said that."

"Why not, it's what you believe, isn't it?"

He nodded slowly, his expression solemn. "Yeah. It's what I believe."

The arms folded across her chest tightened, and it almost seemed to Connor that she shivered in spite of the heat that was sending a steady stream of sweat trickling down his back. He took a step forward, struck by a powerful and unsettling urge to reach out and offer comfort. He could almost feel what it would be like to take her in his arms, to feel the silkiness of her long hair brushing his bare skin and the delicate line of her backbone as he moved his hand consolingly along her back.

He quickly reached for the screwdriver and bent over the engine once more. He was going to loosen that blasted screw if it took him all day. After a minute or so, he sensed her moving and cursed himself for feeling a stupid hope that she was coming closer instead of trying to get away from him. A quick glance up from what he was doing told him she wasn't. That was all the time it took for Murphy's Law to kick in. The screwdriver slipped off the screw, and the pressure he'd been exerting on it was enough to drive his hand forward toward the propeller. His fingers jammed between the metal blades and the casing, and one of the rusted blade edges ripped a four-inch gash across the back of his right hand.

"Ah—" He cut off the epithet as Gaby whirled back to him, her quizzical expression giving way to one of horror as she saw the blood spurting from the open wound. From his vantage point he could see that the blade had sliced all the way to the bone.

"Oh, my God, Connor, what happened?"

"I got stupid," he muttered. He squeezed his eyes shut to see if he could stop his head from spinning. His stomach was doing the same. When he opened them again, Gabrielle was standing directly in front of him looking frantic.

"Sit down," she ordered.

"I'm fine."

"Sit."

He sat, nearly as grateful that sitting controlled the dizziness he was feeling as he was disgusted with himself for feeling it. Hell, he'd been shot, knifed and thrown from a bike doing sixty and never before gone all queasy like this. For an awful moment he thought he might actually pass out. Then the cool touch of Gaby's hands on his face drew him back from the brink of that singular humiliation.

"Let me see your hand," she said.

"Relax." He smiled weakly, the only way he was capable of doing anything at the moment. "It's just a little cut."

Gaby winced as he carefully lifted his left hand, which he had automatically pressed to the gash to stop the bleeding, exposing the injury. With the pressure removed, the blood immediately gushed freely.

"That is not just a little cut," she said. "It looks nasty, Connor, and deep. Lord, I've never seen so much blood."

"This is nothing," he insisted, glancing around and reaching for the rag he'd used earlier. "You want to see blood? You ought to—"

"No," she snapped, snatching the rag from him before he could wrap it around his hand. "That's filthy. I'll run inside and get you a clean towel." She took a step and stopped. "That is, I would run if I had shoes. You'll probably bleed to death before I make it there and back," she added, glancing from Connor to the long, stone-covered driveway that lay between them and the cabin. Blood covered both his hands now, making his good hand so slippery it was hard to exert enough pressure on the cut to staunch the flow.

"Oh, what the hell," she muttered as she grasped the bottom edge of her T-shirt and yanked it over her head. She held it flat in front of him, but Connor barely noticed. As dazed as he was, he had no trouble focusing on the sight of Gaby wearing only the bra he'd bought with her in mind.

"Give me your hand," she ordered.

"Gaby, I'm not going to ruin your—"

"Give it to me," she repeated. Loudly.

"Yes, ma'am."

He placed his hand on top of her shirt, and in a couple of seconds she had it securely wrapped.

"There," she said, tucking the end under. "Hold it against your chest, and I'll help you inside."

. "If you don't mind, I'd rather sit here for a while and—"
And look at you, he'd been about to say when she cut him off.

"You're being stupid again. That cut needs to be cleaned and bandaged in order to stop the bleeding...and you should probably lay down afterward. You look pale."

"I feel fine."

"Really, hotshot?" She stepped back and regarded him with smug impatience. "Then let's see you stand up. Come on."

He quickly got to his feet with his hand still cradled against his chest and was about to flash her a triumphant grin when a wave of light-headedness backwashed so he felt it all the way to his stomach. He instinctively slapped his uninjured hand onto the table to steady himself. Damn.

Connor met her told-you-so gaze and shrugged. "So I got up a little too quickly. What does that prove?"

"It proves," she drawled, reaching out to take his arm and placing it around her neck so that her shoulder was braced under his left arm, "that you're a stubborn, bullheaded...man who doesn't know what's good for him. Come on, lean on me."

"Can't," he muttered even as she pushed him forward. He was amazed at how the combination of sun, hangover and sudden loss of blood made a challenge of the simple act of standing erect and putting one foot in front of the other. "My extra weight on you will only make the stones hurt your feet more."

"Don't worry about me," she told him through clenched teeth, making it sound as if she was the one in pain. Connor straightened so that he wasn't leaning on her even a little bit.

"Not likely," he said, breathing hard, concentrating on reaching the steps, which seemed a million miles away. The initial shock must have worn off, because all of a sudden his hand was throbbing like crazy. "I worry about you all the time, Gabrielle. I have to. Don't you know that?"

"I don't know any such thing. In fact, it's the craziest thing I ever heard."

"Oh, yeah? Well, if I don't, who will? Did you ever ask yourself that?" His voice sounded as languid as he felt.

"No. Never."

"Well, I do. All the time." He grimaced as he reached for the banister with his good hand. "All the, ah, time. I think about you all the time, Gaby."

They climbed the stairs to the deck in silence. Gaby hurried ahead to open the door, and he heeded her command to head straight for the kitchen sink. Following him, she turned on the faucet and let it run until she decided it was the proper temperature before instructing him to hold his hand under the gentle flow.

Connor took pains not to wince as the first drops struck the open wound. He'd already come off looking like a damn wuss, but he could always blame that on heatstroke and initial shock. There was no way he was going to let her think he couldn't handle a little pain. Make that a lot of pain, he thought, wondering if maybe he'd cut a tendon or something. He spread his fingers experimentally. They all seemed to be working all right. It beat him how a cut on the back of his hand could be causing him more aggravation than a bullet he once took in the shoulder.

"Just keep holding it under the water," Gaby told him. "I'll check in the bathroom and see what I can find to bandage it."

As soon as she left the room, he pulled his hand away from the still-running water and took his first close look at the damage. Gaby was right. It did look nasty. And deep. He recalled that the propeller was rusty, but for the life of him couldn't remember the date of his last tetanus shot. Oh, well, it really didn't matter. It was going to take more than the risk of tetanus to get him down from there before he'd found out what he needed to know.

"I found something," Gaby said, hurrying back into the room. She was holding a package of Band-Aids, elastic bandage and a tube of something. "This isn't quite what I would prefer, but it will have to do. I'm going to try to smear some of this antiseptic ointment on there and then we'll just wrap it with the elastic bandage. It's bigger than the Band-Aids and it's still in the package, so it should be sterile. That ought to hold you until we can get you to an emergency room. The question is, do you want to call 911 or try making it there on the motorcycle? Personally I—"

"Neither."

She looked puzzled. "What did you say?"

"I said neither. No emergency room."

"Listen, Connor, I'm sure there are women somewhere in the world who find that tough-guy routine appealing rather than downright ridiculous. It might even come in real handy at times, as a matter of fact, but this isn't a singles bar, I'm not a candidate to be the next notch on your belt and you need to be seen by a doctor. Fast."

"No doctors."

"Are you even listening to me?" she demanded in exasperation.

"I'm listening, are you? I said no doctors."

"Why on earth not?" Her mouth tightened into a thin smile. "Oh, I get it. You're afraid to go to a hospital or see a doctor because that would give me a chance to get away. For heaven's sake, Connor, will you forget about all that? You got what you wanted by stopping the wedding. This way I'll get to go home and see my son and you can still go on with the investigation, but most importantly you'll get proper attention for your hand."

He shook his head as he rewrapped his hand in her shirt. The bleeding had slowed but not stopped completely. Walking into the living room, he looked around, trying to remember where he'd seen that sewing basket. He figured it must belong to Charlie's wife, Marie, and he remembered coming across it when he drove up there earlier and was looking for... He struggled to remember what he might have been looking for when he came across the basket.

A notepad. That was it. He quickly moved to the desk in the corner, pulled open the bottom drawer and reached for the small open wicker basket filled with needles, spools of assorted colored thread and a small pair of scissors.

"...a serious infection. Or worse," Gaby continued, and he realized belatedly that she must have been talking since they left the kitchen. Not that it mattered. There was nothing she could say that would change his mind. "You may have even done nerve damage. That's one more reason you have to have it looked at by a doctor."

He turned to face her, aware of the concern etched on her face. He couldn't help wondering if she was more worried about him or about blowing this unexpected opportunity to make her escape.

"No doctors," he repeated.

"Then I hope you're prepared to bleed to death," she said. "Because while I may not know much about medicine, even I know that cut needs stitches and lots of them."

"Then I'd say I'm a lucky man." He held up the needle and spool of white thread he'd taken from the basket. "Just what the doctor ordered . . . or would order if he could be here."

Her laugh of disbelief held an edge of nervousness, as well. "You can't be serious," she said, her voice suddenly quiet. "You're not really going to attempt to suture your own hand."

"Of course not," he replied, shaking his head. "You are."

Chapter 5

"**Y**ou're insane," Gabrielle told him, shaking her head as she took a step backward, away from the needle and thread he was casually holding out to her. "Certifiable."

She watched, astonished, as his mouth quirked into that lazy, taunting smile she knew too well.

"Why?" he drawled. "Can't you sew?"

"Buttons, yes. Human flesh I've never tried."

"Here's your chance."

"Thanks, I think I'll pass."

"Suit yourself." He tossed the spool of thread with the needle tucked inside onto a nearby table, as if that was that. Gaby was drawing a relieved breath when he continued. "Just a reminder, in case I should develop an infection and become delirious—or worse—watch the bike on those curves going downhill. She has a tendency to spin out around thirty."

Gaby tucked her tongue inside one cheek and regarded him stoically. The thought of riding that monster bike down the steep, endless hill by herself was almost as daunting as the prospect of stitching up his hand, but she wasn't about to reveal that to him. She was all too aware that Connor had a de-

cidedly sharklike mentality, and any hint of weakness would be
like spilling blood in the waters where he swam.

"It's not going to come to that," she told him finally, reaching a decision. "I'm going to call for help whether you like it
or not."

"I don't think so. That is, not unless you've got a mighty
creative way of packing a cellular phone on you."

His insolent gaze drifted over her. Gaby hurriedly crossed her
arms across her chest, acutely aware that she was still wearing
only a bra. True, it wasn't some lacy confection and was no
more revealing really than a bathing-suit top. It was still a bra,
and one that he had chosen for her, no less. Somehow that
added an even more intimate slant. Now that the immediate
crisis had passed, the sacrifice of her shirt left her feeling more
self-conscious than noble.

Connor looked disgustingly pleased with himself as she
flushed in spite of herself.

"I didn't think you were that creative. In which case, you
better take a look around, Gaby," he suggested. "There's no
phone here."

She didn't need to look. How could she have forgotten?
She'd already searched the whole cabin for a phone last night,
the minute he'd left her alone, in fact. There were phone jacks
in nearly every room, but the phones that were there when she'd
last visited were nowhere to be found. Another example of how
very thorough his preparation had been.

Of course, she mused, someone who had planned ahead so
diligently wasn't likely to have left himself open to the possibility of being stranded here incommunicado in the event of a
real crisis. There was every reason to believe that Connor had
a cellular phone hidden around there somewhere. Her gaze slid
to the window and to the acres and acres of thick woods beyond. And, she realized bleakly, almost no possibility of her
getting her hands on it if he didn't want her to.

She turned back just as he was gingerly shifting the position
of his hand against his chest and she saw the slight grimace he
was clearly struggling to squelch.

"Does it hurt a lot?" she asked.

One corner of his mouth tipped upward in an ironic smile. "Define 'a lot.'"

"Never mind, it was a dumb question. Of course it hurts. Damn you, Connor, why do you have to be so stubborn?"

"Look who's talking. It must be contagious," he muttered, adjusting the T-shirt, which was beginning to show blood-stains even on the outermost layer. "To answer your question, it hurts like hell. Sure you won't reconsider helping me out?"

"I can't," she said, unconsciously thrusting her hands behind her back. "Please don't ask me to or look at me that way. I just can't do it."

"Sure you can." He retrieved the needle and thread and smiled at her. "Just pretend I'm a great big button."

Gaby shuddered.

"Same principle," he went on. "In, out, in, out. Heck, I'd do the job myself if I weren't so clumsy with my left hand. Wouldn't want to leave any unsightly scars."

Knowing as she did that his body already bore its share of scars—souvenirs of such past adventures as a motorcycle crash, a diving accident and at least one gunshot wound that she knew of—Gaby could only assume his remark was meant as a joke. Unfortunately she wasn't in the mood to smile.

He moved closer until he was standing only inches away from her, idly tossing the spool of thread in the air and catching it. When he stopped, he looked directly into her eyes without smiling.

"Please, Gaby," he said. "Not for me. I'm sure you don't much care if I lose the damn hand. Do it for your own sake. Think about it...there's no telling what someone like me might do if I get truly delirious."

His grin reappeared, but it was pulled tight at the corners, as if it was costing him a great deal of effort to maintain it. He looked a little pale, too, she noted. At least as pale as skin burned brown by the Mexican sun could look. More to the point, he looked, she decided, like a man in pain. And even though he'd brought it on himself and deserved it, she couldn't stand by like a coward and watch him suffer.

She snatched the thread from his hand. "All right, I'll do it. But only for my own sake."

"I wouldn't have it any other way," he said drolly.

Five minutes later they were seated at the kitchen table, with her trembling hand holding the threaded needle just inches away from the end of the cut nearest his thumb. With his good hand Connor held the skin taut. Thank goodness it was a nice straight slice, she thought, wetting her lips and steeling her nerves for the task ahead.

Once she'd agreed to do it, Connor had become all business, directing her to fetch a bottle of hydrogen peroxide from the downstairs bathroom and instructing her how to sterilize the needle in the flame of his lighter. She had a niggling suspicion he had done this a time or two before. When she had everything assembled on the table, she asked him to wait one more second while she ran upstairs to grab a clean shirt. He'd caught her lightly by the wrist as she passed.

"Don't," he urged, his voice thick, his eyes hooded either with pain or something else. Gaby wasn't sure. "Please. I'm going to need a diversion while you do this, and you're very—" his eyes rested on her chest above the plunging neckline of the brassiere "—diverting just as you are."

Reluctantly she had acquiesced to his ill-mannered request and taken her place in the chair in front of him. Under the circumstances it seemed a bit obsessive to be a stickler about propriety.

It took her the better part of a half hour to do the job. She got through it by focusing on each separate stitch and not thinking about the fact that she was sewing up a man's hand rather than simply a pair of Toby's ripped jeans.

To her amazement, Connor never flinched. Only once did she dare to lift her gaze to see if he could possibly be as relaxed about this as his steady hands suggested. The sight of his rigid jaw and his gaze riveted on her bare shoulders convinced her that *relaxed* wasn't the right word. *Resolute* was more like it.

She had a sudden awareness that there wasn't much Connor couldn't endure if he set his mind to it. Or much he couldn't accomplish. Oh, she had already known there wasn't much he wouldn't do on a dare, but she had always attributed that to stupidity rather than courage. Now she was seeing a different side of his steely determination, and while it might not bode well for her immediate future, Gabrielle couldn't help feeling a grudging new respect for the man.

When it was done, she carefully cleaned the injured area with peroxide, gently applied the antiseptic ointment and bandaged it securely. Straightening at last, she wiggled her shoulders and rolled her neck from side to side. Both her jaw and her back ached from the tension that had collected in the muscles there as she worked.

Connor simply closed his eyes and exhaled deeply and with obvious relief. She would have been hard-pressed to say which of them was more thankful that it was over.

Opening his eyes, he managed to grin at her in spite of the ordeal. "See?" he taunted, "I told you that you could do it."

"Don't look so cocky," Gaby advised, shrugging off his backhanded compliment and the unexpected swell of pride it brought her. "It could still become infected."

"Not a chance. You're the best."

"Yeah. Right."

As she started to get up, he held her in her seat by reaching for her arm with his left hand. "I mean it, Gaby. Thank you."

She shrugged again. "Don't thank me. I did it for myself, remember?"

"Yeah. Right," he said, echoing both her laconic tone and her words, making it clear he wasn't buying her claim for a second.

He released her arm and she stood.

"I do think you ought to take it easy for a while," she told him.

"You might be right. At any rate I seem to have lost my enthusiasm for fixing Charlie's motor."

"What's wrong with it anyway?"

"Good question. I thought if I could get the cowling off I might be able to figure it out, but I can't even get that far. The blasted screwdriver is too long. I can't get the right angle to loosen the screw that's holding it."

"How about trying a smaller screwdriver?" she suggested offhandedly as she gathered together the thread and other supplies.

"Not a bad idea," Connor replied, "except for the fact that Charlie's selection of screwdrivers is a little on the limited side."

"Did you check the basket where you found the thread? I know I keep one of those tiny little screwdrivers in with my sewing stuff. They come in handy for a bunch of things."

"Such as?"

She smiled. "Fixing outboard motors. Sit," she ordered as he made a move to stand. "I'll take a look for you when I put the thread back."

"All right. But I think I'll sit outside for a while. I could use a change of scenery and some fresh air. Let me know what you find."

"I will, but first let me give you a hand getting outside."

His mouthed twisted with annoyance. "I cut my hand, Gaby, that doesn't make me an invalid."

"Excuse me," she retorted, lifting her brows. "It's just that you seemed a little woozy when it first happened, and I thought having the stitches put in might have left you feeling woozy all over again."

"I was not woozy," he declared, indignant. "I never get woozy. Whatever the hell that means."

"Oh, no? Then what exactly were you when you stood up out there and started swaying like a palm tree in a hurricane?"

"Hungover."

Her gaze narrowed. "What?"

"You heard me. I was hungover. Still am a little, although I have to admit that having your hand stitched without painkillers ranks right up there with black coffee for snapping you back to hard, cold reality in a hurry." He eyed her mockingly. "I know you've probably never done anything as wild and reckless as having one drink too many, Gabrielle, but I'm assuming you do understand what a hangover is."

"Of course I know what a hangover is. I just don't understand why you had one this morning."

He looked exasperated. "Then by all means let me spell it out for you. I had a hangover for the usual time-honored reason. Because I drank too much last night. Way too much, actually." His stare drilled into her. "Now, would you like to know why I drank too much?"

"Not especially," she replied, calling on a shrug to hide a sudden feeling of apprehension. "I think I'll just go check out that sewing basket."

Irked, she first went upstairs to grab a clean T-shirt from the bag of clothes he'd provided. The peep show was definitely over. While she was in her room, she heard Connor go outside. The slamming of the door echoed through the cabin just as his sarcastic words still reverberated in her head.

I know you've probably never done anything as wild and reckless as having one drink too many, he'd said.

His smug tone had left no doubt that he hadn't meant it as a compliment. As if she cared. Since when, she asked herself, was it a character flaw not to get drunk and wake up with a hangover? Not that such a comment should surprise her in the least coming from Connor. The man didn't know the meaning of the word *responsibility.* Never had. Never would.

She didn't even need to ask why he'd gotten drunk last night. Because the beer was there and so was he. For a man like Connor that would be reason enough for a party. Wouldn't it? She frowned as she ran back down the stairs. Tugging open the bottom drawer of the desk in the living room, she lifted out the sewing basket and paused with it in her hand. Had he simply been drinking for the heck of it? Or was it possible his drinking too much last night had something to do with her parting shot to him?

I wish it had been you who was killed instead of Joel.

Squeezing her eyes shut, she exhaled mightily, wishing she could simply blow the thoughtless words right out of her memory. It had been a rotten thing to think, much less begin to say to someone. Belatedly it occurred to her that perhaps this morning's peace offering to Connor should have included a small verbal apology.

She slapped the basket on top of the desk, irritated with herself for even thinking that she might owe Connor an apology. Frowning, she hastily rummaged through the basket, pushing aside safety pins and tweezers and a tangled tape measure. She was being ridiculous. She was hardly to blame for Connor's irresponsible behavior.

Or was she? If it was true that her words had caused him to drink too much, which in turn caused the hangover that caused him to be careless and injure himself, maybe she was at least partly responsible. Her eyes narrowed. Tough. She still wasn't about to apologize to the man.

At last spying a tiny screwdriver at the very bottom of the basket, she fished it out and headed for the deck with a triumphant smile.

"Is this small enough?" she asked, holding it before him.

He lifted his sunglasses and squinted at it in the sunlight, then extended his hand, palm up. Gaby dropped the screwdriver into it.

"It's short enough," he said, examining it more closely, "and it looks to be pretty sturdy, too. It just might do the trick." He looked up at her as the dark glasses dropped back into place and he smiled. "Thanks, I'll give it a try later, after the sun goes down."

Gaby responded with a curt nod. She really hated it when he smiled at her. It was so damn . . . distracting. And it had this strange effect on her stomach that made it hard to concentrate on the fact that he was the enemy.

Now that she thought about it, she hated the way he dressed, too. He was wearing an old navy blue T-shirt and a pair of faded jeans that rode low on his hips and conformed to his muscular thighs like a second skin. Granted, there was nothing unusual or sinister about the clothes themselves. What irked her was the effect they had on her senses when he was inside them. Both the shirt and jeans had a soft, oft-washed patina that tempted her to reach out and touch. At least she told herself that was what was tempting her.

She would have loved nothing more than to have been able to say that everything about Connor DeWolfe left her cold and that she couldn't understand why so many women found him irresistible. Come to think of it, she had said exactly that, many times over the years since she'd met him, but always to others, never to herself. She wasn't that good a liar.

Sprawled in one of the two cushioned redwood deck chairs, he had his bare feet propped on the other. Lowering them to the deck, he shoved the empty chair back in order to make room for her.

"Take a load off," he invited.

Gaby hesitated. In the past twenty-four hours she'd discovered that the entire cabin was a powder keg of memories for her. This corner of the deck where he'd chosen to sit, however, threatened to be the most highly charged of all. The last thing she needed or wanted was for those particular memories that lingered there to go off in her face.

"Come on, Gaby," he urged quietly. "Sit with me awhile. It's not like you have anything better to do."

She sniffed. "Actually I have a great deal I could be doing with my time if I weren't being held prisoner here."

He shrugged as if that were a detail beyond his control. "I guess you'd be on your honeymoon right about now."

"That was the plan."

"Where were you headed?"

"We were going to a private island in the Caribbean."

"Tough break," he said, neither sounding nor looking the least bit sorry. In fact, he looked pleased.

Rankled, Gaby added, "I could also point out that even doing nothing alone is better than sitting here wasting time with you."

"You could," he allowed, appearing regally unscathed by her words. "Or else you could just take off your damn armor for a while and join me in making the best of a bad situation."

"A situation of your own making," she felt compelled to add.

"That's still open to debate."

"Of course, how could I have forgotten? Adam is the one to blame for us being stuck up here together. Is that right?"

"That's how it looks to me," he said, matter-of-fact.

"Well, as usual your view of things is skewed."

"Look," he said, leaning forward with sudden animation, "do you really think I like the idea that Adam has been double-crossing us all this time? That he betrayed Joel and might have even been involved in his death?" The sunglasses hid his eyes from her, but his outrage was unmistakable in the rigid set of his jaw.

It was her turn to shrug. "I really have no idea what you like or don't like."

He stared at her, his expression gradually relaxing into the familiar lazy smile. "Don't you, now?" he asked as he settled back in his chair once again. "Well, maybe one of these days I'll get around to telling you. For now why don't we just call a truce and put the whole subject of Adam and the explosion off-limits for the time being?"

"Sure. And while we're at it, why don't you just wave your magic wand and zap me back home and we'll forget this whole thing ever happened?"

He sighed, his head bent slightly forward as he rubbed one temple with the tips of his fingers. "Lord, Gabrielle, you don't know how I wish I could." He lifted his gaze to hers. "Today is Sunday. Just give me until Friday. By then the detectives the state police have working the case should have come up with something one way or the other."

"And if they don't?"

"If they don't," he repeated slowly, as if weighing the options, "then I'll bring you home anyway if that's what you want. I'll just have to figure out some other way to keep an eye on you."

"Fine," she agreed.

Friday was five days away. It seemed like a lifetime, but at least it was something definite she could cling to. As for his intention to keep an eye on her, she would agree to anything to get back home to Toby. Once she was free, she planned to scream so loudly to the police and to file so many charges against him that Connor DeWolfe wouldn't have time to hang around pestering her or anyone else for a long time.

"Now will you sit and talk with me for a while?" he asked.

Gaby hesitated before deciding he was right, after all. It wasn't as if she had anything else to do, and the thought of spending more time shut up alone in her bedroom held no appeal at all. Pulling the chair back a few inches to give herself more legroom, she sat facing him.

Connor immediately reclaimed part of her seat as a footrest, propping one foot up beside her. When she quickly slid over a few inches so they weren't touching, he simply took the space she created as an invitation to prop his other foot there, as well.

"Comfy?" she inquired, regarding him from beneath arched brows.

"Very. Thanks."

Sighing, Gaby resigned herself to sharing the seat with him. "So, what would you like to talk about?" she asked.

"Why don't you tell me about Toby?"

Her eyes flashed warily. "Why?"

Connor appeared startled by the sharpness of her response. "No particular reason. It just struck me that he would be a safe topic for us to discuss...something we don't seem to share a whole lot of," he reminded her in a dry tone. "I figured that since he's someone we both love, we..." He stopped and stared at her, one side of his mouth curving upward in a humorless smile. "Does that come as a shock to you, Gaby? It shouldn't."

"Well, it does. Oh, I know that one of us loves him. I am his mother, after all."

"Right. And I'm..."

"Yes, do go on," she urged when he hesitated. "You're what, Connor?"

"I'm..." He paused again, looking out at the still lake, then finally back to her. "I was his father's best friend. It's only natural I take an interest in Joel's son."

"It may be natural," she agreed, "but if you don't mind my saying so, it seems rather sudden. Where has this loving interest in Toby been hiding for the past two years?"

"Touché." His grim smile was pulled tight. "I guess I deserved that. I'm sure my interest must seem rather sudden to you."

"Meaning it's not?" she asked.

"Meaning it's not," he replied, once again averting his gaze from the undisguised skepticism in hers. His voice was pitched low, a little halting. "Believe it or not, there hasn't been a day in the past two years that I haven't thought about Toby, and about you, and about all I took from both of you."

"Look, Connor, you didn't—"

He lifted his hand. "Stop, all right? I know exactly how you feel about what happened to Joel and about my part in it. So don't think you have to make nice or say things you don't believe to soothe my feelings just because you're stuck here with me."

"Believe me, soothing your feelings is not anywhere on my list of priorities," she assured him with a look of disdain. "Not even close. Honesty is, however. I was simply going to say that deep down I understand that you weren't responsible for what happened to Joel. I know that you never would have intentionally hurt him. I guess I've always known that. I just needed someone to blame, and you were the obvious choice."

His smile was hard and fleeting. "Nice to know you consider me good for something at least." He shrugged. "Anyway the fact remains that I thought about you and Toby a lot while I was away. I used to see little kids around his age and I'd wonder what he was like, if he was anything like Joel was as a kid, and what kind of things he liked to do. I thought about you, too, Gaby. I wondered how you were doing." He glanced at her briefly and shrugged.

"Of course, I knew that you were all set financially. Adam the whiz kid was seeing to that," he continued, his tone suddenly brittle. "But I wondered how you were making out with all the rest of it. And I wished . . . I wished there was something I could do to try and make up for all you lost on my account."

"You sure had a strange way of showing it," she countered, unable to completely conquer the resentment that had been buried inside for so long.

"I tried," he reminded her. "Right after Joel was . . . right after the funeral service. I came by the house to tell you that if there was anything you needed, anything at all that I could do to help, I was there for you and for Toby. You told me—"

"To go to hell," Gaby finished for him, her small smile rueful.

"Yeah, that's about the way I remember it."

"That was inexcusably rude of me. Not that it's any justification, but I was sort of out of it at the time."

"I know. No excuse necessary. Besides, you only said what a lot of people, myself included, were thinking."

She eyed him bewilderedly.

"I mean that hell was the right place for me," he explained. "So I did my best to accommodate everyone."

"By running off to Mexico?"

A weary smiled edged his mouth. "Believe me, most days it felt like hell. When I first got there, I signed on with a road-building crew that was blasting its way through a mountain of solid granite. Combine all that flying rock with a daily temperature of one hundred ten in the shade, and you come as close to hell as I ever want to get."

"One hundred ten in the shade," she echoed, shuddering. "That explains your great tan. But after what happened at the Black Wolf, why on earth would you want to work with . . . ?"

When she hesitated, recalling their truce that was only minutes old, he finished the thought for her.

"Why would I choose to work with explosives?"

Gaby nodded.

He shrugged. "It's what I know best."

"No," she said, studying him closely. "I don't think so. I don't think that's the reason at all. I think you were tempting fate."

She saw his eyes crinkle behind the dark glasses as he gave a short, disbelieving chuckle.

"Oh, really?" he asked. "Tell me, is that an educated guess or simply an ugly rumor?"

"Neither. It's my opinion. I think you were tempting fate," she said again, but with even more conviction this time. "You felt guilty because you survived the explosion and Joel didn't. There's even a name for it—survivor's guilt, I believe it's called.

By running off and playing with dynamite every day, you were giving fate a second shot at you, a chance to even the score.''

"Not quite. Oh, I can't deny that I felt plenty of guilt, survivor's and any other kind you can name," he replied, his jaw suddenly rigid. "I felt guilty believing that the bomb had been meant for me and that thanks to me Joel was just in the wrong place at the wrong time, guilty that I hadn't been able to prevent it or at least get him out of there when I got out. But the rest of your theory is pure crap. Fate can't be tempted, Gaby, I learned that a long time ago." He stared at the water. "And it doesn't stand around waiting for a second shot at anyone. Fate just does what it damn well pleases, whenever it pleases, and if that happens to upend your life in a major way, screw you."

The bitter, strangely contemptuous edge that had crept into his tone surprised her.

"That seems a rather caustic assessment of fate coming from someone who leads such a charmed existence," she remarked.

He jerked his gaze to her. "What the hell is that supposed to mean?"

"Come on, Connor, you have to admit that you're a lucky son of a gun."

"Lucky? You think I'm lucky?"

"Aren't you? I'm not being sarcastic and I'm not talking about the explosion now, either, but about your. . . life-style. You take chances most people would be scared to death to take and you walk away whistling. You do all kinds of reckless, dangerous things, things that I wouldn't dare to even dream of doing and you survive. Hell, you revel in danger."

"That doesn't make me lucky...or brave or even stupid, for that matter. Don't you see? Once you know that fate is in the driver's seat and that, when you get right down to it, it doesn't matter a rat's ass how cautious or reckless you are, it's not hard to throw yourself out of a plane or volunteer to be the one to open a ticking suitcase some jackass left on the courthouse steps. It's not hard at all once you understand that it just doesn't matter."

Gaby's brows were lowered, her tone hushed. "Are you saying it doesn't matter to you if you live or die?"

He grimaced impatiently. "If you're asking whether you're stuck here with a suicidal maniac, the answer is no. I'm saying that what I choose to do, the risks I take or avoid, have nothing to do with whether I live or die."

"That's absurd. We may not have any control over the actual moment of our death, but we can certainly better our odds of living a longer, healthier life by taking care of ourselves and not taking unnecessary chances."

"Wrong, Gaby, none of us has a damn thing to say about the odds."

"Don't give me that smug look," she retorted. "Everyone knows that the more often you play with fire the more likely you are to get burned. The same principle holds true for sky-diving and drag racing and . . ."

She stopped. He was shaking his head more vehemently now.

"You're wrong," he told her. "I know you're wrong."

He stood abruptly, and for an instant Gaby thought he was going to stalk off. Instead, he took a couple of steps away from her and leaned on the deck rail, looking out at the lake where a couple of mallards swam in lazy circles, the swirl of green feathers along their necks gleaming like emeralds in the sunlight.

For several minutes neither of them spoke. The tension radiating from his hunched shoulders was almost palpable, making Gaby wish for some tactful way of changing the subject. How had they ever gotten into so murky a philosophical realm in the first place? And how had a conversation begun merely to pass the time turned into such an emotional clash of ideas?

"I was six when my mother died," he said suddenly, without preamble and without turning his head to look in her direction. "It was August and we had been out shopping for back-to-school clothes. I was going to be starting the first grade the next week. My three older brothers hadn't wanted to go. They didn't want to waste one of their last afternoons of freedom trying on clothes for school, but I was excited by the whole idea of school and everything about it. Probably because my mother made it seem so exciting, like an adventure."

Gaby heard him draw a deep breath. There was no mistaking how much of an effort it was for him to talk about this, and she was tempted to tell him to never mind, to say that maybe she was wrong and he was right about fate and risks and that he really didn't have to try to convince her by dredging up details from his past that were obviously painful to him. It was too late for that, however. She sensed that for her to speak now would be to intrude on what had become a private moment, one too emotionally charged to be short-circuited.

"It was one of those hot, humid August days when the air is almost too heavy to breathe," he went on. "As soon as we got home, my brothers all took off to play with their friends in the neighborhood. I was upstairs with my mother, helping her sort all the new socks and underwear into piles when all of a sudden it got dark outside, real dark, almost as if night had come early. We turned on the radio, and the announcer was talking about a thunderstorm heading our way. Right away my mother ran to the front door and started yelling for my brothers to come home and to put their bikes in the garage so they wouldn't blow away.

"I remember thinking about *The Wizard of Oz,*" he continued, "and about the scene when Dorothy's house is spinning through the air and the witch comes riding by on her bike with the wind blowing all around her. The way the air felt that day, I could imagine exactly how that could have happened. It was so hot and heavy that you could feel it in your chest and you knew something was going to happen, something had to happen, or else the whole world would just explode."

He exhaled, still hunched over the railing, one hand gripping it tightly. Gaby felt as if the air around them was heavy and charged in exactly the way he described. She could almost feel the pressure building inside him, and it made her fingers curl so tightly her nails bit into her palms. The moment held a sense of inevitability. She'd ridden a roller coaster only once in her entire life, but she would never forget the feeling that had churned inside her as the car made the long, slow climb to the top of the track, knowing that a violent drop was coming any second and that there was no way to avoid it no matter how much she wanted to. She felt that same way now.

"After she called them home, my mother ran out back and began dragging in the patio furniture," he said, his voice a slow, steady monotone. "I helped her with the cushions, throwing them down the cellar stairs. My brother Jake—he was thirteen—he came home then and helped her drag the table close to the house where it would be safe. My brother Chris was rushing around picking up the bats and other stuff laying all over the yard. When the rain started, she yelled for us to go inside. Justin still wasn't home, so she went out front and called for him again. Then she ran to take the clothes off the clothesline. I watched her from the kitchen window, and up over her head I could see this giant wave of darkness coming closer and closer and I was excited and scared all at once."

Gaby's lips were pressed tightly together, her arms folded across her chest as she listened with a grim feeling of helplessness growing inside her.

"I remember her running into the house and dumping an armload of clothes on the kitchen table. By then she was really upset with Justin for not heading home as soon as he saw a storm coming. Jake wanted to ride his bike down to the ball field to see if he was there, but my mother wouldn't let him and he went off to his room in a huff. I remember she dragged out the phone book and looked up the number of Justin's friend Brian and called to see if he was there. He was at Brian's, and she told him he better stay there until the storm passed. Then she ran back outside to get the rest of the clothes.

"That black wave was right up over our house by then, and I could hear thunder in the distance getting louder with every crack. My mother was still grabbing the clothes off the line, and I remember wondering why she was bothering because it was so hard they were already wet. And I remember wishing she would just come back inside because I was getting really scared and I . . . I just wanted her to be there with me.

"I had never seen it so dark in the middle of the day," he continued. "The next thing I knew, she was yelling for Jake to bring in the dog. 'Get the dog, get the dog,' she shouted. I knew

Jake couldn't even hear her upstairs with his radio blasting, so I ran to the back door to do it. By the time I got there, she was already tossing the last of the clothes inside.

"She said to never mind, she'd get the dog herself. She was out of breath, and I knew she was upset with Jake for taking off to his room instead of helping. And then Knight—that was the dog's name, Knight—he wouldn't come when she called him. He was a huge German shepherd that would charge anything that set foot on our property, but he was crazy scared of thunder and he was cowering behind the shed. My mother ran back out to the yard to get him. It was raining hard by then, and I watched her bend down and grab his chain and . . ."

He stopped abruptly and Gaby closed her eyes. Comprehension, which had been hovering closer and closer, rose up suddenly to fill her throat. She unconsciously pressed her hand there, her teeth clamped over her bottom lip. When she opened her eyes to look at Connor, he had turned at last and his gaze found hers.

"You've probably never seen anyone struck by lightning." He said it matter-of-factly, with no trace of the emotion that had been lurking in his voice just a few seconds earlier, and that made his words all the more horrifying.

"Most people haven't," he went on. "It's fast and there's a sound like the earth splitting open, only it's happening up above you and right in front of you at the same exact instant." He shrugged. "Or maybe I just imagined that. It's just . . . it's not.." He paused and for a moment Gaby had the strong and eerie sensation that she was seeing not the Connor she'd always known—or rather, thought she had—but a six-year-old boy, overwhelmed and struggling to make sense of something that was beyond understanding at any age.

"It's something you don't forget," he concluded finally, softly. "You don't ever forget."

"Oh, Connor," she said on a ragged breath. "I had no idea. Joel never mentioned . . ."

"He didn't know," he interjected. "I never told him." A smile drifted ghostlike across his lips. "I never told anyone before today."

Please don't let her ask me why, Connor pleaded, silently calling on a God he wasn't even sure he still believed existed. Faith didn't fit very neatly into his view of life, so he preferred not to think about it. He couldn't explain to Gaby why he had told her about that day when he had never spoken about it to another living soul, because he didn't know why himself. He had never discussed what he saw with his father or his brothers or the child psychologist he had been taken to see every week for months after "the accident"—as it came to be known in his family—had occurred.

They could refer to it as an accident all they wanted. Connor had always understood that it hadn't been an accident. *Accident* implied something inadvertent, something that wasn't supposed to happen. He stopped believing in accidents the day his mother died.

Call it fate or destiny or anything else—it's just the way it was. Written in the stars. The way it was meant to be. That's all. Acknowledge and move on. And he had no idea why, after all these years, he had suddenly begun talking about it, and to Gaby of all people. He didn't want to think about the reason for that any more than he wanted to think about God.

He watched as she got to her feet and walked the few steps to where he was standing by the railing. Her touch on his arm was so light he saw more than felt it, and still it was enough to cause an immediate and portentous tightening of all the muscles in his stomach and chest. His response to her, swift and primal and beyond his control, was something he understood all too well.

"I'm so sorry, Connor," she said quietly. "That was an awful thing for a little boy to have to witness."

He tried to force a smile and found it harder than he expected, like a weight too heavy to lift. Giving up, he shrugged instead. "Yeah, well. It was a long time ago."

"Of course." She dropped her arm to her side, her expression rueful. "And time heals all wounds, right? I've heard that line more times than I care to count in the past couple of years, and you know what? I don't buy it. Time doesn't heal a damn thing. It doesn't erase the pain or lessen it, it simply gives you more practice at hiding it from everyone else." Her smile deepened with self-deprecation. "And from yourself, too, sometimes. Then one day, when you're least expecting it—"

"Wham," he broke in. "Right in the gut."

She nodded, her small smile edged with sadness in a way that tore loose something buried deep inside him.

"Wham. That says it exactly," she said. "Sometimes when Toby does something funny or clever, I look at him and out of nowhere comes this massive wall of pain and I just miss Joel so much it takes my breath away."

"Yeah, I know." He managed a feeble smile at last. "I never buy new socks or underwear without breaking into a cold sweat."

She tipped her face up to look at him, her beautiful eyes slightly narrowed, her soft mouth pursed thoughtfully. As if, it seemed to Connor, she had been presented with one of those psychedelic-looking posters that contained a hidden picture and she couldn't quite figure it out.

He sighed, his smile sardonic. "You're wondering why I told you about this when I never even told my best friend."

"Yes," she said, nodding. "I am wondering about that. Among other things."

"I can't explain it," he told her. "I certainly didn't plan on talking about it when I asked you to sit with me. Maybe I was just ready to talk to someone and you were handy."

She looked skeptical. He didn't blame her.

"Then again," he continued, "maybe it's because I've always known how much you disapprove of me and of my 'lifestyle,' as you put it, and when you made that remark about me tempting fate I just wanted to set the record straight once and for all."

"You certainly don't owe me any explanations about how you choose to live your life."

"Don't I? Seems to me I owe you something. I gave you some rough times through the years, when I wanted Joel to come along on some crazy stunt or another that you thought was too dangerous."

"That I *knew* was too dangerous," she corrected. "And you always dismissed my concerns as if they were nothing."

"Now you know why."

Her smile slipped away. "Yes. Now I know why."

"My mother was a very cautious woman, Gaby. She never left the house without checking to see that the stove was off and grabbing an umbrella just in case it should rain. And Joel, hell, Joel carried a spare key in his pocket and had a spare for the spare tucked inside his wallet."

They both laughed, and when their eyes met they both fell abruptly silent, as if caught in some transgression. Gaby looked away first, awkwardly dropping her gaze to the deck below. Connor moved restlessly toward his chair.

"No doubt about it, Gaby. If being cautious was enough to keep you safe, they'd both be alive today." He sat down, leaning his head back against the chair cushion with a weary sigh. "Instead of me."

His eyes were closed, and he wasn't aware she had sat down again until she spoke. Her tone was soft and warm and when he opened his eyes to look at her, she was leaning forward in her chair and smiling at him.

"He's a lot like Joel," she said. At his confused glance, she added, "Toby. You said you wondered if he was like Joel. He is. His smile, his laugh, even his sense of humor. Of course, he's still only five, but Toby is...exceptional." She raised her hand as if to ward off any protest, her smile both sheepish and proud. "Oh, I know, I know, that's what every mother says about her child, but Toby really is special. He has this air of serenity that seems to come from someplace deep inside. As if he's centered somehow."

"Like Joel," Connor said, his voice gruffer than usual.

Gaby nodded. "Like Joel. I think that being so sick for all those months added to his tendency to be self-reliant."

Connor levered forward, feeling as if someone had just swung a hard right at his gut and connected. "What are you talking about? When was he sick?"

She looked startled briefly, then shook her head. "I'm sorry. I just assumed you knew but, of course, how could you have?"

"Knew what, for God's sake? Is Toby all right or isn't he?"

"Yes. Well, at least we think he is. The doctors..."

He shot to his feet, unable to sit quietly for this. "Hell, Gaby. Why didn't you call me or send a message if the kid was sick?" He caught her wry expression and grimaced. "All right, all right. I guess I'm not exactly your idea of a knight in shining armor. I still wish I had known."

He forced himself to sit. "What was wrong with him?" he demanded.

"You remember he had that heart problem when he was born? A small hole near—"

Connor nodded impatiently, cutting her off. "Yes, but that was all taken care of before they sent him home from the hospital."

"So we thought," she said ruefully. "A few months after Joel was killed, Toby passed out on the jungle gym at the playground. When they examined him at the hospital emergency room, they discovered that in addition to the concussion and bruises he suffered from the fall, his heart was malfunctioning. That's what caused him to black out in the first place."

"Hell," he muttered, roughly dragging the hair back off his forehead. "You must have been half-crazy with worry."

"More than half, actually. He had to have emergency surgery. Twice," she amended, shuddering at the recollection in a way that sent frustration shooting through Connor, along with an all-too-familiar desire to go back and change the past. "It was touch and go for a while afterward. He was kept in the hospital for weeks of recovery—no easy thing for a three-year-old, believe me—and then confined to bed at home for a long time after that."

He shook his head at the thought of as active a little kid as he remembered Toby being restrained for all that time. "And now?" he asked, his clipped tone urgent. "How is he now?"

"Like I said, he seems to be fully recovered. The doctors still want to see him for periodic checkups, but they tell me that he's as good as new. Correction," she said, smiling happily. "Make that better than new."

Connor relaxed his fists, aware for the first time how tightly they'd been closed and how badly his hand was throbbing as a result. "Good. That's really good." With a small shrug he dropped his hands to the arms of the chair and sat back. "I wish I had been here for you. There might have been something I could have done. Some way I could help out."

"Thanks. We managed fine. Toby and I make a great team, and I had my mother and my sister to help. And Adam, of course."

Connor felt his blood temperature plummet so low it was inevitable that the sudden iciness would spill over into his voice, as well. "Of course. Good old Adam."

"I know you have your suspicions about him, Connor, but I have to tell you he was wonderful to Toby and me when we really needed him."

He smiled tightly, his soul feeling like a dart board.

"He never left my side when Toby was in the operating room and he handled all the hospital forms and bills so I didn't even have to look at them. And later, after Toby was allowed to come home, he spent hours at our place entertaining him, playing checkers and the Batman game and anything else Toby wanted to play."

The softness of her expression made Connor feel like punching Adam Ressler right in the jaw. "Like I said, good old Adam."

"I owe him a lot, Connor."

"Is that why you agreed to marry him? To pay him back for playing checkers with the kid?"

"I resent that," she snapped. As always there was no trace of that sweet-hearted softness in the look she aimed at him.

"You ought to," he drawled. "It's a hell of a lousy reason to marry someone."

"That is not the reason I'm marrying Adam."

"Then what is?"

"There are several. Not that it's any of your business. It so happens that I do think he's an excellent role model for Toby, and there's the restaurant to consider, and the fact that we get along beautifully. We always have." Her mouth curled. "Unlike you and me."

"You forgot to say you loved him."

"Did I?" She shrugged.

"Go on, Gaby, say it. Tell me that you're in love with Adam Ressler."

"I . . ."

He watched her chest rise and fall as she drew a deep breath. Her eyes glinted with resentment.

"Say it, Gaby."

"I. . . Love will come," she insisted. "For now we share other things just as important to a good marriage as love. Things like friendship and respect and something you wouldn't understand, a mutual concern for our future and Toby's."

"A mutual concern for your future, huh? That sounds more like a merger than a marriage to me."

"I told you that you wouldn't understand."

"So enlighten me," he urged, arching back into the seat, his long legs stretched in front of him. "Better yet, tell me this, does Adam know about the friendship-mutual-respect angle of the deal?"

"Of course," she replied, clearly indignant. "We've discussed the matter openly, like two mature adults—another concept beyond your understanding, I'm sure—and we've agreed that we have ample foundation for a sound marriage and that in time we can learn to love one another."

"Gosh, that sounds romantic."

"Maybe I'm not looking for romance."

"What are you looking for, Gaby?"

"Safety, security, a decent future for my son," she replied without hesitation. She crossed her arms in front of her, a defensive move if he'd ever seen one, Connor thought with satisfaction. "And companionship. Adam is a kind, decent man, who—I might add—is no doubt worried sick about me right this very minute."

"Well, hallelujah," he exclaimed, throwing his hands in the air and grinning. He glanced at his watch. "Just over twenty-four hours. That's got to be some sort of record."

"Record for what?" She eyed him suspiciously. "What on earth are you ranting about now?"

"About the fact that it took you that long to express some concern for your poor, worried intended."

"What do you mean?"

"I mean that all afternoon yesterday you carried on about Toby and your family and the guests invited to the wedding, but this is the first time you actually mentioned feeling any concern for Adam or the fact that he might be worried about you, as well."

"Don't be ridiculous, of course I mentioned..." She stopped, her brows lowering thoughtfully. "I just assumed that you would assume that... Oh, stop giving me that look."

"What look?" he asked, still grinning.

"That stupid gloating look. For your information, this isn't high school. How many times I mention his name in a day isn't any indication of my feelings for Adam."

"Of course not," he agreed. "So how about sex?"

Her eyes widened. "What?"

"Sex. I asked about sex."

"Are you asking about sex between Adam and me?"

"If you're willing to answer, then I'm definitely asking. But I was actually referring to the fact that you ticked off a whole long list of things you're looking for in this marriage, and sex wasn't on it. So I can't help wondering..."

She scowled at him, evidently hoping to scare him off with the silent threat of her everlasting wrath. Obviously, he thought, she didn't remember him nearly as well as she claimed.

"I can't help wondering," he said again, sliding forward in his chair until his knees bracketed hers, "if Adam can make you shiver on a hot day just by bringing his mouth real close to yours. Like this."

Chapter 6

"Stop," Gaby ordered.

"Stop what? I'm not doing anything. Yet."

Connor was whispering, leaning forward so that his mouth hovered barely an inch from hers. As she'd backed away from him, he had moved in on her, bracing his hands on the arms of her chair for support. Now, with her body already pressed to the back of her chair, she had nowhere to go.

"This isn't funny," she told him.

He pulled off his sunglasses and tossed them on the chair behind him. "No, it isn't. Better be careful, Gaby, we're beginning to see eye to eye on things."

"For God's sake, Connor..." She put her hands on his arms to push him away.

"Why don't you answer my question?" he asked, refusing to be pushed.

She made an exasperated sound. "What question?"

"Can Adam make you shiver on a hot day the way I can?"

"You can't make..."

Even as she spoke, he brought his mouth a fraction of an inch closer to hers and let his breath warm her lips. Her eyelids fluttered shut, concealing the confusion behind them, but there was no hiding the tiny goose bumps that erupted on the smooth flesh of her shoulders and arms. Her protest remained unfinished.

"I can," he said with quiet satisfaction.

"Don't."

"I want to kiss you, Gaby," he told her, his whisper growing hoarse and urgent. He hadn't expected her to smell so good or feel so soft, and the combination was causing what had started out as teasing to spin out of his control. "Just like I wanted to kiss you the last time we were here alone like this. Do you remember that day?"

"No," she said quickly. Too quickly.

He chuckled. "Liar."

Her chin came up fiercely, causing their mouths to bump. Immediately she jerked away, but the defiance remained in her voice. "What's the matter, Wolf?" she asked. "Did I bruise your ego?"

He laughed again at the scalding inflection she gave to his old nickname.

"Does it irk you to think that not every woman who meets you finds you unforgettable?" she taunted.

"Not at all," he replied. "I don't much give a damn about every woman I meet. But it does bother the hell out of me that you don't remember that day when the memory of it has cost me a few sleepless nights in the years since."

Her eyes widened in surprise, signaling that his words had struck their mark.

"So, seeing as how you don't remember that day and I do, and in great detail," he added, "I guess I'll just have to refresh your memory for you."

"Don't bother."

"No bother at all," he assured her, pulling back just enough so that he could watch her face as he spoke. "I'm sure you haven't forgotten the week we all planned to spend together up here. It was before Toby was born, so it must have been at least six or seven years ago. We spent a lot of time together back then. You and Joel, Adam and . . . what was her name?"

She stared at him in silence.

Connor shrugged. "It doesn't matter. You might recall that my date canceled out at the last minute. It wasn't a big disappointment except for the fact that I'd really been looking forward to the week up here and I didn't want to come alone and be a fifth wheel. Would you like to know why I was looking forward to that week so much?" he asked her.

"No," she replied.

"I'll tell you anyway. It was because of you, Gaby. I was looking forward to being around you for a week."

"Now who's lying?" she retorted. "Admit it, Connor, you've always barely tolerated me and for the same reason I barely tolerated you. For Joel's sake."

He shook his head, a self-mocking smile on his lips. "No, I'm afraid *tolerate* isn't quite the right word to describe how I felt about you. Oh, I won't deny that you rubbed me in about a dozen wrong ways right from the moment we met, but for some insane reason that never affected all the other feelings I had for you. Tolerated? No. Fascinated. Now, there's a much better word to describe what I felt."

She shifted in the chair, making a move to stand, but Connor held his ground.

"I'm not finished."

"Well, I am. I don't think I want to hear any more of this," she told him.

"That's too bad, because all of a sudden I want you to hear it. I want you to know how I felt now, even if you really didn't know back then."

Their gazes locked in silent warfare. Had she shared something of what he'd felt that long-ago day? Connor wondered. Or had he simply wanted to believe that she had? Whatever she might have felt, along with whatever she remembered of that day, was locked behind the stare of pure blue ice she was training on him right now. Connor refused to back off. He wasn't sure why unlocking the truth mattered so much to him. Only that it did.

"Around about Thursday of that week I finally decided that fifth wheel or not, I was coming up for a few days. It was a day a lot like today. Hot. Muggy. The air heavy and full of the smell of the trees all around." He shifted his weight so he was squatting in front of her, his outstretched arms still barring her escape.

"When I got here the cabin was empty. You were all off fishing further upstream," he continued, indicating the path of the stream that fed the lake. "I went for a swim, had a few beers."

He chuckled as Gaby rolled her eyes smugly.

"Like I said," he went on, "it was a day a lot like today. I sat out here on the deck to wait, and the next thing I knew I saw you coming through the woods, right over there."

He pointed to the spot, but Gaby refused to turn her head to look.

"You were wearing cutoff denim shorts and a flimsy white top that let me see a little of your skin and your bra when the sun hit it just right." He half smiled, wondering if he should tell her how, when he went shopping for her a couple of days ago, he had searched hard for a bra that reminded him of the one she'd been wearing that day.

"So you're a voyeur along with everything else," she said, lifting one slender shoulder in an elegant shrug. "It doesn't surprise me."

He decided against mentioning his shopping excursion.

"No?" he countered. "This might. I took one look at you that day and my blood started rushing. Just like it always did when I saw you. I felt the way I always felt when you walked into a room, excited and like a bastard at the same time. Happy and guilty, always the two together, all mixed up inside of me in a knot. You belonged to Joel, and Joel was the best friend I ever had. Hell, he was more like a brother than my own brothers. I knew without any doubt that you were way off-limits, I just never knew what I was supposed to do with all those feelings I couldn't stop myself from feeling."

She was silent, her gaze averted, her jaw rigid. Good thing he didn't put much stock in body language, Connor thought, or he'd just slink off into the woods and shoot himself right then and there.

"When I saw that you were alone, I was..." He paused, grasping for words to express the feeling. His mouth curving grimly, he finally settled on "Euphoric. Then I realized you were hurt."

"I cut my toe," she said quietly, still not looking at him. "I thought I was getting too much sun so I decided to come back to the cabin ahead of the others and I cut my toe on a rock on the way. I didn't expect anyone to be here."

"You mean you didn't expect me to be here. I'm sure if you had, you never would have come back alone."

She met his gaze. "That's right."

"As it turned out, you were lucky I was here. It was me who patched you up that day."

"True, but at least I didn't need stitches."

"No, just a shot of whiskey."

"Which you poured on my toe," she continued, almost giving in to the smile that threatened to form on her lips.

"To sterilize it," he reminded her. "You said you didn't want it to become infected."

"I didn't. But I never expected you to pour whiskey on my toes or to..."

She stopped, memories and secrets moving in a heated swirl behind her shuttered gaze. Connor's heart lifted in his chest.

"Kiss it better?" he prompted, his words rough and raspy as he moved closer and slid his hand down her leg to caress her bare foot.

"That was just a joke."

"Not to me."

He lifted her foot to his mouth and kissed her toe the way he had that afternoon years ago. His mouth was slow and warm and wet. And just as she had back then, Gaby gasped and stiffened but didn't pull away. He smiled at her, running the thumb of his uninjured hand back and forth along her instep. "I wanted to kiss you that day, Gaby. I wanted it real bad. I still do."

She took an uneasy breath, her brow furrowed. "Please, Connor...what do you expect me to say to that?"

"The 'Please, Connor' part was a good start," he replied, moving up so he was leaning over her once again. "Try saying . . . 'Please, Connor, kiss me.'"

She shook her head. "I can't."

"That's what you said to me the last time. The difference is that you were right back then. You couldn't. God knows I shouldn't have even tried." He shook his head, remembering. "Afterwards I tried to shake it off by blaming it on the beer or temporary insanity and I swore it would never, ever happen again."

"Nothing happened that day, either."

"Right. Technically nothing did happen. Just the same, ever since that day I've carried the scars on my conscience to remind me of what a bastard I can be." He put his hand against her cheek, the smoothness of her skin sending a ripple of pleasure through him. "Back then there was a reason to stop. Joel."

"There's still a reason," she insisted, nervousness in her tone. "Adam."

"I don't give a damn about Adam," he growled.

"But I do," she said. "I'm supposed to marry the man . . . I would be married to him right now if it weren't for you."

"That marriage is never going to happen," he told her with utter conviction. "I'm right about Adam. I know I am. Adam is not a reason for us to stop."

"All right, have it your way. Leave Adam out of it. But you can't just forget about Joel. Neither of us can," she said frantically just as his mouth lowered to slant across hers.

Connor froze, then pulled back. "Gaby, Joel isn't here. I wish to hell he was, but he's not. He's gone."

"He's still between us," she insisted. "He always will be."

Running his hand through his hair, he lowered his weight to one knee, his somber expression gentle. "He'll always be with us, I believe that, but I also believe that Joel would want you to go on living, Gaby. He'd want you to be happy."

"What Joel would want," she said, taking advantage of his relaxed position to leap from the chair and push past him before whirling around to face him, "is for me to put his son's welfare ahead of everything else. I can do that by marrying someone who'll protect him and set a good example for him, someone decent—"

"Like Adam?" Connor interrupted angrily.

"Yes, someone like Adam. Joel certainly wouldn't want me to get mixed up with a man I wouldn't trust to baby-sit my cat for a weekend . . . a man who once made a play for me behind his back, for heaven's sake."

Gaby spun toward the door to the cabin, but not before she saw Connor recoil as if she'd lashed out at him with a spiked whip rather than simply the first words that flashed to mind. She made it to the door and yanked it open before her sense of decency and fair play grabbed her and jerked her to a halt.

Pausing with the door still open, she allowed the rapidly building wave of second thoughts to crash over her, waiting for them to sweep past before she tried to swim back to the surface. She'd gone and done it again. She'd let Connor get to her, let him trap her inside a storm of her own emotions, emotions she didn't want to feel and couldn't understand. And once again she'd reacted by blurting out nasty, hurtful things she would never ordinarily say to another human being. Two days alone with the man and she was turning into someone she didn't even know.

He'd provoked her, to be sure. Once again, however, she couldn't ignore her sense that all his many faults didn't justify what she'd said to him. As much as it pained her to admit that to herself, much less Connor, she'd be damned if she'd slink off and spend more hours cooped up alone in her room with a guilty conscience.

Drawing a deep breath, she let go of the door and turned back to face him. He'd reclaimed his seat, his feet once more propped up on the empty chair, his face tilted up to the sun.

"Look," she said, coming to a halt a few away from him. "I'm sorry. That was a rotten thing for me to say."

He shoved his sunglasses to the top of his head and squinted at her as if she'd just woken him from a long nap. "What was?"

"Knock it off, Connor. I shouldn't have made that crack about not trusting you to baby-sit a cat and . . . and about you making a play for me."

"Oh. That." He dropped the glasses back into place. "Forget it. No blood, no foul."

"Don't do that," she snapped.

He sighed. "What am I doing wrong now, Gaby?"

"You're closing up again, playing the part of the big, strong tough guy whom nothing can ever hurt."

He unleashed an insolent smile. "I am a tough guy, remember?"

"Even tough guys have feelings."

"Honey, if I didn't know you better, I'd think you were worried about hurting my feelings."

"Maybe I am."

"Is this the same woman who once called me a no-good, low-life jerk? The same woman who said I—"

"Yes, yes," she said, cutting him off. "And I still hate you for keeping me here and I don't share your suspicions about Adam, but deep down I guess I know that you believe you're doing the right thing and that your motives are sincere."

"Careful, Gaby, you're getting mighty close to calling me your hero."

"Don't hold your breath, DeWolfe. I just want to say that I know how hard it was for you to open up to me about things in your past that were extremely painful and I wasn't very gracious in return."

"Forget it. I'm not the only person in the world whose mother died."

"I wasn't talking only about your mother's death. I'm sure it was also hard for you to talk about your feelings for me."

"My feelings for you," he repeated, as if trying to figure out what she was getting at.

"Yes. You trusted me, and I repaid your trust by overreacting and I'm sorry."

"My feelings . . . Oh, you mean about you being an itch I never got to scratch?"

Gaby flinched. "I suppose that's one way of putting it."

"I'll live," he said, shrugging. "You can't blame a guy for trying when you're everything he likes in a woman." The dark glasses did little to conceal the hungry look he ran over her before casually adding, "Not that there's very much I don't like in a woman."

"You're impossible," she said, not sure whom she was angrier with, Connor for his insolence or herself for turning around and apologizing in the first place. After all, you could hardly fault a panther for pouncing on raw meat. "I don't know why I waste my time talking to you."

"My irresistible charm maybe?"

"Hardly. It's probably because for one brief shining moment I thought there was a scrap of something redeemable inside that obnoxious shell."

"Don't take it too hard, Gabrielle. We all make mistakes."

She resisted the urge to punch him. "Just tell me one thing, Connor, if you're really so tough and nothing anyone says gets to you, why did you drink too much beer last night?"

"Why?" He tipped his head to the side carelessly. "Why else? Because it was there."

Liar, she thought as she strode away. *Liar, liar, liar.*

Inside the cabin she paced for a while, eventually finding an old mystery novel on a shelf in the living room, and carried it down by the lake to sit and read. Or tried to. It was nearly impossible to concentrate on the words on the page when her own thoughts were in such turmoil.

Connor could say he drank too much simply because it was there, but she wasn't buying it. Not for a second. She knew differently and she'd be willing to bet he'd gotten drunk to escape an old and persistent demon. She knew because the same old demon haunted her, as well. She'd just never tried to hide from it in a bottle.

For years she'd relied on self-control, ignoring her demon, denying it, locking the mere thought of it away in a safe place where she didn't have to acknowledge the truth to herself, much less to anyone else. It was just too upsetting to think that she could ever, in any way, be attracted to a man she disdained as vehemently as she did Connor. But Lord help her, she was attracted to him. That was her demon . . . and his, she suspected. She knew it now just as she had known it that afternoon years ago when he had kissed her toes and made her shiver with a longing she had no right to feel.

That day, too, she had left him alone on the deck and run off feeling guilty. And afraid. Afterward she had wanted to tell Joel what had happened. She'd wanted to hear him laugh and tell her in his levelheaded way that just because they were married didn't mean they were immune to a little temptation now and then. She'd wanted him to dismiss the whole incident, reassuring her that he trusted her and that she hadn't done anything wrong.

Because she hadn't. She'd loved Joel with all her heart. She was never unfaithful to him and never would have been. Still, what had happened that day with Connor had felt wrong, and she'd known that was because it hadn't happened simply as a result of too much sun or too much beer. That moment on the deck had been a long time coming. And the aftershocks of it had lingered long afterward. In fact, she realized, they were still being played out today, years later.

Beneath the irreverent retorts and the low-level animosity that characterized their relationship, something else was always simmering between Connor and her. It had been there from the start. If she was totally honest, she'd have to admit that in part her resentment of Connor was due to this other feeling, this attraction or chemistry or whatever it was. "The lady doth protest too much, methinks." That line could have been written for her, she acknowledged wryly.

She'd always kept Connor at a distance, professing to find him irksome and irresponsible, because deep down she was afraid. Not afraid of Connor, but of a side of herself that he alone seemed to understand and that his very existence silently threatened to unleash. In subtle ways he made her aware of a reckless, uninhibited side of herself that had been systematically shushed and squelched by parents and teachers and society's expectations . . . by life itself, she supposed.

It was a side of her that wasn't afraid to ride a fast motorcycle or let the wind mess up her hair, that wasn't afraid to take

a chance or to sometimes choose having fun over being responsible. A side of her that wasn't afraid of the way a man like
Connor could make her feel. Worse, that other, alien side of her
wanted to feel that way, she wanted it all and she didn't care
who or what stood in the way.

At least that's the way it had seemed to her sometimes when
Connor was around, and so she had gone to great lengths to
hide that reckless streak inside from herself and from others.
She'd played it safe by keeping that other side submerged inside the more sensible, practical Gabrielle, and by always staying out of Connor's way. She became the perfect wife and
mother, standing on the sidelines, watching and worrying and
making sure that the grocery shopping got done and the beds
got made and that everyone had clean underwear.

And for what? she thought now as she let the mystery novel
fall to her lap and stared out over the quiet lake. Her heart was
twisting inside her. Clean underwear and nutritious meals
hadn't stopped Joel from being killed or Toby from getting
sick. She thought of what Connor had said about his mother
never leaving the house without an umbrella and then she
thought about the folding umbrella always tucked under the
seat of her own car, and her mouth curved into a sad smile. If
she had only a short while to be with those she loved, would she
rather be remembered as the woman with the umbrella or a
woman with the wind in her hair, a woman who knew how to
laugh and how to live?

Gaby drew a deep breath. Making the choice was easy. It was
living it that took courage. She had always shaken her head in
disapproval whenever Connor had involved Joel in one of his
exploits. She'd never acknowledged, not even to herself, how
easily she could have been swept up in one of those adventures
and loved every second of it. She'd accused Connor of bringing out the "worst" in Joel because she was able to see so
clearly how easily he could bring out the "worst" in her, too.

Only all of a sudden the worst didn't seem so bad. Connor
didn't seem so bad, she thought, shocking herself. Even his
philosophy of life, which she had always dismissed out of hand,

was understandable when you considered the events in his past. And in her own, she realized, sighing heavily.

They had a lot in common, Connor and her, and yet she'd always been wary of him. Guilt and fear, all of it kept carefully hidden beneath the surface—that's what had shaped her relationship with Connor through the years. Guilt over the fact that part of her connected with him in a way that she didn't even connect with her husband. And fear of what might happen if that part of her was ever set free.

She could see now that the guilt had been misguided. She had been singularly faithful to Joel and she would be still if he had lived. In the end that's what counted. She had done nothing to be ashamed of and she'd been wrong to blame herself for a feeling. She'd also been wrong a little while ago when she snapped at Connor about the kind of man Joel would want her to fall in love with now that he was gone. The fact is that Joel would never have presumed to tell her such a thing. What Joel would tell her was to follow her instincts and do whatever made her happiest and damn the consequences. As solid and dependable as he was, she thought, smiling gently, he hadn't been Connor's best friend all those years for nothing.

Guilt and fear. She lay back on the grass, the book forgotten as she felt a long-held tension draining from her. Guilt and fear. Such a waste of time and energy. Her eyes closed and the warmth of the sun relaxed her muscles, making them feel like jelly. All those years of guilt and fear. Oh, well, she thought, letting go with a yawn, at least now the guilt was gone.

She felt herself drifting off to sleep and didn't fight it. She awoke gradually, aware of Connor calling to her from the deck. Sitting up, she twisted around and peered at him through the low-hanging branches of the willow tree behind her. The angle of the sun suggested she had been asleep for several hours.

"What is it?" she called to him, reluctant to rouse herself further unnecessarily.

"Are you hungry?" he shouted.

She was, Gaby realized suddenly. Very. Although she'd eaten a late breakfast, they had skipped lunch and that cinnamon muffin seemed ages ago.

"Yes, starving."

"Then come on. Dinner's ready."

She stood, brushing grass from her shorts, and walked toward the cabin, staying on the grass and avoiding the crushed-stone path that was murder on her bare feet. As she crossed the deck, she caught a whiff of something so delicious her mouth watered and stomach growled. Inside, the aroma was even more tempting. She paused just inside the kitchen and stared at the table.

White plates had been set atop a dark-blue-and-white-plaid tablecloth. There were matching napkins folded beside each of the two plates, and chunky dark blue wine goblets and white candles in rustic wooden candle holders. There was even a bunch of wild daisies stuck in an old metal jug. But what caused Gaby to stare in amazement was the dinner set before her. There was salad in a wooden bowl, a platter of crisp barbecued chicken and corn on the cob, and a basket of buttermilk biscuits. It was obviously a meal that had been carefully planned and prepared with as much attention to detail as the table setting. It was also a long way from the grilled hot dog or peanut-butter-and-jelly sandwich served on a paper plate that she'd been expecting since Connor yelled to her.

"You can cook," she said, dragging her gaze from the table to where he was uncorking a bottle of wine.

He finished twisting the cork loose before turning to her with a shrug. "There wasn't a whole lot of cooking involved in this meal, but yes, I can cook. You don't have to look so shocked," he added dryly.

"I am shocked. It's easier to picture you jumping out of a plane than wearing an apron."

"Real men don't wear aprons," he retorted, deadpan. "And I look on cooking as sort of the ultimate survival skill. You ought to taste my Shanghai shrimp."

"Right now I can't wait to taste this. It smells wonderful."

"Then have a seat and dig in," he urged.

He followed her to the table, holding her chair for her as she sat. As if, Gaby couldn't help thinking ironically, they were a couple dining at a posh restaurant instead of captor and capive, stuck together in the middle of nowhere. He poured the wine and lit the candles, holding the lighter aloft afterward.

"I told you we might need this later."

"Silly me," she retorted, "I had no idea there were candlelit dinners in my future. You're just full of surprises, Connor."

He grimaced as he reached for the platter of chicken.

"You really don't like being called that, do you?" she asked, already knowing the answer.

"Connor? No, as a rule I really don't."

"Why?"

He held the platter in front of her. "Chicken?"

"Thank you." She took a piece. "Why?"

"You don't back off gracefully, do you?"

Gaby lifted one shoulder. "I figure I don't have anything to lose by being persistent. If you get irked enough, you just might take me home early."

"I don't irk that easily." He helped himself to chicken and corn, then lifted his head to meet her waiting gaze. "It's no big deal about the name. My mother called me Connor. Everyone else always called me Con. After she died, I went through what I guess you'd call a stage. That's when my brothers started calling me Wolf, short for Lone Wolf, which a few years later was changed to Black Wolf because I had this black T-shirt and jeans that I wore a lot."

She arched one brow.

"All right, I wore them nonstop for about six months," he admitted, his expression sheepish.

"Another stage?" she asked, her nose wrinkling at the picture he'd presented.

"I guess. I was thirteen," he added as if that explained everything.

"I see."

"I suppose I got used to being called Wolf by everyone. At some point that just became who I was, how I thought of myself, how I introduced myself. The name Connor was part of the past, a whole other lifetime and . . ."

"And it brings back memories of your mother," she finished softly when he trailed off.

His mouth quirked. "Yeah, it does."

"I understand." She flashed him a smile. "Wolf it is, then."

"No," he said quickly. He shrugged. "Over the past couple of days I've gotten used to hearing you call me Connor and I sort of like it."

"Then why did you grimace a minute ago?" she asked, skeptical.

"Because I brushed the back of my hand against that hot platter." With a rueful expression he held up his bandaged hand. "That's the last time I go messing around a rusty motor with a hangover."

"Does it hurt a lot?"

He shrugged. "Only when I cook over a hot grill. Or splash boiling water on it when I'm dropping corn in the pot. Or touch a hot platter. Or..."

She broke off in the middle of a commiserative wince to eye him warningly. "Connor DeWolfe, are you looking for sympathy?"

"Is it working?"

"Yes," she admitted, laughing.

"Then I'm looking."

Gaby shook her head, still laughing. "Just be quiet and eat your dinner."

"Is that what you say to Toby?"

"Yes, as a matter of fact, but he always listens."

Grinning silently, he picked up his fork, and for a while they both ate without talking.

The meal tasted as good as it looked and smelled. Gaby even succumbed to seconds and then groaned when he offered strawberry shortcake for dessert. He refused to accept her polite protests that she was full, tempting her until she finally gave in and tried a small piece. It didn't even surprise Gaby to find that the sweet, flaky biscuit beneath the fresh sliced strawberries was homemade, any more than it surprised her to learn that he had made a special trip to the cabin to stock the pantry the night before bringing her there. She didn't think anything could ever surprise her again where Connor was concerned.

He wasn't what she'd thought, she realized, or maybe he was exactly what she'd thought and had struggled so hard to deny. She wasn't sure yet, and it was going to take some time to figure it out. She only knew that if a woman had to be stuck in a cabin with a man, she could do a lot worse.

Now that she wasn't constantly looking for him to do or say something wrong, he was actually very easy to be with, funny and talkative and utterly attentive, as if every word she spoke was of the greatest importance to him. It didn't hurt any that he was also gorgeous and sexy and armed with enough seductive charm to make a woman on the verge of turning thirty feel like a teenager on her first date.

No wonder the man never lacked for female companionship, she thought dryly. Recalling the many lean, leggy blondes she had seen him with through the years, Gaby couldn't help wondering why he had ever looked twice at her at all, never mind had the kind of intense, sustained interest he claimed. There was only one explanation, she told herself as she helped clear the table after dinner while he loaded the dishwasher. The lure of the forbidden.

He'd been interested in her precisely because she was Joel's wife and therefore off-limits. A classic case of the spoiled little boy who wants the one thing in the toy shop that he's been told he can't have. Once he got it, of course, he would quickly lose interest. So, she told herself with a small smile, if she really wanted Connor to leave her alone once and forever, the solution was as obvious as the effect he had had on her earlier this afternoon. A very intriguing idea.

"What's so funny?"

"Hmm?" She paused in the middle of her thought, halfway between the table and counter with the empty wine goblets in hand, and peered at Connor quizzically.

"I asked what was so funny," he explained. "You have this sort of secret little smile."

"That," she told him, "is because it's a secret."

"You're also blushing, which only makes me more curious."

"Sorry, like I told you, it's a secret."

"Oh, no." He tossed the dish towel aside and moved toward her. "No secrets around here. It's a house rule."

He kept coming toward her with slow, measured strides, his eyes narrowed in an expression of mock menace. A flutter of anticipation deep inside, a feeling that was both delicious and long forgotten, made Gabrielle giggle softly.

"I see," she said. "And when precisely was this house rule instituted?"

"Precisely one minute ago." He took the glasses from her hands and placed them on the counter behind her. "So are you going to give up gracefully, or am I going to have to tickle the truth out of you?"

She laughed, her eyes widening and her hands instinctively lifting to fend him off. "No, Connor, you wouldn't."

"A dare?" he said, reaching for her. "Hell, Gaby, you know how I am about dares."

"I know, I know," she half cried, half laughed, squirming frantically as his fingers roamed over her ribs, tickling her mercilessly. "Stop...I hate...I hate..."

"I already know all about how you hate me," he declared. He was holding her with one arm while he tickled her. "I want to hear about that smile."

"No, not you." She gasped as he let up momentarily. "I hate being tickled."

"Then tell me what I want to know. The truth, Gaby, why were you smiling?"

"Because..." Laughing hard, she tried to slip to the floor to escape him, but he easily hauled her upright so that she ended up pressed tightly against him from chest to thigh. "Because..."

She broke off abruptly, a sudden awareness of him making it difficult to breathe, much less speak. Her entire body softened as the effect of being so close to him slowly commanded total control of her consciousness. Excitement filled her. The heat and smell and feel of him swamped her senses, and when she lifted her gaze and looked into his eyes, what she saw there made her tremble against him.

She saw desire. Strong and forthright and a little wild. Like the man himself. Connor wanted her. The look in his eyes declared that without restraint or apology, and God help her, at that instant she wanted him the same way.

He lowered his head.

She lifted hers.

And their mouths came together as naturally and spectacularly as water tumbling over a waterfall, the motion smooth and graceful and endless. Their parted lips slanted and angled in a series of delicate brushes. Each touch was butterfly soft, eager, as they learned the taste and feel of each other.

With his hands in her hair, Connor kissed her mouth and her cheeks. He used the pressure of his thumbs to tip her head back so he could kiss her throat gently, oh so gently, as if she were something fine and rare. He bent his head to trace the line of her collarbone with his tongue. Gaby felt his touch in a burst of rapid-fire sensations, hot and wet and rough. A sweet-sharp jolt made her arch against him as he sucked lightly on the skin at the side of her neck.

Laughing softly, he bracketed her face with his hands and stared at her, his eyes dark with passion.

"Oh, God, Gaby, this feels good. So good."

"I know," she whispered, touching his face hesitantly, as if she couldn't quite believe she was doing it, as if she couldn't quite believe this was Connor holding her and making her feel this way. "I know."

Everything about him was familiar and at the same time entirely new to her. It was all there in the chiseled planes and hard ridges of his face. All the pride and arrogance and determination, along with a reckless need to prove he wasn't afraid of anyone or anything. She ran her fingertip over the black silk arch of his eyebrow, prompting his mouth to curve with indulgence.

His forehead was broad, his eyes deep set, his jaw as square and solid as they came. Connor looked exactly like what he was. A tough guy, he had called himself, and she wouldn't argue with that. But there was tenderness there, too...in his eyes and in the full, brooding lips that could make her shiver and melt simply by coming close to hers. How could she have been so blind for so long to the tenderness in him?

Recalling what he had asked her to say to him on the deck earlier, she leaned into him slightly and whispered, "Please, Connor, kiss me."

He looked surprised. Then he grinned and jerked her flat against him as his mouth again laid claim to hers. This time, however, there was none of the tentative experimentation of a moment ago. This kiss was hard and fast and hungry. When his tongue pushed inside her mouth, Gaby moaned and felt her knees go weak.

Connor made a rough noise at the back of his throat, something between a groan and a curse. His hips moved against hers, rhythmically, suggestively, matching the rough thrusts of his tongue. Gaby clung to his shoulders, lost in a spiraling pleasure. She felt suspended in the moment and in herself. Dazed and at the same time acutely aware of every touch of his hand, every sound he made, every bit of sensation that whirled within her.

She felt alive. As if she'd been sleepwalking, she thought, and Connor's kiss had woken her once more. He was right. This felt so good.

Connor pulled her closer still, absorbing the restless movement of her hips against his. He was aware of the exact instant when Gaby surrendered the last shred of her resistance. Like a race-car driver knows engines, he knew women and he knew in that instant that after all this time, Gaby Flanders was his for the taking.

It was heady knowledge, a blessing, a gift, a dream about to come true. Desire surged inside him, like something untamed and trapped that needed to break loose.

With his tongue buried deep in her mouth, his hands moving impatiently beneath her T-shirt, he backed her up to the kitchen counter and pressed against her, hard. She responded and sent pleasure streaking through him in an unbroken arc from his groin to his brain.

He lifted his head with a rough groan, glancing around the kitchen in search of a place to lay her down. The table, the floor, like an animal searching for food or shelter from the cold, he silently hunted for the best and quickest solution to his needs.

Like an animal.

He shuddered, still holding her tightly, and closed his eyes as his chin came to rest on the top of her head.

Like an animal.

The thought made his insides lurch.

Damn it, what was he doing? This was Gaby he was holding, Gaby he was grinding himself against, Gaby he was thinking of tossing right there on the kitchen floor. Gaby, whom he had no more right to hold now than he'd had five years ago, or yesterday or this afternoon out on that deck.

"Connor?" she said quietly. "What is it? Are you all right?"

"Yeah." He lifted his head and met her bewildered gaze. *Don't look at me like that,* he thought, staring into her eyes, wide and bright with longing. *Don't make this harder than it already has to be.*

"Then why...?" Her voice dropped and halted.

"Why did I stop?" he finished for her.

She nodded, her expression growing watchful.

"I stopped because I suddenly got to wondering...." He paused as he loosened his hold on her and leaned back, his eyes narrowing speculatively as he struggled to shut down the need still roiling inside him. "Have you ever done it on a kitchen floor before, Gaby?"

She stiffened, her delicate jaw taking on a firmness he knew well. The flash of resentment in her eyes was almost a relief. *That's right, get mad,* he thought. *Push me away.*

"No," she replied in a stiff voice. "Have you?"

"As a matter of fact I have. On more than a few occasions. That's why you have to believe that I know what I'm talking about when I tell you it's not the kind of thing you ought to be doing."

"Let me see if I'm getting this," she said slowly. "You can, but I shouldn't."

"You're not me. You're Joel's wife."

Her head shot up defiantly. "Wrong, Connor. I'm Joel's widow."

"Same thing," he said, releasing her with a shrug.

"No. No, believe me, it's very different."

"You're right. You were a lot smarter as a wife. For instance, back then you saw me for what I am and you knew enough to keep away."

"Oh, Connor." Her eyes softened as she lifted her hand toward his face. "Are you really that afraid of letting someone close to you?"

Connor grabbed her wrist to stop her from touching him. "Like I told you when we were in the back of that van, Gabrielle, I'm not afraid of anything."

He thrust her hand aside as he turned to go. "Leave the rest of the dishes," he said to her over his shoulder. "I'll get them in the morning."

Letting the door slam behind him, he crossed the deck in a few long strides and headed toward the lake, a glossy stretch of ebony under the almost starless sky. He didn't stop until he passed a thick stand of cedar trees that formed a natural barricade between the cabin and lake at that spot. As if, he thought sardonically, he needed a barrier to block the force drawing him back to the cabin and to Gaby. A place to hide him from the thoughts that had followed him out, pounding at his heels with each step, telling him to go back and finish what he'd started, that it was what he wanted, what Gaby and he both wanted tonight. And that he was being an idiot.

Alone in the blackness between the cedars, he did what he'd seldom done in his lifetime—put thoughts of tomorrow ahead of tonight. By his own code of living for the moment and damn the rest, that, too, made him an idiot. So be it. He understood that sometimes it took an idiot to risk doing what had to be done. This had to be done. Tonight, tomorrow, the next day... until the end of the week. It wouldn't get any easier after that, but at least then he'd have distance on his side. After Friday he wouldn't be stuck here alone, watching over the one thing he wanted most in the world and couldn't have.

Talk about the wolf getting into the henhouse, he thought with a morose smile. Worse, for some insane, unnatural reason the hen had decided to invite him in. Crazy woman. And who could blame her with all he'd put her through in the past couple of days? She wasn't thinking straight. She couldn't be.

Which meant, Connor told himself, that it was up to him to make sure things stayed under control around there. That meant that somehow, no matter what it cost him, he was going to have to find a way to keep his hands off Gaby for the next four days..

Chapter 7

By the time Connor returned to the cabin, the kitchen was clean, the dishwasher running, the leftovers wrapped and put away. He had to admit he was glad. While not a fanatic by any means, he did disprove the conventional wisdom that said all bachelors were slobs by nature. He much preferred his surroundings to be clean and reasonably orderly.

Like his decision to learn to cook a decent meal, it was probably a reaction to the condition of his own all-male home after his mother's death. If Gaby had taken him at his word and left the dinner mess for the morning, he would probably have decided to deal with it before turning in and he really wasn't in the mood.

As he reached to turn out the kitchen light, he noticed the note propped between the now unlit candles in the center of the table. It read, "Sweet dreams, tough guy." Beside it Gaby had placed his lighter. He must have left it on the table earlier, he realized, slipping it into his pocket and smiling in spite of himself at her note.

So. She wasn't angry. He'd fully expected her to be, at the very least, annoyed and quite possibly furious with him, either for kissing her or for stopping. It was a call he couldn't make with any certainty. That was another thing he knew about women. You could never be sure of the details. That didn't alter the fact that the basics were carved in stone. Or so he'd thought.

He glanced again at the note, thinking how most women would have been angry with him, if only to hide their bruised feelings. Gaby had said he was full of surprises, but it seemed to him she held a few of her own. The note was written in a clean, feminine hand, and on impulse he folded it and slipped it into his pocket along with the lighter. Then he took two aspirins in hopes of calming the throbbing in his injured hand and headed for bed.

Sweet dreams, tough guy. The words ran through his head as he climbed the stairs. Sweet dreams. Not likely, he thought, not tonight. And he didn't feel like such a tough guy, either, as he passed Gaby's tightly closed door.

For no particular reason Gaby had set the alarm on the clock radio beside her bed before going to sleep. It clicked on at exactly seven o'clock, drawing her awake with the soft sounds of an old Bette Midler song. It was one she'd always liked. "From a distance..." Even half-asleep her mind supplied the rest of the words: "God is watching us, from a distance."

She rolled onto her back, stretching her arms wide and smiling even before she opened her eyes to discover that it was a gorgeous morning. It was the sort of clear, sunlit morning that made it easy to believe there was a God watching over the world, in spite of all the evidence to the contrary presented on the nightly news.

Actually ever since Joel had died, she'd felt she had a little extra action going on in the watched-over department. She usually thought of it in regard to Toby. It helped to believe she wasn't raising him entirely alone, that in some way Joel was still looking out for him and that he would never let anything bad happen to his son. It hadn't been easy to maintain that belief when Toby was sick, but she had held on to her prayers and her trust. And in the end, when Toby pulled through against all odds, her confidence in the power of love, from all directions, was stronger than ever.

At times she suspected that Joel wasn't only watching over Toby, but over her, as well. She couldn't define the feeling and she never tried explaining it to anyone, convinced it would simply be dismissed as a natural part of the grieving process, of her coming to terms with her loss. Maybe that's all it was, but Gaby didn't think so.

Whenever it happened, which wasn't often, she got this strong, absolutely clear sense of what she ought to do at that moment, as if someone was speaking to her and guiding her from within. She might have considered that it was her own common sense, except for the fact that when it happened, she felt a certainty and confidence she rarely felt as she muddled her way through life as a single parent.

That sense that Joel was watching over her was partly why she had accepted Adam's proposal even though they weren't in love with each other. Though she had to admit, she'd never quite felt that crystalline sense of certainty where Adam was concerned. It had been more like a gentle current washing her in his direction.

He'd been one of Joel's closest friends, after all, and he'd been there at the hospital with her the whole time Toby was sick. That proved his concern and that he could be counted on. Everyone told her so. Marrying Adam would mean that Toby wouldn't have to grow up without a father. Everyone said that was very important, too. And merging their interests in the Black Wolf would secure Toby's future even further. With his health always a lurking question in her mind, in spite of the doctors' assurances that he was fine, his future security was very important to her. Marrying Adam had seemed like the wise thing—the right thing—to do at the time. Now she wasn't so sure.

And why? she asked herself sheepishly. Because Connor DeWolfe had blown back into town, kissed her and made her knees buckle? That had never happened when Adam kissed her. But, she reminded herself, weak knees were not essential for a successful marriage. Especially not the second time around.

Hadn't she made a conscious decision to opt for security over romance?

Sighing, she looked out the window at a sky of solid blue and cowardly shifted her thoughts to Toby instead of the prickly problem of what to do about Connor. It had only been two days, and she missed Toby like crazy. She missed his smile and the sweet smell of him, still half baby, half little boy. She missed him running in to wake her in the morning, full of plans for whatever he wanted to do that day, his eyes sparkling with an innocent assurance that today was going to be the best day ever.

Lord, how she'd had to struggle in the weeks and months following the explosion not to let her own sadness overwhelm his spirit. They'd been together constantly, and there had been times when she'd barely managed to tuck him in at bedtime before the pain that she'd been holding at bay all day came crashing in on her, the harbinger of another tear-filled, sleepless night. In the morning, puffy eyed and exhausted, she would once more haul herself out of bed and rustle up a smile for Toby's sake.

Sometimes she had longed to escape for a while and would wish she had a job she could go to where she could perform some mindless task and forget she'd ever been a wife and mother. Looking back, however, she saw how lucky she was to have been able to stay home with Toby, where she had an ever-present reason to smile even when she didn't feel like it.

Before her marriage she'd worked restoring antique stained glass at a gallery in Boston. She enjoyed the sense that she was creating something new and rescuing something old and beautiful at the same time. After Toby was born, she continued to work at home on a free-lance basis, accepting projects that interested her and that could be adapted to her unhurried pace. Joel had deemed it a labor of love, since her income in no way reflected the hours she devoted to each restoration, painstakingly matching colors and cutting intricately shaped pieces of glass to replace those that had been lost or damaged over the years.

Fortunately they hadn't been dependent on her income to pay the bills, and that remained the same even after Joel's death. The money from his life insurance, along with their share of the restaurant income, more than took care of her living expenses, enabling her to continue working at home. She worked for enjoyment and to keep her skills sharp for the day when she could return to it full-time. For now, being there for Toby, to take him to the playground and teach him to ride a bike, was her top priority.

She glanced at the clock, wondering what Toby was doing right then. Seven-fifteen. He was probably eating breakfast. Sugar-coated Crunchies cereal, no doubt, his favorite, which she seldom bought because it was too sweet and which his grandmother always had waiting on the cupboard shelf as a special treat. At least she didn't have to worry about his well-being while she was away. He adored his nana and she doted on him. The two of them had been looking forward to spending this week together while Gaby was away on what was to have been her honeymoon. They had made grand plans for how they would spend each day.

Her mother would no doubt go ahead with all their plans for strawberry picking and the zoo and the rest. Although she was probably worried sick about Gaby, she would hide her concern from her grandson and do all she could to keep him happy and entertained. If anything, Gaby thought ruefully, he would be too well cared for, and it would take her a few days after they returned home to ease him back into a routine that didn't include Crunchies cereal and unlimited cartoons.

She thought wistfully of the serene pattern of their days together, of rainy mornings spent finger painting and how they saved bread crusts for their weekly trip to feed the ducks and their spur-of-the-moment picnics in the park. She had a sudden, unbidden image of Connor in the middle of all that simple domesticity and she grinned. It was almost as hard to picture the Black Wolf feeding ducks as it was to picture him wielding a spatula. Yet he had learned to cook, she mused, lending credence to that old adage that where there's a will, there's a way.

Not, she told herself sharply, that she was entertaining any notions that Connor would be fitting himself into her daily life. Or that she even wanted him to. The opposite was in fact true. She wanted to get through this and get back to her life and away from him as quickly as she could. Friday, she thought. Four more days after today. Three if you didn't count Friday itself. Surely she could survive a few more days. Couldn't she?

Unconsciously she lifted her fingertips to her lips, recalling last night and the way Connor's mouth had felt on hers. It occurred to her suddenly that perhaps survival in the classic sense was not what should concern her most. Maybe what was at risk for her here was not her safety or her temper, although so far both had been tested. Maybe something more elusive and infinitely more portentous hung in the balance. She'd glimpsed hints of it. It was there in the air whenever Connor came close to her and it was hidden between their words whenever they talked about anything more serious than the weather.

She wasn't sure exactly what that something was, only that her thoughts and feelings about Connor were shifting so quickly it was hard to know what to hold on to and what was mere illusion. Was this what it felt like just before an earthquake, she wondered, faint rumblings from below as the earth gets ready to split wide open?

She stroked her fingers across her lips, purposely trying to recapture the way she had felt last night in Connor's arms. It was impossible. She'd never experienced that sort of wild, instantaneous desire before, so how could she hope to recreate it all by itself, as if it were something tangible, like a stained-glass panel she could study and analyze and duplicate with near perfection? This was all new and more than a little intimidating.

For just a second she felt a stab of disloyalty for admitting even to herself that she had never felt as excited as she had last night when Connor was kissing her. Her marriage to Joel had been happy and fulfilling in every way, but their passion had built over time. They had been much younger when they met, coming together in a predictable pattern of dates and incremental intimacy, with no preconceived notions of each other to add the kind of tension that made the air between Connor and her seem to crackle with invisible sparks.

The difference between last night and the first kiss she ever shared with Joel was like the difference between a flash flood and a lawn sprinkler.

A good thing, too, she thought, smiling a little self-consciously. If she'd been exposed to Connor's passion twelve years ago, she would surely have drowned. Or at the very least run away.

And now? she challenged herself. Was she really so much more worldly and self-possessed now? Could she handle this...whatever "this" was? Was she ready to deal with the way Connor made her feel? Hungry and womanly and...alive. Very much alive, she thought, recalling and savoring the exhilarating way it had felt to be caressed and held in his arms, to respond to his blatantly male demands with a matching fervor she hadn't known she possessed.

It was rare these days for her to feel so intensely any emotion that did not involve Toby. Over the past few years she had developed a shell to protect her from feeling too much... too much pain, too much anticipation, too much need. She'd blocked out the highs and lows, steadily narrowing the span of allowable emotions. It was a self-defense mechanism obviously, and a darn good one if she did say so herself.

It was also one that Connor had managed to blow through in less than forty-eight hours. He had made her feel intensely again, and not only when he kissed her. It occurred to her that since he'd snatched her off the church steps she'd been more frightened, more furious, more confused, more resentful and more aroused than she had been in years. More alive, in every sense of the word, good and bad. Now that she thought about it, she supposed that's what being alive meant. All she knew was that it felt great. How long, she asked herself, since she'd woken up smiling?

She must have needed that shell as a buffer or she never would have created it. Adam, for all the time they spent together, had never threatened it. Connor had not only threatened it, but he'd also cracked it wide open and left her with a choice as to whether she wanted to try to patch it up and stay safely inside or come out and live again. Really live, that is, with all the risks and the pleasures and the uncertainties that life encompassed, instead of simply going through the motions.

She could see now that's what she had been doing. That's why she had felt so unsettled as she waited on those church steps for the ceremony to begin. She had been going through the motions. She'd become an expert at it, at performing all the tasks required for living life on the surface. Be a good mother, refinance the mortgage, marry a stepfather for Toby, all without really feeling anything...except where Toby was concerned. She had never shut down her feelings around him. He had been the only real joy or pleasure in her life for the past two years, safe inside the shell along with her.

Until last night.

Last night, she thought, picturing it all at once as some sort of monumental dividing line in her life. There was the past behind her and the future ahead, and last night like a bold red slash separating the two. She bit her bottom lip. Regardless of how the investigation into Adam turned out, there was no way she could cross back over that line and return to a life of going through the motions. Last night she had come alive again, and whatever happened next, she had Connor to thank for that.

What would happen next? she wondered. In a way it was up to Connor. After all, he was the one who had rejected her and walked away last night. Ordinarily that would have left her feeling humiliated and mad as hell. Except she hadn't felt rejected when he pulled away. She'd felt sorry for him. She knew the kind of guilt and doubts he was wrestling with. Hadn't she felt their talons in her earlier in the day, when she'd run from his honest admission of how much he wanted to kiss her?

Last night she had been suddenly, miraculously freed of the last of that guilt and self-doubt. She had responded to Connor with an unfettered heart...with that mysterious crystalline sense of certainty, she thought, grinning. A certainty that had nothing to do with common sense, but rather with something she couldn't explain.

She wished she could, she thought, sliding from the bed and walking to the window to gaze outside. If she could explain it to Connor, maybe she could help him find freedom, too. As it was, all she could do was be patient and wait for him to find it on his own . . . with maybe just a little help from other sources.

Glancing up at the bluest sky she'd ever seen, she smiled wistfully.

"If you're listening," she whispered, "I have another little job for you. . . ."

After showering and dressing in white shorts and a yellow tank top, she went downstairs. The kitchen was deserted, the coffee not yet made. Evidently Connor was still sleeping. Shrugging off her disappointment, she made coffee and looked around for the book she'd started yesterday. She carried it, along with a cup of coffee and a muffin, to her grassy spot just above the shoreline. There was a warm breeze blowing off the water, and the scent of the lilacs and wild lilies growing all around sweetened the air.

She ate her breakfast as she watched the birds swooping low over the water in search of their own. She had just brushed the crumbs from her shorts and opened her book when she heard footsteps and turned to see Connor walking toward her, carrying two cups.

His hair was still damp from the shower, and the black stubble that had seemed to be permanently affixed to his face was gone. Without it, his combination of high cheekbones and dark, deep-set eyes was even more striking. He also looked younger, she noted, and even more handsome. He had on faded jeans and a clean white cotton shirt open at the collar, and her heart turned over at the sight of him.

"Morning," he said, squatting in front of her and offering her one of the cups that she could see contained hot coffee. "I figured you might be ready for a second cup about now."

"Your timing is perfect."

"Good. And since it seems to be my turn to make the morning peace offering, I brought you this, too."

She hadn't noticed the daisy stuck in his pocket until he reached for it and handed it to her.

"Thank you," she said, smiling. "But you have nothing to make peace for."

His mouth quirked. "Don't I? After the way I came on to you last night and then called a halt?"

"So which one are you making peace for, coming on or calling a halt?"

"Good question," he said, shrugging, his smile self-mocking. "Which should I be apologizing for?"

"Oh, no, you don't. This is your peace offering—you decide." She took a sip of coffee. "Of course, I could give you a hint if you like."

He lowered himself to the ground a little in front and to the left of her. "I think I could use one."

"It seems obvious that what we have here are two diametrically opposed actions. Kissing and stopping," she explained. "My thought is that you shouldn't be sorry for whichever of them you wanted to do, whether it was kissing me or stopping."

"That's easy. I wanted to kiss you. The last thing I wanted to do last night was to stop."

"Then you shouldn't have," she said, meeting his gaze, letting the silence that followed speak for her. Finally she added, "As for the rest, if there's any apologizing to be done, I'd say you owe one to yourself for not trusting your own instincts."

"My instincts," he echoed, a small, sardonic smile playing at the edges of his mouth. "Would you like to hear what my instincts tell me where you're concerned, Gabrielle?"

He said her name softly, turning it into a caress that sent a shiver of excitement dancing along her spine, making it impossible for her to do more than nod.

"My instincts tell me to take you," he said bluntly. He watched her reaction closely, as if expecting her to be shocked by his directness, perhaps even to be scared off. When she wasn't, he continued, "My instincts tell me that you want me almost as much as I want you. And that if we made love, it would be good. Real good. For both of us."

"I see," she managed to say, her heart pumping so furiously she felt out of breath. "And for some reason you feel you can't follow that instinct?"

He frowned impatiently. "Damn it, Gaby, you know I can't. And you know the reason why."

"No." She shook her head. "I'm not sure I do."

He exhaled sharply and stared at the lake. "You said it yesterday. Because of Joel," he said without looking at her. Before she could protest, he continued. "Maybe it would be different if I hadn't wanted you the way I did while he was still alive, while you were still his wife, for God's sake. But I did and I can never go back and change that."

"No. You can't," she agreed, looping her arms loosely around her bent knees.

Something in her tranquil tone drew his attention. He peered at her, his expression guarded but curious.

"It's like almost everything in life," she went on, "or at least, it seems to me, all the things that matter most. You can never go back and change them no matter how badly you want to. All you can do is accept them and move on and hopefully learn from the past."

"You're looking at the master of accepting and moving on," he told her.

"You're thinking of your mother."

He nodded, plucking at the long blades of grass growing beside him. "My mother, and the way my family just seemed to fall apart after she died." He squinted, as if the sun hurt his eyes even though the branches overhead shielded them from its direct glare. "And Joel, too."

"Are you really sure you're all right with all of that?"

"Sure I'm sure."

"Then how come you never got married?"

"What?"

"How come you never got married?"

"I never found the right woman."

She lifted one shoulder and gave a dubious nod.

"What does that mean?" he asked. "That look."

"It means a psychiatrist would have a field day with the fact that after losing your mother so suddenly and at such a young age, you've never really bonded with another woman."

"I've bonded with plenty of women," he retorted, his lip curled at one side.

"I'm talking about one special woman."

"What if I told you they were all special? All right, all right," he added at the despairing rolling of her eyes. "I get your meaning."

"Plus you say your family fell apart when she died. That seems to have bothered you a great deal, and yet you've never tried to start a family of your own. Maybe you're afraid of losing all over again." She stopped suddenly and shook her head, aghast. "Gosh, I'm sorry, listen to me. I sound as if I'm a psychiatrist, sitting here analyzing your whole life. I am sorry, Connor."

"Don't be. There's probably a whole lot of truth in what you said. Maybe what I should have said before was that I've accepted the things that have happened in the only way I know how to."

She nodded, her small smile self-effacing. "I can't argue with that. In some ways I'm still coming to terms with what happened to Joel."

He met her suddenly teary gaze, his lean face unsmiling, his silence conveying an understanding deeper than words could express.

"You know," she said, blinking back the tears that had threatened briefly, "right after Joel was killed, I packed up everything of his that I could find. His clothes, his books, all the papers and stuff from his office. I intended to throw them away or give them to Goodwill, but my mother convinced me to hang on to some of it, at least his trophies and sporting equipment and his personal papers, if only for Toby's sake. I separated that from the rest and stored it in the basement. Now I'm glad I did, but back then I just wanted any reminder of him gone. I was so miserable and so angry with him for dying and leaving me." She gave a broken, forlorn laugh. "Crazy, huh?"

He placed his hand on top of hers where it rested on the grass between them. "I don't think so. Not at all."

For a minute Gaby just savored the feeling of his warm, rough palm, the very act of connecting with someone who could hear her grief without mouthing sunny platitudes. Finally she gave a soft chuckle.

"I even put away all the pictures of him," she revealed. "Can you believe it? And whenever Toby asked about his daddy, I gave him the shortest answer I could. Eventually, with no reminders and no encouragement, he sort of stopped asking. I know that's awful," she said hurriedly, seeing his pained expression, "but at the time it was the only way I could deal with it."

"I don't think it's awful. Just real sad." He lifted his hand from hers, dragging his fingers roughly through his hair. "You never should have had to go through that, and I'm going to make sure that whoever's responsible pays for it."

She shrugged, her lips pressed tightly together. She knew he was thinking about Adam and the investigation, but she didn't feel like dealing with that right now. They would know one way or the other soon enough.

"Anyway my point is that I didn't handle it well at all back then," she confessed. "I even moved out of our bedroom into the smaller one down the hall." She hesitated. "When I started dating Adam, I avoided going to any place where Joel and I used to go and later..." She searched for the right words. "Later, when he wanted us to become...intimate, I told him I couldn't sleep with another man in that house. Joel's house."

"That was your right," Connor said, a note of what sounded like satisfaction in his deep voice. "A decent man would honor your wishes without question."

"He did. He tried to, anyway. What made it hard was that I also couldn't spend a night away from Toby to stay at his house or at a motel. It made things rather...difficult."

"So where did the big event finally take place?" Connor asked, his full lips tight and barely moving.

Gaby stared at her knees and mumbled, "It didn't."

"What did you say?"

Her head jerked up. "It didn't. I said it didn't take place anywhere, all right? We never . . ." She stopped. He was grinning like a kid on the last day of school.

"What a shame," he said. "In that case I'll bet old Adam was really looking forward to his wedding night."

"We both were," she snapped.

Black sparks flashed in his eyes. "Then I'm damn sorry I interfered."

"You're nothing of the sort, Connor DeWolfe, and you know it."

"You're right. I'm not." His smile could have melted concrete. "I just thought I'd be polite and say I was. The truth is I couldn't be happier that you never went to bed with Adam."

He sure looked happy, Gaby noted, overjoyed actually. Against her will she found herself returning his smile.

"So tell me," he said after a minute, "why do you think you never slept with him?"

Gaby shrugged. "At first I just wasn't ready. Then I told myself that waiting for our wedding night would be symbolic of making a clean break with the past and starting fresh. Maybe it was because he had been Joel's friend and partner and all, but I always felt as if I had to make it clear to Adam and myself and everyone else that this was an entirely different relationship. That I wasn't simply trying to replace Joel with a reasonable facsimile, that this was something completely and utterly new, with no relation to what I had shared with Joel. I guess I thought that was the way to protect and preserve what Joel and I had together."

"Sounds reasonable."

"It shouldn't," she replied. "Because it's really dumb. Especially coming from me."

"What do you mean?"

"I'm thinking about my work. I've spent my whole life trying to meld the old and the new. People bring me old panels of stained glass that have been treated less than kindly by the years, and it's my job to salvage what can be salvaged and replace what's missing. It's not easy," she went on. "Colors fade, lead seams shrink and grow brittle. But with a lot of skill and patience and luck, the end result can be something stronger and richer and sometimes even more beautiful than either the original panel or an entirely new piece. You see, it's the blending of the old and the new that makes it unique.''

She glanced at him self-consciously. ''Sorry. I tend to rattle on about my work.''

''Were we talking about your work?'' he asked her quietly, the intensity in his gaze suggesting he knew her remarks had been more cogent and complicated than an impromptu lecture on restoring stained glass.

''No,'' she admitted. ''I guess I was really talking about my life.''

''Well, then, as long as we're on the subject,'' he said, seeming to come closer without moving. It was his eyes, Gaby thought; the look in his eyes made her feel he was closing in on her without him moving an inch. ''What are your instincts telling you to do about me, Gabrielle?''

A half a dozen glib, evasive replies came into her head and died there. She didn't want to be glib and she didn't want to lie to him. The question was, did she have the guts to tell him the truth?

''I...you...'' She looked away from his searching gaze and blew out an anxious breath. Coward, chided a small voice. Ready to climb back into your shell so soon, are you? it taunted. Lifting her chin, she turned back to him.

''I want to give myself to you, Connor. I know that sounds corny,'' she continued in a rush. ''Old-fashioned, I mean, but that's how I feel. That's what I want. You said your instinct was to take me. Well, mine is to give myself to you, free and clear, with no strings and no expectations on either side. I mean it,'' she said as his expression turned frankly skeptical.

''You're not that kind of woman,'' he told her.

''What kind? The kind who knows what she wants and reaches out for it? The kind who just once wants to put that first and let herself feel . . .everything there is to feel,'' she finished, a note of desperation creeping into her voice.

Connor rubbed his jaw, frowning as if she'd presented him with a ten-line algebraic equation to solve.

"Let's face it," she said to him, her expression rueful, "anything that happens between you and me is bound to be stormy and fraught with questions and...complications. It comes with our history. And maybe we'll realize it isn't worth the bother of trying to sort it out and decide what's salvageable and figure out how to fit in all the new pieces. Why go to all that trouble just to find out that we're not...compatible?"

His mouth curved into a bemused smile. "If by 'compatible' you mean what I think you mean, believe me, we will be very compatible. My instincts in that area are never wrong."

She lifted her steady gaze to his. "Prove it."

Gaby heard his sharp intake of breath and watched his eyes darken and heat.

"Hell, Gaby," he muttered, leaning closer, "you know how I am about dares."

"Right. I do."

He stopped with his face very close to hers, his dark gaze intense and just slightly amazed. "All I wanted was to do right by you."

"Here's your chance, tough guy."

He raised his hand, and she felt it close on the back of her neck, drawing her toward him. Her eyes closed. Her mouth lifted to meet his. It was so easy, so simple and uncomplicated, just the way she told him it would be. Just the way she needed for it to be. She couldn't bear to think of all the *shoulds* and *ought tos* and *what ifs* right now. She refused to think of them.

It was easy to let all other thoughts drift away when she was being kissed by Connor. He filled her senses, overwhelming her, leaving no room for anything but the heat and scent and feel of him. His mouth moved over hers, slow and easy, savoring that first heady kiss as if it was fully as pleasurable and important as anything that might follow. His tongue stroked her lips, warm, rough strokes that made her tremble even before he pushed inside her mouth, letting her feel him the way she yearned to.

She lifted her hands and clasped his shoulders. Her head tilted as she sought to fit her mouth to his even more closely, and her tongue moved against his in an age-old game of thrust and parry.

Gaby was breathing hard by the time he pulled back to look at her, studying her face, already flushed with pleasure, as if it was something rare and remarkable that he might never see again.

"Tell me, Gabrielle," he said in a slow, husky drawl that sent a tingle racing down her spine, "have you ever made love outside in the grass before?" Before she could reply, he pressed his fingers to her lips. "No, on second thought don't answer that. What happened in the past doesn't matter. It won't change the fact that unless you tell me to stop pretty damn quick, you're about to."

An eager smile bloomed on her lips and in her eyes. "Stop stalling, Connor. I have no intention of telling you to stop."

"You're sure?" he asked simply, asking everything with those two words. "You're sure, Gaby?"

She nodded. "I'm sure."

This time when he kissed her he leaned into her with his body, letting his weight bring her down on her back in the grass, which felt both soft and prickly through the thin cotton of her top. He came to rest half on top of her, their legs entwined, his body a welcome anchor as need, deep, dark and turbulent, rose up inside her, threatening to sweep her away.

The strength in him was unmistakable. She felt it in the lean hardness of his thigh when it pressed against hers, and in something as innocuous as the movement of his hands on her face, his rough palms framing her, his thumbs rubbing across her lips before his fingers arrowed into her hair to hold her still for another kiss. His strength excited her even further, reminding her that he could be ruthless if he needed to be, that he was a man who went after what he wanted without fear or restraint. He was a fighter, and that triggered something untouched inside of her.

Last night she had marveled to discover how tender he could be. But today it was his ruthlessness she wanted, she realized, his toughness. The honesty of his desire, of a give-and-take without pretense or reservation, thrilled her, and she arched beneath him with the sudden urgency of her need for him.

She wanted him to crush her into the soft earth, to sweep her away with the force of his passion. Instead, his touch at that moment was strangely gentle, even hesitant. Her fists clenched restlessly as his lips lightly brushed hers and his fingers trailed across her throat, tracing a delicate pattern at odds with what he was and what she needed. He slid one long, sun-browned finger beneath the narrow shoulder of her tank top, but made no move to lower it.

He was holding back, she realized. And the cost of his restraint was revealed in the shudder that gripped him when she once again instinctively shifted her weight beneath him.

With a soft groan he dipped his head and touched his tongue to her breast, just long enough to leave a wet circle on her shirt there. Gaby shivered, her teeth coming down hard on her bottom lip as desire clawed at her.

Connor lifted his head and looked down at her, misreading her response. "Are you afraid of me?" he asked.

Gaby shook her head. "No."

His smile was ruefully decisive. "You are. You ought to be. I'm not sure I know how..."

His words trailed off uncertainly, but when she looked in his eyes there was no uncertainty there, no ambiguity. There she saw only hunger, bright, hard-edged, urgent—everything she wanted and needed to feel alive.

"You said you wanted to take me," she reminded him. "Do it."

He hesitated, watching her, a sort of frantic uncertainty still hovering about him, like a man handed a newborn infant for the first time.

"Do it," she urged. "Do it, Wolf."

Instantly his gaze narrowed in surprise, either at the fervor in her voice or her unconscious use of the nickname she'd previously shunned.

Conscious or not, the use of the name seemed appropriate now since it was the danger and recklessness in him that had earned him the name Wolf and it was that dangerous, reckless side of him that she wanted to make love to her.

She wasn't looking for promises of tomorrow or trying to recreate a lost love from her past. She wanted right now, today, that very moment. She wanted to be reminded that she was a woman, a woman with desires too long denied. She wanted to be pushed to the very edge of what it meant to want and need and feel. She wanted Wolf, with her, over her, inside her.

Her breath caught as his expression changed, darkening, reflecting the exquisite danger that was the other side of passion. His hand wound slowly, roughly through her hair. His hips pinned her to the grass, and her eyes widened at the sudden feeling of being overwhelmed by his power.

But it wasn't fear that made her tremble as his mouth slammed into hers. And the sound that vibrated deep in her throat as she met the driving thrusts of his tongue was one not of surrender, but triumph.

Chapter 8

He wasn't a needy man. Self-reliance and independence and a take-it-or-leave-it philosophy that ran right to the bone—those were the qualities he had been honing to perfection ever since he was six years old, the attributes he prided himself on.

But he needed something now, Connor realized as he sought to devour Gaby's soft mouth, and he needed it bad.

He needed to make this woman, who stood apart from all others in his memory, scream and tremble and melt beneath him. He needed to bury himself in her, to lose himself and find himself and make it to the other side. He had a sense, haunting and vague, that if he did, then maybe, just maybe everything would be all right.

And he needed to bring her with him every step of the way. He needed the sweet, hot taste of her all over his tongue and the liquid fire of her fingers moving on his skin. He needed to conquer, to overwhelm, to possess.

He needed to win this, without even knowing what "this" was.

With desire like a saber at his back, he left her mouth wet and swollen and dragged his teeth along her throat and the curve of her shoulder. Hooking one finger in the neckline of her top, he jerked it down to expose the sweet, secret valley between her breasts. He licked her there and groaned. She tasted of soap and salt and woman, and he couldn't get enough. He was afraid if this moment went on forever, he would still never get enough.

Gaby twisted under him as he stretched the neck of her shirt lower still, snagging the upper edge of her bra and dragging it down, too, until her breast was bared to his hungry mouth. He felt her hands in his hair as he captured the hard pink crest between his lips, her fists clenching and holding on.

Her hips lifted and fell as he sucked and licked, using his teeth and his tongue and the heat of his breath to make her shiver, make her moan, to draw from her the small, half-formed whimpers of pleasure that fed his excitement and fueled the towering need inside him.

Take her, take her, take her, it roared.

It was what she wanted him to do. She'd said so.

Take her. Put an end to it.

The command pounded inside his head, urgent and compelling. But Connor wasn't sure he wanted it to end. Only that he wanted it. He wanted it fast and furious and he wanted it to last forever and he wanted it all, all she would give him. All that was hers to be taken.

He lowered his hands to her hips, grasping her tightly and stretching out on top of her, holding her still as his pelvis slowly rocked against hers. Desire, white-hot and sparking, hissed inside him.

He buried his face in her shoulder, inhaling her scent, like wildflowers, like yesterday, inhaling, drinking her into his senses until it hurt to breathe.

He thrust his leg between hers and felt a shudder that began in her and traveled through him, as though they were one, sharing flesh and sensation. It thrilled him and scared him and made him tighten his grip on her. He bent his head and again suckled her breast, harder now, as Gaby groaned and groaned, her head turning from side to side on the pillow of summer grass.

She tossed her arm across her face, hiding her eyes from him, and drew her knee up. It angled outward just a little, just enough to draw his attention to the soft, pale flesh of her inner thigh. He was instantly riveted. The movement, at once so guileless and so utterly erotic, made his blood run hot and thick.

He moved to touch her there, discovering the taut muscle beneath the softness, his fingers stroking upward, drawn to that spot where her silky flesh disappeared inside the loose leg of her shorts. The spot that had become for him in that second the most mesmerizing and mysterious in the entire universe.

His fingers curved into her, greedy, wanting. Needing. Needing this. Needing her. Needing more. He shoved his hand fully inside her shorts, his fingertips butting against the elastic band on her panties, clawing it aside until he uncovered the soft nest of curls between her legs.

Heaven.

Gaby froze, her eyes still covered, her breath seeming to catch deep in her throat.

His own breath came in short, harsh pants as he followed the path of heat and dampness, ruffling through her silky curls, parting her flesh hurriedly, wanting, craving, too deep into her now to slow down, to wait, to do more than feel and let the feeling take him.

He gasped as his fingers at last uncovered what he sought, the core of her. Hot. Wet. She quivered against his fingers, and he was lost forever.

She was dying. She had to be, thought Gaby. It wasn't possible to feel this good and live. Sensations bombarded her from everywhere. Her mouth, her breasts, the ultrasensitive flesh between her legs, all of her was burning up, melting in the frantic inferno of Connor's touch.

His hands were on her shorts now, ripping open the snap, tugging on the zipper. He went up on his knees, his eyes hot and bright as he watched her watching him strip off her shorts and her panties and toss them aside. His movements were quick and efficient as he reached for her top and pulled it over her head. He dealt with her bra by curling his fingers around the narrowing where it dipped between her breasts and ripping it from her.

Then she was naked and he was grinning and reaching for her, murmuring to her, rough, urgent words. Gaby didn't know what he was saying. Didn't care, as his hands moved over her body, her breasts and tummy, her hips, sliding between her thighs, parting them to make a place for himself there.

His clever, dangerous fingers stroked her, making her tremble, turning everything inside her to liquid that pooled right inside the place he was touching her, stroking her.

She closed her eyes, and lights danced inside her head. Her senses were humming, supercharged. She felt herself being lifted, carried out of herself. Strong. He was so strong.

"Yeah, like that," she heard him say. "Just like that, baby."

He'd called her baby. Gaby smiled. She always thought she hated being called baby.

His touch changed suddenly, the pressure and texture all different, still good, just so different and wonderful. Her eyes fluttered open, and she gasped to see him bent over her, her legs propped on his shoulders, his head buried in between.

He was...

She'd never...

She had to stop him... his mouth... his tongue...

She levered upright, her gaze locked onto the top of his head, on the streaks of sunlight dancing on his dark hair. She reached for him as wave after wave of pleasure radiated out from where his mouth was doing such incredible, unspeakable things to her. Magical things. Making her shimmer inside. Making her crazy.

"Connor. Please..."

She wasn't sure if he heard her. She wasn't even sure she was speaking out loud.

Connor, oh, Connor.

She reached for him, clutching his shoulders, her head thrown back as the pressure inside wound tighter and tighter until she was arching her hips and gasping for air.

"Please, please."

Please stop. Please don't. She couldn't think.

He was devouring her, frightening her, thrilling her.

She cried out. Grabbing at him, dragging him back up, unable to bear whatever was happening to her. Desperate for more.

Connor grinned at her again, a wicked grin. She reached for his shirt, scratching at the buttons that held it closed, as frantic now as he was, maybe more. She wanted to touch him, to feel his flesh rubbing against hers all over.

"Forget that," he murmured, his grin fading as he grasped her wrists firmly to pull her hands away from the buttons. "I can't wait that long."

He dropped his hands to the front of his jeans. They were stretched tight across his arousal, underscoring the accuracy of his claim.

They were both kneeling now, facing each other. Gaby pushed his hands aside and opened the metal button at his waist, then tugged on the zipper. He winced as her knuckles pressed against him, sucking air between his clenched teeth.

"Oh, baby," he whispered, clamping his hand on top of hers and holding it there for a few seconds, his head thrown back.

Gaby turned to cup her fingers around him, feeling his responsive jerk through the layers of cotton and denim. His response sent her back to work on the zipper with a frenzy, lowering it, wrestling his snug jeans and shorts over his hips at the same time. She stopped, holding her breath, spellbound as his manhood sprang free, intimidating to behold.

As she swayed toward him, it brushed against her tummy, a touch like velvet, like fire. She reached for him, fisting him, cupping him, reveling in the shudders that racked him. At last, groaning, he pulled away. His gaze held hers as he quickly dealt with his jeans, kicking them aside even as he was pushing her back into the grass.

Still kneeling, he hooked his hands behind her knees and parted her legs.

Gaby wound her arms around his neck, lifting to meet him as he sank down and into her.

He was out of control, he thought. Almost, anyway. So close to losing it. How could he help it? She was like heat and water, drawing him deeper, drowning him and burning him alive at the same time.

Her supple body closed around him like a satin glove. He could feel her muscles clenching. Tight. So tight. Nothing was ever so tight. Or warm. Or right. Her body sheathed him, rippling around him, milking him.

He buried his face in her neck and found her skin there coated with a slick sheen, like his was all over. Of course, he'd been working harder than she had. At the start she had been responsive but quiet, relinquishing control, allowing him to take the lead. But suddenly she had come alive, matching him thrust for thrust, lifting, straining, moving beneath him with a raw, sinuous energy that sent his senses soaring.

Her passion inflamed him. Never had a woman displayed such a reckless desire for him. Her hands were everywhere, all over him, sliding under his shirt to knead his back, caressing his hips and the backs of his thighs.

She raked her teeth across his shoulder, then turned her face up in search of his mouth. Curling her fingers around the back of his neck, she pulled him into a long, deep tongue kiss that left him hanging by a thread at the very utter edge of his control.

Frantic to make it last a little longer, he locked his arms around her and rolled onto his back. Gaby cried out in surprise, clutching at him, then laughed in exaltation as she discovered herself on top, poised to ride him.

She took full advantage, leaning forward to brace herself on her hands on either side of his head, enabling her to lift herself almost free of him, then sink back, slowly, slowly, so slowly he had to grit his teeth to keep from grasping her hips and forcing her to match the pace set by the frenetic hammering of his heart.

Only one thing stopped him. The delight and exhilaration that played across her face as it slowly dawned on her the extent of the power she wielded over him. Connor watched the delight that danced in her eyes as she played with him, moving first faster and harder, her full breasts swaying just out of reach, bringing him dangerously close to the brink, then sliding up until he was barely inside her and making him wait until she deigned to rescue him, lowering herself again in slow, minuscule increments of relief.

She trailed one finger along his cheek, down his neck and into the open collar of his shirt. He caught her hand and carried it to his lips, pressing his mouth to her palm before quickly pulling her other arm out from under her, as well, throwing her off balance so that she came tumbling down on top of him.

"Do you enjoy teasing me?" he demanded, his voice rough, his hands gentle.

She lifted her head, laughing. "Yes. You look so sweet and fierce."

He scowled. "Sweet?"

"And fierce," she added soothingly.

"You want sweet? I'll show you sweet."

Clasping her to him, he rolled again. This time Gaby was ready for him, however, and she leaned into the roll, sending them farther than he intended. They ended up crashing against a tree, but he was where he wanted to be. On top, between her open thighs, poised to claim her once again.

He met her gaze and held it. "I am not sweet," he told her. "This..." He paused, still watching her, and very deliberately ran his finger along the dewy cleft between her legs before bringing it to his mouth and licking the taste of her from it. "This is sweet. The sweetest in the world."

They were the sexiest words anyone had ever said to her. No, Gaby thought, they were the sexiest words anyone had ever said to anybody anywhere.

The beginnings of a satisfied smile gave way to a gasp as, without warning, he bracketed her hips with his hands and entered her with one swift thrust. He was a big man, and it had been a long time for her. Yet, just as the first time he'd moved inside her, her body welcomed him without reservation. As if, she thought hazily, she had been waiting all this time for Connor to fill her the way she was meant to be filled.

He rocked into her, his pounding pace and rigid expression signaling that whatever had gone before, he was now beyond teasing, beyond waiting.

Yes, now, Gaby thought, wrapping her arms around him, instantly catching his fever. She was like a volcano. All pent-up heat and energy. She rose with him, arching, reaching, wanting it harder, faster, hotter. They slammed together and pulled apart, their sweat-slick bodies straining, grasping together for something just out of sight.

"No," Connor growled as her eyes fluttered shut. "I want you to see. I want you to watch. I want you to know this is me loving you."

His tone was sharp and insistent.

"I know who you are," Gaby assured him gently, lifting her hands to caress his face. "Connor, Wolf, my nemesis."

He smiled at that, understanding mingling briefly with the heat in his gray eyes before giving way, as everything else they were or had been gave way, to the magnitude of that moment. Still she kept her eyes open and locked on his, her hands on his face.

Only when the rushing pleasure inside her came faster and faster did she drop her hands to his broad shoulders, holding on to him as the storm inside drove her higher, its primitive, lusty rhythm beating just beneath her skin, until there was nowhere higher left and all she could do was let go and feel herself falling, endlessly, helplessly, falling and glorying in it.

She felt the wild, rippling contractions of her muscles as she climaxed and then heard his rough gasp of pleasure as he found his own release, and a feeling came over her like that which comes with a safe landing following a very rocky flight.

Connor collapsed on her, feeling spent and boneless and as though he might never breathe normally again. Damn, he thought, he'd climbed mountains that had taken less out of him. Beneath him he felt Gaby gulping air, too, and he reluctantly summoned the energy to roll to his side beside her. The last thing she needed was the strain of his added weight on her lungs.

He placed his hand on the gentle swell of her stomach, fingers spread. "That was..."

He stopped, stymied, realizing that if there was a word big enough, magnificent enough, to hold all he wanted to say, he didn't know it.

As it happened it didn't matter.

"Yes," agreed Gaby. "It certainly was."

And that was that.

Connor stared at her in amazement as she lay there with her eyes closed, a contented smile on her lips. She could have waited while he struggled to find the word he was looking for. A lot of women would have. A lot of women he'd known would also right this instant be pressuring him for details, asking if he was happy and if it had been good for him or—the absolute worst on his list of postcoital downers—if he was sure he didn't think she was too fat. Instead, Gaby had surprised him all over again.

Yes, it certainly was, she'd said. Period.

And just like that, for the first time in his life, he fell in love.

As a feeling it was a bit daunting. Hell, he thought, watching with fascination the way she breathed, it was downright scary. There were times in the past when he'd wondered if maybe he was in love with Gaby. As crazy as it seemed, he'd wondered if maybe that was why no matter how hard he tried he couldn't shake the invisible hold she had on him. He'd been driven back then to figure out exactly what the feelings she incited in him were...other than forbidden. It had seemed to him that naming them was the first step to getting rid of them.

But he hadn't loved her, he realized now. He couldn't have, because until the past few days he had never truly known her. That only made it all the harder to understand. It was nothing as simple as envy. A casual observer might think differently, but it wasn't in him to want her just because she belonged to another man, especially Joel.

He'd known Joel a long time before Gaby came into their lives, through cheerleaders and prom queens and girls-most-likely-to... and they'd never even come close to clashing over any of them. He'd also never craved Joel's fancier house or more expensive car or even his happy family, so why would he have suddenly started craving his best friend's woman?

It didn't make sense to him, yet he couldn't deny that the connection between Gabrielle and him had been there right from the first instant they met. Their gazes had collided in a silent storm of heat and eerie recognition that swept away their polite smiles and had them both throwing up a protective wall that had stayed up until...until a few minutes ago, he thought ironically. When it had come down with a vengeance.

That connection had been real and it had been mutual. Connor knew that in his heart, although he would never again even attempt to make her admit it.

Real and unexplainable, right up there with UFO sightings and déjà vu. Which, as far as he was concerned, left the matter hanging out there in a sort of mystical realm he didn't even want to try to figure out. Whatever was between them was real. Pure and simple. That was good enough for him, he thought, leaning forward to kiss Gaby's hair, avoiding the question of whether it would be enough for her.

Connor's lips on her hair roused Gaby from the drifting, half-asleep zone where she'd been languishing. She happily rolled to her side so they were lying face-to-face and opened her eyes to look at him, thinking what she sometimes thought when she looked at Toby—that she could easily go on looking at him forever, infinitely fascinated with each small nuance of him.

He brushed the hair from her face, touched her cheek and her breast and smiled. "You're beautiful," he said.

"Not really."

"Really."

"Thank you."

"Thank you." At her quizzical look, he added, "For simply saying thank you and leaving it at that. For not feeling obligated to recite a litany of every perceived flaw on your body."

She shrugged. "What's the point? I'm laying here naked, in full sunlight. I've had a baby and I'll turn thirty in a week or so. I figure this is what I've got to work with, and you've seen it all."

"Damn right," he said, the smile becoming a full-fledged grin. "And liked every minute of it. I like your attitude, too, lady."

"Yes, well, I guess whatever else you say about traumatic experiences, they have a way of putting things like stretch marks in perspective."

She believed that. Just the same, her hand unconsciously drifted to cover the pattern of shiny threadlike lines on her hip, a souvenir of her pregnancy. Connor intercepted her halfway and brought her hand to his mouth instead, planting a warm, open-mouthed kiss in her palm.

"I've already seen them," he said. "I love them, too."

"Too?"

"Yeah. I also love your—" he ran his insolently appraising gaze over her body "—smile."

"What a coincidence," she drawled, opening her eyes wide with mock surprise. "It so happens I love your—" she narrowed her eyes assessingly, doing a very credible imitation of the way he had just perused her body by sliding her gaze slowly, slowly over his, then concluding with a satisfied leer "—smile, too. I also love your—" she leaned closer "—ears."

He looked startled. "My ears?"

"Mmm-hmm," she said, blowing gently in his ear. "They're so . . . sexy."

"Let me see if I've got this right. You're saying I have sexy ears?"

"That's right. And your jaw, that's sexy, too." She kissed his jaw, a slow, lazy, meandering kiss that started at the bone just below his ear and ended somewhere beneath his chin. "And your Adam's apple," she said, kissing that, too. She felt the rumble of his amused chuckle beneath her lips.

"Now, that much I knew," he said. "I've always thought my Adam's apple may just be my best feature."

"Oh, no. Your best feature is situated a bit lower. In fact," she continued as her fingers fell to the top button on his shirt, "I'd say that . . ."

Instantly his hands covered hers, stopping her.

"Why do you do that?" Gaby asked.

"Do what?"

"Stop me every time I go to take off your shirt. I know you're not shy, Connor."

"Does it matter if my shirt is on or off?"

"I suppose not. Although now that I think about it, it does somehow make me feel even more naked with you still half-dressed and apparently determined to stay that way."

He let go of her to drag his fingers through his hair. "I wouldn't exactly call wearing a shirt being half-dressed."

"All right, how about too dressed? You're too dressed. Is that better?" She purposefully moved her hands to the button once again.

"Gaby, wait." This time he simply laid his fingers lightly atop hers. "It's not about the shirt. It's just...I have...scars."

"That's why you won't take your shirt off?" she asked, staring at him in disbelief. "Do you actually think I'd care about something like that...that I would want you less because your body isn't perfect?"

"Maybe not."

"Maybe not?" she countered, her voice rising in direct proportion to her displeasure.

"All right," he said. "Definitely not."

"You got that right," she said. "This wasn't about scoring with a perfect 10."

"What a relief," he muttered.

"If it was, I could have saved myself a lot of aggravation and just hung around outside the stage door of some male strip club. And besides," she added as he appeared to be searching for an appropriate response to that, "I've seen your scars before, remember? In fact, as I recall, DeWolfe, you used to wear them like badges of honor."

"You haven't seen these," he said quietly.

"It doesn't matter. One scar is pretty much—"

He cut in. "Gaby, the scars on my chest are from burns. They're from the explosion."

She went silent, letting his revelation sink in. "I see."

"Do you?" he countered, sitting up and grasping the front of his shirt, yanking on it and sending buttons shooting in all directions. "I kept my shirt on because I didn't want you to see this for the first time when we were about to make love. I knew you would ask about it and I didn't want to have to tell you. I didn't want to have to see the look on your face when you saw them and realized that I'm a walking reminder of everything you want to forget.''

Gaby stared at his badly scarred chest, at the patches of puckered skin, at the varying shades of red, enough to comprise their own scarlet rainbow. She stared and didn't flinch or look away until she lifted her gaze to meet his, finding it shuttered and unreadable.

"I know what you said about wanting to meld the past and the present," he said. "This just didn't strike me as the best time to start . . . if such a thing is even possible," he finished grimly.

"How . . ." she began, and halted. "I didn't know . . ."

"That I'd been burned?" he finished for her, releasing the edges of his shirt so that it fell closed, leaving visible only a narrow ribbon of scarred flesh.

Gaby nodded. "At least not badly enough to leave those scars. I thought you had . . ."

A cynical smile edged his lips as she halted once again, her expression awkward. "You thought I'd walked out of there scot-free and left Joel to die."

"No." She shook her head vehemently. "No, I knew you wouldn't have left him, that you would have done everything you could to save him if it was possible. I just thought you had somehow been standing in the right place when it happened, near a door or something and that you lucked out. . . ."

"Again," he interjected, his drawl heavy with sarcasm.

She refused to deny it. "Yes, again." She shook her head. "I never even thought to ask how badly you were hurt. I guess I was too wrapped up in my own pain. I'm so sorry, Connor."

"It doesn't matter," he said, smiling for her sake. Toby might not recognize a manufactured smile when he saw one, but his mother did.

She rested her hand on his shoulder. "It does to me. Tell me about it, Connor."

"There's nothing to tell. The whole ceiling came down on us. Something—a support beam, I think—landed on my chest, pinning me to the floor. By the time I managed to move it off me, the place was filled with smoke. I tried..." He stopped and lay back down beside her. "I got out somehow, but I don't remember doing it. I woke up in the hospital and—" he shrugged "—you've seen the results. My own fault really. They tell me it would have healed better if I hadn't checked myself out of the hospital early."

"Why did you?"

"For the funeral."

"Of course." She closed her eyes, wincing. "And after all that I told you to go to hell. God, what a bitch I must have seemed to you."

"No. You just seemed like a woman who'd been dealt a lousy break that she didn't deserve."

Gaby wrapped her arms around herself, cold suddenly in spite of the sun overhead. "I was scared, Connor, so scared."

"I know, Gaby," he said quietly, wrapping his arms around her, as well, pulling her close to him.

"I think in some ways I've been scared ever since."

She felt him nod.

"Connor?"

"Hmm?" he responded, his warm palm pressed flat on her back, rubbing gently.

"I can't marry Adam Ressler."

"Good. 'Cause I don't share."

No, he wouldn't, Gaby thought, affection for him curving her lips just a little as she laid her head against his chest, against his open shirt and that narrow ribbon of warm flesh and closed her eyes.

"And Connor?" she said after a minute.

"Yeah?"

"I don't care about your scars," she told him, the drowsy remark punctuated by a yawn. "Not any of them."

Not any of them. Connor thought that over as his own eyes closed, wondering what her words meant, sleep sneaking up on him before he figured it out.

When they woke, Gaby fixed lunch for him using the leftovers from the night before—sliced chicken sandwiches and a marinated salad of tomatoes and corn. Connor tried to guess which spices had gone into the marinade, showing off his culinary wizardry, she teased. Gaby couldn't deny it, however; when it came to spices, the man knew his stuff.

Watching him chew, his expression as intent and discriminating as a wine connoisseur's, she was struck by a sudden vision of a big old house with a kitchen roomy enough to accommodate a center island and her and Connor cooking there together. Chopping and stirring and tasting, side by side until the Connor in her imagination cleared the countertop with one violent sweep of his arm, grasped her by the waist and lifted her up there, going to work on her instead.

Of course, whatever food they had been preparing just conveniently disappeared, the way such details do in daydreams, and then the vision in her head became involved and so erotically compelling she had to blink and ask the real Connor, sitting across from her, to repeat whatever he had said before she could tell him that yes, yes, it was tarragon that he was tasting.

Later they went for a walk along the shore and up into the woods where it was cool and dark and where Connor backed her up against a tree and pulled aside her shorts and panties, unzipped his jeans and made love to her with the same abrupt air of dominance as the Connor in her daydream. His manner excited her, his lovemaking left her weak and the whole incident made her wonder if he could somehow read her mind.

The afternoon encounter was simply a hurried prelude to what lay ahead. Inspired, Gaby scoured the cabin, gathering all the candles she could find and arranging them in every available nook and cranny in the spacious upstairs bathroom. After dinner she sneaked upstairs alone to light them, tossing scented bath oil into the roomy tub and filling it to near the top. When everything was ready, she took Connor by his uninjured hand, ordered him to close his eyes, and led him into the fragrant, flickering fantasy she had created.

He rose to the occasion admirably, magnificently, repeatedly. Spice-smarts and great stamina—what more could she ask for in a man? she mused later, much later, long after the water had cooled and her poor, overworked muscles had grown too limp to move.

Connor obliged by carrying her to bed, where he joined her and somehow managed to arouse her all over again.

Afterward he lay beside her, his legs entwined with hers, murmuring as he nuzzled her throat, something he seemed especially fond of doing.

"The perfect end to a perfect day," he said.

"You mean it's over?"

"If it's not," he retorted dryly, "I won't live till morning."

"Well, in that case I suppose tomorrow's another day."

"Mmm." He smiled, thinking about the possibilities a whole new day with Gaby presented.

"There's just one thing I wish," she revealed with a sleepy sigh. "One thing that really would make it perfect."

Connor opened his eyes, frowning, fully prepared to move whatever mountain necessary to indulge her. "What's that?"

"I wish I had taken my purse with me."

She said it with a sort of wistfulness, as if regretting her own thoughtlessness in leaving it behind rather than the fact that she'd been brought there without warning and against her will.

"Your purse," he repeated stoically, thinking he knew more about dealing with mountains.

"Mmm."

"I have a comb you can use," he offered.

"Thanks, I found a comb and a few other essentials in the bathroom."

"I suppose you want your makeup," he said, prepared to tell her she didn't need it.

"Not really." She touched her lips. "Although some lip balm would be nice. I think the sun burned my lips. They feel so raw and puffy."

"Mine, too," he said, a hint of laughter in his deep voice. "But I don't think the sun is to blame."

"Oh?" she countered a half instant before his mouth settled on hers and lingered, making his point most eloquently. "Oh."

He hugged her to him, loving everything about her, loving her with an absoluteness he hadn't known possible. "So why do you want your purse?"

"Actually it's my wallet I wish I had with me."

"Your wallet." He thought of all the new possibilities that presented and ran through them out loud. "Money? Credit cards? License?"

"Pictures."

"Pictures?" Connor felt cheated. He never would have thought of pictures. There were no pictures in his wallet.

"Pictures of Toby," she explained. "I really miss him. I thought if I had a picture of him to look at, maybe I would miss him a little less."

Connor folded his hands behind his head and stared at the ceiling. He had planned their stay there meticulously, location, supplies, everything down to the last detail. He'd anticipated every possible contingency and planned for them, as well. If a true emergency arose, he would be ready. As far as he was concerned, fetching a five-year-old because his mother missed him didn't constitute an emergency.

Just the same, he was going to do it, along with just about anything else it might take to make her smile. Gaby had shown him a mountain he could move and, part of the original plan or not, he was going to move it for her. It was, he thought with a resurgence of the cynical self-awareness he had managed to stay one step ahead of most of the day, the least he could do for her.

"In that case," he said, "I guess we'll just have to make a trip back to the city."

Gaby lifted up on one elbow to peer at him in confusion. "You're kidding, right?"

"Wrong."

"You mean you're willing to drive me all the way home to get my purse?"

"Not your purse. The real thing. First thing in the morning we're going to drive to your mother's to get Toby and bring him back here with us."

The look of utter amazement and dawning joy on her face was worth every bit of the aggravation he knew this little deviation from his plan was going to bring him before it was over.

"Oh, thank you, Connor," she cried, reaching for his hand.

He winced as she squeezed it too hard.

"Oh, I'm sorry...your sore hand!"

"It's okay," he told her, smiling through the sudden pain.

"I was so excited I forgot all about your stitches."

"It's fine now."

"Really?"

"Really."

"Good. I would never hurt you. You've made me so happy...and I love you for it."

He held on to her as she squirmed with excitement and rattled on about how wonderful he was to do it. He wasn't accustomed to such lavish thanks or praise, and it made him uncomfortable for reasons he couldn't name. He mostly kept his head down and just let her talk until she wound down.

Only one thing she said stuck with him, refusing to be shrugged off as lightly as the rest. *I love you for it,* she'd said.

Not *I love you,* period, he noted, but *I love you for it.* Not that it meant anything. It was just an expression, no more to be taken literally than *Let's do lunch* or *The check is in the mail.* He understood that. Still, it got him to thinking and hoping that maybe, just maybe...and those maybes were enough to keep him awake and dreaming long after Gaby had fallen asleep in his arms.

Chapter 9

The trip to Providence to pick up Toby turned out to be not quite as simple as Connor had made it sound the night before. It didn't matter. Gaby didn't care how complicated it became or how long it took as long as she could have Toby with her. She was grateful to Connor for going to so much trouble when he didn't have to, and she loved him for offering to do it.

It was, she came to realize as she lay awake in the first pink light of morning, watching him still asleep by her side, only one of the things she loved about him. Why she had fallen so hard so fast for this man she'd once thought she hated, she couldn't begin to understand, much less explain. She could, however, make a list long enough to launch a kite of all the things she had come to love about him in only a few short days.

She loved his strength, and how his hair was thick and ramrod straight, so different from her own soft, loose waves. She loved his deep voice and the snuffly sound he made when he dozed off with his head on her breast. She loved how stubborn he was about getting his own way and the wicked grin he often flashed as he went about getting it. She loved him for being

afraid to show her the scars on his chest and she loved him because of his scars, both inside and out.

He'd feared those from the explosion would be too painful
a reminder of the past, but Gaby wasn't afraid of the past, not
any longer. She wasn't afraid of the future, either. It felt good
to shed her ever-present layer of apprehension, and she had
Connor to thank for that, too. She'd finally figured out that
like him, she was a survivor.

The actual ride back to the city was considerably more fun
than the trip up there had been. For one thing she no longer felt
obliged to sit erect on the back of the bike, making only enough
contact with Connor to keep from being thrown off. Now she
savored the thrill of riding with her arms wrapped around his
waist, her pelvis snuggled up close behind him, free to rest her
cheek against his solidly muscled back whenever the wind became too much for her.

With the physical attraction between them still fever hot and
compulsive, it was nearly noon by the time they actually got on
the road. They talked it over before leaving the cabin and decided that, since they obviously couldn't make the return trip
with Toby on the bike, they would first stop at her house and
pick up her car. Now, riding down her street behind Connor,
she giggled as she imagined the reaction of her neighbors if they
saw her.

She doubted any of them considered her the motorcycle
type . . . if there was such a thing. Why should they? Since she
had never before thought of herself that way. Quite the opposite, in fact. She'd always considered herself too sensible, too
conservative, too cautious to enjoy flying down the street with
the wind whipping her hair around her face.

"It's too dangerous," she had insisted to Joel that time years
ago when Connor had tried to talk him into buying a bike so
they could ride together.

"Life's dangerous," he had told her before eventually heed-
ing her objections and passing on the deal.

So Joel had never had the chance to join Connor on one of
his legendary bike rides and he'd ended up being killed anyway. Fate. She shivered, regret welling up inside her. She tight-

ened her hold on Connor's waist. As a mother she wasn't prepared to completely toss caution to the wind when it came to living, especially not when it involved Toby. But she vowed, for both their sakes, to think long and hard before she arbitrarily dismissed a chance for them to feel the wind on their faces.

Connor needed no directions to her house. He turned into the driveway of the brick-front Colonial with the black shutters and slowed to a stop before the double garage doors, leaving the engine running.

"Can you open the garage door from out here?" he asked over the engine noise.

"Yes. I can override the alarm at the keypad and open it from there."

"Good. Can we get into the house from the garage?"

Gaby shook her head. "No. That door is bolted from the kitchen side. But I have a key hidden in the toolshed out back that will let us in the front door."

"All right," he said, glancing around, his expression guarded. "That will have to do."

Puzzled by his demeanor, Gaby looked around, as well, not surprised to find that there was no one in sight. It was a quiet neighborhood of elegant, well-spaced houses, all with large yards, many with in-ground pools and lavishly landscaped for privacy. Most of her neighbors worked full-time. The few who were home during the day reserved their outdoor activity for early morning or after dinner, when it was cooler.

"Go on and open it," he directed after peering down the street in both directions. "The sooner we get inside and out of sight, the better I'll feel."

Gaby waited until she had the garage door open and he had pulled the motorcycle into the spot beside her white station wagon where Joel had once parked before asking him to explain his caution.

"Adam has no idea I'm back," he told her as he pushed the button to lower the door once again. "I'm hoping that he bought your story about needing time to think and that he believes all he has to worry about is a bride who's having some second thoughts. It would be nice to keep the element of surprise on our side, and if he's watching the house and sees me or my bike hanging around, it's blown.''

The air in the garage was warm and musty smelling from having been closed up tightly while she was away. It added to the otherworldly feeling she got as she listened to Connor talk about Adam as if he was some kind of B-movie gangster.

"Do you really think Adam is watching the house? It's hard to picture him sitting out there in his fancy sports car, around the clock, without arousing suspicion . . . or without us noticing him as we pulled in, for that matter.''

"Maybe he's not watching around the clock," he responded with a negligent shrug. "Maybe he drives by from time to time just to check the place out, maybe he pays someone else to drive by . . . or to sit out there somewhere and wait for you to show up.''

Gaby shivered, finding the possibility alone creepy.

Connor took her chin between his bent index finger and his thumb and smiled gently at her. "It's not anything you have to worry about, Gabrielle. I'd just rather that Adam not know I'm involved in this for as long as possible. Okay?''

"Okay." She took a deep breath, finding that the accusations against Adam that had seemed so outrageous when she first heard them were seeming more and more believable, and that it was becoming more and more difficult to keep from dwelling on them.

"I'll get the key from the shed," she said. "As long as we're here, there are a few things inside I'd like to pick up, a few things for Toby and for myself . . . like shoes.''

He feigned disappointment. "Do you have to? There's something about a barefoot woman that really gets to me.''

"I'm sure you'll adjust," she retorted.

Connor followed her out to the backyard, waiting while she retrieved the front-door key from its hiding place under the wheelbarrow.

"Was all of this Joel's?" he asked, looking around at the peg boards that lined the walls and the assortment of rakes, shovels and gardening tools hanging there.

"Most of it. The Mickey Mouse sprinkler belongs to Toby."

His mouth lifted in a quick smile before he resumed his perusal of the shed's contents. "I never knew he had so much . . . stuff."

"And this is just the outdoor 'stuff,' " she told him. "Once he built that workroom in the basement, there was no stopping him. Every new tool or hardware gadget he came across had to be added to his collection."

She smiled affectionately as she led the way around to the front of the house. "My favorite was something called the stud finder. I used to kid him and say that if we ever got divorced I wanted that included in my half of the property settlement . . . for obvious reasons. Joel would always hug me and say that if I were ever unattached, I wouldn't have to find studs, they'd find me."

"Looks like he was right," Connor said lightly as he waited for her to unlock the door. "Though I'm not sure I care to be lumped with Adam Ressler under the heading of Studs."

Swinging the door open, she turned back to him and looped her arms around his neck. "I really can't comment with any authority on Adam, but you, sweet Wolf, have a great many decidedly studlike qualities."

"Oh, yeah?" he drawled as he backed her over the threshold and kicked the door shut behind him. "Name one."

"Your name," she said when he finished kissing her. She was just a little breathless. "Wolf is definitely a studly name."

"Studly?"

"Mmm-hmm."

"Names don't count. What's another of these studly qualities you say I possess?"

Laughing, she slipped from his grasp. "I don't think I should tell you. It will only serve to inflame your already overheated libido."

"You inflame my libido," he said softly, trailing her as she backed into the living room and scooted to put a table between them. "Come over here, Gabrielle."

"I can't. We've already wasted enough time." She circled the small cherry accent table, moving at the same pace he was so that they remained on opposite sides of it. "That's what you said when we got a late start this morning, remember?"

"No," he said, tiring of her game of cat and mouse and reaching across the table to grab her. "I said come here."

"Connor, be careful...my vase," she cried as his elbow bumped the crystal vase centered on the table and it began to tip. Reaching under his arm, she managed to grab it with her free hand and steady it. She exhaled loudly. "Whew. That was close."

"Forget the vase. I'll buy you a new one." He was still holding on to her, the dark glint of intention in his eyes.

"I don't think so...at least not one like this," she said airily. "This is Lenox. It was a wedding present, and the style has been discontinued, which makes it even more valuable."

Connor felt as if he had just had his hand slapped for reaching into the cookie jar.

"I see." He released her abruptly and dropped his arm to his side. "In that case I guess I should be careful. Go ahead and get your things, Gaby. I'll wait here...and I won't touch anything," he added, turning away from her to gaze around what even he could tell was a very carefully and expensively decorated room. "I promise."

Connor felt her come up behind him, her touch on his shoulder hesitant.

"Connor, I'm sorry if I sounded...picky. I didn't mean it that way. I just didn't want the vase to get broken. I'm probably so used to warning Toby to be careful that it was automatic."

He smiled sardonically, not at all cheered by her explanation. "Right. I understand. You have a great place here, Gaby, with lots of valuable, irreplaceable things. You have a right to expect guests in your home to be careful. Now, go get whatever it is you want to bring with you. Like you said, we've already wasted enough time today."

Still looking troubled and apologetic, she disappeared up the stairs, leaving him alone with the discontinued-style vase and the handmade Oriental rugs and the collection of porcelain figurines that he seemed to recall had been in the Flanders family since . . . he didn't remember exactly. The invention of porcelain, probably.

Squinting, he hunkered down for a closer look at the assemblage of gently rounded, softly colored birds and flowers and strangely elongated people . . . all of them probably irreplaceable, too. Yep, he thought, straightening and glancing around, just about the only thing around here that wasn't irreplaceable was him. If he checked into it, he'd bet he'd find that even the mouse sprinkler in the shed was probably some sort of limited, commemorative edition.

Restless, he paced across the living room to the double glass-paneled doors that opened into the dining room. There, too, everything was in perfect order, a lace cloth arranged on the gleaming dark wood table, silver candlesticks all in a row.

Funny, he mused, trailing his finger along the edge of a silver tray that held a crystal decanter and some glasses, he must have been in this house hundreds of times before, on holidays and for parties and just to hang out and watch a game with Joel on the TV in the den, but he'd never noticed how . . . settled it was here. How filled it was with permanence and details, how structured and heavily weighted a life lived within these solid walls must be.

He'd never really thought about what Joel did when they weren't together, when he wasn't playing poker with the guys or watching a game. Now he did. He thought about him entertaining his boss in this dining room and using the tools out in the shed and living the life that came with a house like this . . . with a woman like Gabrielle. And he was in awe of the friend he had loved and lost.

He wandered out of the dining room and into the kitchen, stopping to look at the finger paintings hanging on the refrigerator, some signed Toby and some Mommy. He smiled, only slightly less intimidated by the mother-son projects as he was by the porcelain figurines in the other room. On the calendar hanging nearby were pencil notations for dentist appointments and swimming lessons and birthday parties. He read a few and turned away. If he were to wander into the bathroom, he wondered, would there be things there, too, to make him feel like an interloper?

Hitching his hands in his jeans pockets, he stood by the window and stared out at the relatively open space of the backyard. He couldn't shake the feeling that had followed him from room to room, growing steadily stronger. It was hard to put into words. It was almost as if the walls of the house were closing in on him. No, he thought, that wasn't it. It was more as if, as spacious as it was, the house was too small for him, as if there was no room for him within its solid walls. He felt trapped, caged.

It wasn't the first time he'd felt that way. Once, a while after his mother died, right after the locked-trunk-in-the-attic incident, to be precise, his father had gotten the bright idea that he was too young to be left alone with his brothers after school. He had arranged for an aunt, a distant relative of his who lived across town and whom Connor had never even met, to pick him up at school each day and look after him until his father could get him on the way home from work.

Aunt Grace, he was instructed to call her. She lived in a house a lot like this, settled, filled with things he was too reckless and clumsy to be trusted around. One day he tripped over a little footrest she had near her chair. He could still see it, covered in red velvet and with ugly, spindly legs that curved out at the top. One of those spindly legs snapped off when he caught his foot on it. Before he could say he was sorry, almost before he'd regained his balance, Aunt Grace slapped him across the face and called him a buffoon. A great, lumbering buffoon, he recalled, his lips narrowed and curved dangerously as he also remembered how much the slap had stung and how the pale red imprint of her hand had still been on his cheek when he went to school the next day.

After it happened, he had run out of her house and kept running all the way home. Later, when his father stormed into his room and demanded to know what had happened, he'd told him that he would rather let his brothers lock him in the trunk in the attic and forget about him all over again than have to stay with that aunt who wasn't even his aunt, and that he was never going back to that place where he didn't belong ever again. And he never had.

He exhaled roughly, wishing Gaby would hurry up. It was hot in there, and while he knew the temperature had nothing to do with how out of place he felt, it did provide him with an excuse to holler up for her to get moving.

Almost immediately she came rushing down the stairs, her face flushed, wisps of shiny dark hair slipping from the braid at the back of her head, the braid he'd watched her arrange as he'd lain in bed that morning. He had to admit, the memory of that moment, along with the smile she now flashed at him coming down the stairs, went a long way toward wiping out the uneasiness he'd felt since walking in there.

She was carrying an oversize tote bag, denim blue with pink roses scattered across it, along with an armload of children's books.

"For Toby," she explained. "I don't like him out in the sun during the middle of the day, and these will help me persuade him to stay put in the shade for a while. And I want to bring some snacks I know he'll like. Some Fun Fruits and animal crackers. Maybe I'll even steal the box of sugar-coated cereal from my mother's," she said, talking more to herself than him as she headed for the kitchen.

Before she was through, she had filled two shopping bags with more things to bring back to the cabin.

"That should do it," she told him.

Connor surveyed the pile by the back door. "I'm beginning to see why you drive a station wagon."

"Stop grumbling. You've never had to pack for a five-year-old."

"No," he admitted, feeling the words like a lance near his heart. "I never have, at that. If you're ready to go, there is one last thing I'd like to do before we leave."

"What's that?"

"I'd like to take a look at those boxes of Joel's things you said you packed away in the basement."

Her face lost most of its color. "But why?"

"You mentioned that you saved the personal papers from his office."

She nodded, still looking stricken. "It was mostly correspondence and his old date books. There were also some notes for a book on household economics that he wanted to write, and a few notebooks he had hanging around. Do you think there might be something there to shed some light on what happened?"

"I don't know. But it's worth a try. I do think that Joel knew exactly what was going on, he just didn't know how vicious it was going to get. As painful as it will be for you to look through his things, Gaby, it's as close as we're going to come to hearing what Joel has to say, and I don't think we should pass it up."

"No," she said, the delicate muscles in her throat flexing as she swallowed and lifted her chin resolutely. "I don't, either." She reached to open the door to the basement and flipped on the light over the stairs. "Come on. I'll show you where I put them."

The boxes were on shelves in the storage area behind Joel's workshop. They were unlabeled and shoved all the way to the back, behind more boxes filled with clothes and toys that Toby had already outgrown in the time since she'd packed Joel's things away.

"I should have done a better job," she confessed. "I could have at least labeled the boxes. I usually do, but I just wanted to get it done. Out of sight, out of mind," she added as she slit the packing tape and opened the first box Connor lifted down. It was filled with pictures, some in albums, some loose, some still in the frames that had once been scattered throughout the house. "Only it never quite worked out that way."

He watched as she sifted through the uppermost pictures in the box, stopping to press the back of her hand to her eyes at one point. Connor resisted the urge to gather her in his arms. It wasn't his place to intrude. Gaby knew he was there if she needed him.

She pulled from the box a picture of Joel that Connor remembered well. It was taken when they were still in high school. In it Joel was wearing his old red-and-white high school bas-

ketball uniform and spinning a basketball on the tip of his finger, a trick he could do and Connor couldn't, and that Joel
never tired of demonstrating.

Gaby stared at the picture for a long time, as if it held some
sort of secret she wanted to uncover. Connor didn't rush her.
Finally she placed it carefully back on top of the others in the
box and turned to him.

"I don't think there are any papers in here," she told him.
"Why don't we try another box?"

They located the box containing the things from his office on
the third try. She readily agreed with Connor's suggestion that
they bring it back to the cabin, where they would have more
time to look the contents over thoroughly. She appeared relieved to put the task off for a while longer, and Connor re-
gretted having to make her do it at all. It must have shown on
his face, because she stopped him as he hoisted the heavy box
and turned toward the stairs, placing her hand gently on his
arm and going up on her toes to kiss him on the mouth.

"I'm glad I did this," she said. "And I'm glad you were here
with me when I did. It feels right." Smiling, she held up the
picture of Joel in his uniform. She must have removed it from
the box of pictures, along with the handful of others she was
holding, when he was busy restacking the other boxes. "I think
it's time Toby had some pictures of his father around. He has
this collage of his favorite sports stars in his room, and there's
the perfect place for this picture of Joel right at the top."

"I think that's a great idea." He grinned as he started walking. "So Toby's a sports fan already, huh?"

"What can I say? It's in the genes."

"Really? I never knew you were a sports fan," he teased,
intentionally misunderstanding.

"Very funny."

"Seriously who do you like in the Pazienza fight next week?
All right, all right, don't hit, I'll stop. And don't push," he
added, pausing on the stairs. "I can't see where I'm going."

"Then let me take the lead."

"Never. Men lead, women follow."

"Oh, really? As I recall, that's not what you said this morning, in bed, when you wanted me to—"

"That was different," he interrupted.

"Says who?"

"Me. It's a guy thing that you wouldn't understand."

They kept the banter up as they loaded the box of papers, along with all the things Gaby was bringing with them, into the back of her car. By the time they pulled out of the garage, the harmony that had miraculously developed between them during the past few days had been pretty much restored and Connor had almost forgotten the uneasiness he'd felt inside her house.

Almost, but not entirely. A small piece of that uneasiness remained embedded in him, like a splinter that slips beneath the skin, hidden from sight and only hurting if you move the wrong way, until it inevitably festers, without warning, forcing you to pay attention.

The drive to Gaby's mother's house took about fifteen minutes. Gaby had called ahead and explained that she would be coming for Toby, warning her mother not to mention it to anyone, especially not to Adam. She'd assured Connor that it was best to call ahead so that Toby would be ready and that her mother could be trusted not to let anything slip.

When they arrived, Toby was waiting in the window. He came tearing through the front door and across the porch and landed in Gaby's arms the instant she was out of the car. She bent down and gathered him close as Connor stood apart from them, watching.

Joel's son, he thought, taking note of the little boy's familiar sandy hair and intense brown eyes. Joel's son. The realization was like something much stronger than he was, gripping his heart and squeezing. It was impossible to stand there—watching Gaby laughing and hoisting Toby in the air, pretending that he had grown bigger in just the short time she'd been gone—without thinking about Joel and that he should be the one witnessing that moment, sharing in it.

Countless times after the explosion, Connor's thoughts had turned to moments exactly like this one, dwelling on all the moments Joel was going to miss out on, all the summer days and birthdays and graduations. And inside of him there would rise up a burning resentment that steadily, inevitably was edged out by guilt and by the belief that when you cut right through to the bone, it was his fault that Joel had to miss out on all of it, his fault that Joel was dead.

This time was different. This time it was the guilt that was edged out and overwhelmed by other feelings. Watching Toby laugh at something Gaby had whispered in his ear, Connor felt only sadness for the little boy's loss, and the same steely, single-minded determination to exact vengeance on his father's behalf that had brought Connor home in the first place.

They moved inside, where Gaby dealt gracefully with the introductions, referring to Connor as an old friend.

"What's wrong with your hand?" Toby asked him matter-of-factly.

Connor held up the hand, freshly bandaged by Gaby that morning, and briefly explained how he'd injured it, but not who had stitched him up or how.

Gaby's mother was a pretty, silver-haired lady whom Connor remembered from get-togethers they had both attended at Gaby's house in the past. He could tell she remembered him, too, and not entirely favorably, judging from the wary look she wore as Gaby briefly explained what was going on.

With Toby present it was necessary to skim over most of the details of her disappearance from the church and the renewed investigation into Joel's death. It was obvious to Connor that the boy was happy to have his mother back with him and was looking forward to spending time at the lake. It was just as obvious that Gaby didn't want to alarm him. Finally she sent him to fetch his things from the bedroom and took the opportunity to hurriedly fill in some of the missing pieces.

"Oh, my," her mother said when Gaby had finished, pressing her fingers to her throat. "If what you say about Adam is true, he could be dangerous. Maybe we should call the authorities."

Gaby touched her hand reassuringly. "Mom, Connor is the authorities . . . at least he was. And they're already working on it."

"But he's not with the force any longer," her mother argued, giving Gaby a warning look that wasn't lost on Connor. "So why would they ask him to look after you and Toby?"

"They didn't, ma'am," Connor replied before Gaby could. "I asked them to let me handle this end of it. I figured I knew Gabrielle and I knew Adam and, to be honest, I trust myself to do the job more than I trust anyone else. I won't let anything happen to your daughter or your grandson. I promise you."

"I'm going to hold you to that," the older woman replied, looking him right in the eye, leaving him no doubt how Gaby came by her stubbornness.

Connor offered her his hand. "Deal," he said, and they shook on it.

When Toby returned with his overnight bag and another bag full of toys, Connor enlisted his help in loading them into the car. Gaby kissed her mother goodbye and held the door to the back seat open for Toby to climb in.

"Seat belt," she said, shutting the door after him, and Connor noticed that as she slid into her own seat in front she turned to make sure he had heeded the reminder to fasten it.

The whole procedure was done smoothly and efficiently, as if she had done it hundreds of times before. Which, of course, she had, Connor realized, seeing her at that instant not simply as the woman he had fallen in love with, but as a living, breathing, integral part of something much bigger than anything the two of them alone might share. She wasn't simply his lover and never would be, but someone's mother and someone's daughter, a sister, a friend and probably a lot of other things he wasn't even aware of.

She had a whole other life he knew nothing about, and thinking about that other life made that sliver of feeling he'd carried away from her house shift inside him, sliding in a little deeper.

He thought about that other life of hers most of the way back to the cabin, with Toby chattering to his mother about all the great things he and his nana had done while she was gone. He thought about where he might fit into that life of Gaby's, amid all the swimming lessons and gardening tools and irreplaceable possessions. He thought about it and he realized that the uneasy feeling he'd had back at her house, the feeling he'd at first thought was fear of being trapped by everything the house symbolized, wasn't really fear of being trapped at all. He could see now that it was something much worse.

What he was really afraid of was failing, of trying to find a place for himself in her life only to discover there wasn't one, or worse, that one existed but he didn't have what it took to fill it. He wasn't like Joel. He never had been. And he was afraid of letting Gaby down all over again.

How did that old saying go? he thought as he drove on into the deepening afternoon. "Better to have tried and failed than never to have tried at all." That wasn't it exactly, but it would do. Better to have tried and failed than never to have tried at all. The problem with all those old sayings was that they never went far enough.

Better to have tried and failed—even if it might mean screwing up other people's lives and hurting a woman who, God knew, had already been hurt more than enough—than never to have tried at all. That version came a hell of a lot closer to the truth, and he wasn't buying it, not for a minute.

When they pulled within sight of the lake, Toby whooped with excitement and strained at his seat belt to see as much of it as he could. Listening to him, Connor was struck by how differently a five-year-old perceives things. To Toby the medium-sized lake was "the ocean," the cabin "a cowboy's house," the surrounding woods a whole new world he was champing at the bit to explore.

"Later," Gaby told him, stretching her legs after the long ride.

"You always say later," Toby grumbled. "I want to touch the water now. Please, just my toes, Mommy?"

She shot Connor a resigned smile. "Do you mind? He's been cooped up for a while and—"

"Go ahead," he said without letting her finish. He opened the door to the cargo compartment in back. "I'll bring this stuff inside."

"If you wait a few minutes we can—"

"I said go ahead," he told her. "I don't mind."

It was true. He didn't mind. In fact, he preferred to do it alone, making several trips from the car to the cabin rather than having to work alongside Gaby, joking as they divvied up the boxes and bags, brushing against each other each time they passed in the doorway.

The fact is he was used to doing things alone. He worked best that way. A few days and some great sex didn't alter the habits of a lifetime. Or anything else, for that matter. As he grabbed her open-topped tote, the books she'd brought along for Toby slid out. Connor hurriedly grabbed them and jammed them back into the bag. What did he know about storybooks and garden tools and kids? Nothing, that's what, and at thirty-five it was a little late to start learning. For everyone's sake he had to reestablish some distance between himself and Gaby, and unloading the car by himself was as good a place as any to start.

He had the job done before she and Toby came racing back from the water. From his chair on the deck he noticed how Gaby slowed slightly as they reached the steps, just enough so that Toby touched the top railing first.

"I won," he shouted. "I beat you."

"You sure did. I'm going to have to start eating my Wheaties if I'm going to keep up with you, kiddo."

"Uh-uh." He shook his head emphatically, his silky hair lifting like a halo around his head. "I'll still beat you, cause you're a girl and boys are always faster than girls."

"What?" Gaby gasped, her expression one of mock horror. "Who told you that?"

"Aunt Lisa's boyfriend, Jack. Jack says boys do everything better than girls except cook."

"Well, it so happens Jack is wrong, and I can prove it."

Connor sensed her turning to him and he kept his gaze focused on the lake.

"Tell him, Connor," she said.

He slanted a glance her way. "Tell him what?"

"That some boys cook better than girls."

Connor shrugged. "Beats me."

He could feel the surprise that jolted her at his coolness, feel her perplexed gaze resting on him even as Toby was whispering to her. All Connor heard was the last part of his plea. "Ask him. Please, Mommy, ask him."

Connor braced himself as Gaby ambled closer to where he was sitting, standing between him and the water so that he was forced to look at her.

"Connor," she began in a tone that wrapped around him like a silk sheet, "Toby and I were checking out the boat down there by the water and we wondered if maybe later you'd take us for a little spin around the lake."

"It's broken," he said. "Remember?"

The brightness in her eyes clouded over. "I thought you had gotten the motor going."

"I did, but the cowling keeps lifting up and letting water spray in and she stalls out."

She turned to Toby, who was standing by her side listening intently. "Sorry, kiddo, it looks like the boat is out of commission. But I have an idea. How would you like to take your dinosaurs down to that sandy patch over there and build your own Jurassic Park?"

Instantly the boy's face brightened. "Okay."

"Come on, I'll help you find them."

They went inside, reappearing a few minutes later, both with their hands full of plastic dinosaurs of various sizes and types. They carried them to a small area near the edge of the trees, where Gaby lingered for a few minutes before straightening and brushing the sand from her legs.

The second he saw her move, Connor abandoned his chair on the deck and went inside. Distance, distance, he reminded himself as he grabbed a can of cola from the refrigerator, intending to drink it upstairs in his room.

Gaby intercepted him just as he reached the stairs.

"Connor, hold on. I need to talk with you about something."

"What's that?"

"The sleeping arrangements. There are only two bedrooms up there and, well, I know Toby is only five, but I still wouldn't feel comfortable having him know that we're sleeping together."

"No problem."

"So I thought I'd just keep my stuff where it is and put him in the room with me."

"Fine." He moved his foot up a step.

Gaby shook her head, eyeing him with a look that was part wounded, part bewildered. "No, it's not fine. It sucks, frankly." Moving closer, she lifted her hands to his waist. "I loved spending last night in your bed. As far as I'm concerned, spending all night, every night there would be...heaven. It just wouldn't be reality. Not my reality, anyway."

Connor felt his insides tighten.

"Toby is my reality and I have to think of what's best for him. But," she continued before Connor could again say *No problem* and extricate himself, "fortunately he is a very heavy sleeper. Once I tuck him in, he's gone until morning. Which means there will be all those long, lovely hours in the middle of the night when I can—"

"Can sneak off to spend a little time with me?" He removed her hands from his sides. "Thanks, Gabrielle, but I don't think that will work."

"Connor, please..."

"No, you're right. You have to put Toby's needs first. I understand that. Honest. The fact is, we both have responsibilities to attend to. I ought to be keeping my mind on the reason we're here in the first place, and I can't do that the way I should with you in my bed."

"I see."

"Good. Then it's settled. You and Toby stay in your room, and I'll stay in mine."

There wasn't anything to add to that, or if there was, Gaby couldn't think of anything. Not anything civil, at any rate. Once before, she had made the mistake of believing she knew everything there was to know about Connor DeWolfe. The past few days had proved how wrong her simplistic view of him had been, revealing to her new and utterly unexpected aspects of the man. It seemed, however, that she still had more to learn about him.

It was true the subject of children had never come up, other than his casual queries the other day as to whether Toby was at all like his father. She had just assumed that, like most people in the world, he liked kids and got along with them reasonably well. It had never occurred to her that Connor was the type to be jealous of a five-year-old.

Shaking her head, she started to turn away then stopped suddenly, her eyes narrowing thoughtfully as she stared at the empty staircase.

Either jealous, she mused, or afraid.

Chapter 10

They decided to wait until after Toby was in bed to look through the box of Joel's papers. Actually Gaby mentioned to Connor that she would prefer to wait until Toby wasn't around, unsure as she was of what they might find, and he said, "No problem."

That seemed to have become his answer to everything. Waiting to look through the box was no problem. Pasta and tomato sauce for dinner was no problem. Sleeping by himself while she was in the next room was no problem. The irony of it was that his black expression and brusque manner made her think he was definitely a man with a problem.

She just hadn't yet figured out exactly what it might be. Or what she was going to do about it when she did figure it out.

They spent the hours between dinner and Toby's bedtime mostly staying out of each other's way. Connor short-circuited all attempts at light conversation. Willing to give him the benefit of the doubt, Gaby considered that he might truly be preoccupied with the situation that had brought them there. Perhaps his sense of duty had kicked in as he sensed that things were about to start developing quickly and this was the way he acted when he was working. Perhaps, but Gaby didn't really think so.

She would have just asked him what was the matter straight out if Toby wasn't always within hearing. In case it was the investigation troubling Connor, she didn't want Toby overhearing too much. However things with Adam turned out, she was determined to shield her son from as much of the fallout as possible.

It was true that Adam and Toby had never become as close as she wished, in spite of Adam's best efforts, playing games and buying Toby outrageous presents. He had still come very close to being Toby's stepfather. Toby was bound to be hurt and confused if he had to face the fact that the man his mother almost married was in some way responsible for his father's death.

She sighed as she sat on the side of the oversize tub and watched Toby splash around, blessedly oblivious to the dark undercurrents that might be rippling beneath the surface of his life. In her fantasies of late, Toby's bonding with Adam was one more thing that would miraculously take place after the wedding, right after she and Adam learned to fall in love with each other and after she somehow managed to overcome the niggling suspicion that what Adam found most alluring about her was her share of the Black Wolf. She had been really dumb, she realized now. There had been so many signs that she was making a mistake. How could she have missed or chosen to ignore them all? If it hadn't been for Connor...

She yelped and feigned horror as Toby emerged from the water near her in a surprise attack, a sudsy warrior with dirt behind his ears and a sprinkling of freckles across his nose. If it hadn't been for Connor, she thought as she grabbed her son with one hand and the washcloth with the other, who knows what would have happened to them?

Once Toby was safely tucked in bed, she decided to take a quick shower herself. It had been a long, hot, sticky day. Besides, she hadn't lost hope that Connor would renege on his earlier stance on separate beds, and vanity demanded that if he did, she should be wearing something silky and fresh scented, rather than the shorts and T-shirt she'd worn chasing Toby around all afternoon.

Not wanting to risk waking Toby before he was in a deep sleep, she opted to use Connor's room to dress after her shower. She didn't even bother to ask, deciding it wouldn't upset her if he walked in while she was rubbing the rose-scented lotion she'd brought from home onto her skin, finishing with a splash of the same fragrance on her wrists and behind her ears, followed by a nightgown that was no more than an ivory silk tube secured by two narrow straps at the shoulders. The bodice pooled in a soft U between her breasts. She checked her reflection in the mirror and smiled. All right, DeWolfe, she thought as she ran her fingers through her hair to tousle it, resist this.

Covering her handiwork with a midnight blue, kimono-style robe, she hurried downstairs.She found Connor in the living room, seated in one of the two chairs flanking the sofa, the unopened box on the floor in front of him. Just the sight of it was sufficient to instantly clear her head of all frivolous thoughts of seduction.

"I hope I didn't take too long," she said. "I felt sticky all over."

His eyes collided with hers, their dark luster reminiscent of tangled sheets and hot, damp places.

"I mean . . ." She faltered.

Connor shrugged. "I know what you meant. Forget it. It's—"

"No problem," she finished along with him. "I know."

Settling herself in the corner of the sofa nearest him, she tugged on the sash on her robe, aware that it had loosened to reveal the bodice of her nightgown beneath. Connor was aware of it, as well, and his smoky gaze lingered there as she pulled the robe shut and secured it.

"So," she said, "have you found anything interesting?"

"I haven't looked," he replied, dragging his gaze up to meet hers. "These papers belong to you, after all. I thought it only right that I wait for you to go through them."

"Thanks. I appreciate that. I guess we should start before it gets any later." She reached for the cover of the box and removed it. "Maybe we should divide it up. It will go more quickly that way."

"All right. What do you want to start with? Date books or notebooks?"

She bit the edge of her lip. Neither, she thought, dreading the mere act of holding in her hands something that Joel had once held, reading the words that he had written with no inkling of where those words would end up or the tragic circumstances that would one day lead her to read them in search of clues . . . clues that might not even exist, clues to an act of betrayal that might not even exist.

"I'll take the date books," she said.

The process was every bit as emotionally wrenching as Gaby feared. After only a few pages she was tempted to tell Connor she'd changed her mind, that they should switch and he should do the date books or, better yet, that he could do all of it. She didn't, however. She gritted her teeth and pressed on, starting with the year before Joel was killed. Connor had explained that since they had no idea of when his suspicions were first aroused, they had to look at everything.

January, February, March. She read entries for lunch dates with friends and clients, appointments to get his hair cut and reminders to himself to bring her flowers on the third of every month . . . the day of the month that Toby had been born. She recognized his *p*s that looked like *g*s and the unique brand of shorthand he used. Joel's life unfolded on the pages before her, and it broke her heart all over again.

Only one thing kept her going when she wanted to quit, to throw the book across the room and run upstairs to hug Toby to her and pull the covers up over their heads. The knowledge that she owed it to Joel to see this through. And to Toby. And in a way to herself, as well.

The family they had once been had been shattered forever by the explosion that ripped apart the Black Wolf. For Joel and Toby and her there would be no more family outings, no more Christmas mornings, no little brothers or sisters for Toby or a smiling family portrait snapped at his wedding on some distant future day. There was no future for them period.

She understood now how the obliteration of that future made it all the more important that she not surrender their past. For all their sakes, but especially for Toby. She'd been wrong to put away Joel's pictures and discourage Toby from talking about him. Joel was worth remembering, no matter how painful the remembering could sometimes be for her. She knew now that she was strong enough to handle it. And hopefully, in spite of what she had claimed to Connor, time would lessen the pain, leaving behind only her memories of the joy they had once shared.

She would have to work at it, she knew, and the first step was the one she was taking right now. In a way this was the beginning of the complicated and sorrowful process of letting go while holding on, of looking back in order to move ahead. It was closure. It was the last act they would make as the family they once were, with Joel's own words and notes helping her to uncover the truth, a truth that sometime in the future, when he was ready, their son was going to want to hear.

Connor's agitated sigh intruded on her thoughts, startling her. She had been feeling so alone it was almost a surprise to look up and find him sitting there. A welcome surprise.

He was kneading the back of his neck, his dark brows arrowed down in a deep frown.

"No luck?" she asked.

"I can't even read some of this," he complained. "I thought doctors were supposed to have bad handwriting, but if Joel is any indication, then accountants could give the medical profession a run for its money."

"He did have a tendency to squeeze his letters together a little," she conceded.

"A little? Take a look at this." Carrying the notebook he'd been looking through, he moved to sit next to her on the sofa. "These are so tightly packed they don't even look like letters."

Amused, Gaby peered at the passage he indicated. "It says, 'Profits equal expanded client base plus expansion versus profits equals selective client base with application focus. The big question is how to convince Higgins and Clarke to act.'"

She looked up triumphantly.

"You're making that up," Connor declared.

"I most certainly am not."

He took the notebook from her and studied the scribbled paragraph again, squinting and angling his head to the side in concentration. "No way," he pronounced. "Those words you read are just not there."

"Of course they are," Gaby said, laughing. "I admit that Joel used his own style of shorthand when he wrote, but they're all there. Look, I'll show you."

She leaned closer in order to see the notebook balanced on his lap and once again read the passage out loud, following along with her finger.

"Plus?" he interrupted at one point. "Where is the word *plus?*"

"Right here."

"That's *plus?*"

"Yes. Pretend the *g* is a *p*. See it now?"

He shook his head. "Thank God we weren't pen pals, or it would have been the shortest friendship in history."

Smiling, she continued to read.

He stopped her again. "I don't see the word *with*. Show me *with*."

"Right here."

"Ha," he said loudly. "I knew it. You're faking. You can't read it, either."

"I can so."

"No way. You can tell me to pretend a *g* is a *p*, but there's no way you can convince me that is the word *with*." He stabbed the page with his finger.

"All right, I admit it. It's not exactly the word *with*. It's actually the medical transcription symbol for *with*."

"Run that by me again."

"Joel's father was a doctor," she reminded him. "Who knows? Maybe Joel inherited his poor handwriting from him. But along with it he picked up some of the common symbols used in transcribing doctors' orders and he incorporated them into his own writing. A *c* with a straight line over it is the symbol for *with*. I guess I picked them up from Joel so completely

I forgot that I use them, too. For instance," she continued as he listened, looking only half-convinced, "if I wrote a note to Joel telling him I left the keys with the baby-sitter, I would write 'Keys, *c* with a line over it, sitter.' See?"

"Would you also write a *d* and pretend it was a *k*?"

She laughed. "Not quite. But you get the general idea. Trust me, that paragraph says exactly what I told you it says."

"In that case," he said, pulling the low table in front of the sofa closer and placing the open notebook on it so it was half-way between them, "you're a genius. I think we ought to go over this together . . . and we better start back at page one. Just to be sure I didn't miss anything."

They worked for the next hour and half without stopping. It actually went faster working together. Partly because she was so much better than he was at deciphering Joel's scrawl and partly because having Connor to talk to kept her from sinking into her own thoughts.

Not that his company was enough to keep the bad feelings at bay entirely. It wasn't, and she was certain that Connor understood how difficult this was for her. Time and again he casually rescued her from the clutches of her own memory with a remark or insight that quickly tugged her back to the here and now, and to his intoxicating blend of charm and humor. And Gaby knew that at that moment in her life, it was exactly where she wanted to be.

They broke for coffee sometime around ten-thirty, both a little discouraged and doing their best to hide it from the other. Neither of them was ready to confront the possibility that they might be pursuing a dead end . . . that there might not be any evidence against Adam buried in Joel's copious notes . . . and that the reason it might not be there was because Adam was innocent of any wrongdoing.

Gaby only knew that she wanted the matter settled, and quickly. Her feelings about how she wanted it settled were not so clear-cut. If it turned out that Adam was involved in something illegal and had arranged to have Joel killed to stop him from revealing it, it would mean that Connor was what she had always believed Joel to have been: an innocent victim who happened to be in the wrong place at the wrong time. It would mean he could let himself off the hook for the explosion the way she already had in her heart. She hadn't discounted the possibility that a guilty conscience was behind his suddenly black mood and his lack of interest in sharing his bed with her again.

However, Adam's guilt would also mean that Joel had been savagely betrayed by a man he trusted and called his friend. A man she had nearly married. That would be a bitter pill to swallow. Gaby sipped her coffee, acknowledging the fact that however it turned out, it was going to be ugly.

Exactly how ugly began to come together for them in the early hours of the morning as they were nearing the point of exhaustion, both yawning and dropping hints about calling it a night soon.

Gaby's discovery of a reference to Adam in the notebook that they'd discovered was sort of a work diary—Joel's detailed running account of all he did professionally—instantly reenergized both of them.

"Force?" Connor repeated after she had read the brief entry out loud. "You're sure that he used the word *force?*"

"Yes, I'm sure. It says 'Adam, Black Wolf, 6 p.m. Bring printout. Force issue.' The rest is a little tough to make out even for me, but I think it says, 'No stalling. No more bull.'"

"No more bull," Connor echoed softly, contemplating each word separately. "No more bull from Adam." He rubbed his jaw. "Printout—that could have something to do with the restaurant's books."

"He kept all that information on his computer," she told him. "He would have made a printout of something if he wanted to bring it along and show it to Adam."

"His home computer?" he asked, growing excited. "Do you still have it?"

"It's in his office. I figured Toby would grow into it soon enough. I know his work for the restaurant is all on it because... Damn."

"What?" he demanded. "What, Gaby?"

"Because Adam called one day a while after the explosio
and asked if he could stop by with the new accountant he hire
so they could take a look at Joel's computer files and see whicl
ones they needed."

"And you said yes."

"Of course I said yes," she replied, defensive even though h
tone had been more resigned than accusing. "Adam doe
manage the restaurant, after all. He had a right to any file
pertaining to business. I had no idea what they needed, so I jus
showed them to Joel's office and excused myself."

"Think back, Gaby, this is important. Did they take an
computer disks with them when they left?"

"They may have. I really didn't pay attention."

"Did they say anything about copying or removing any
thing from the hard drive on Joel's computer?"

"They didn't say anything to me, and I didn't ask, all right?"
She shook her head, her mouth twisting with irritation. "Prett
stupid, huh? I may have handed over to them the proof w
need . . . maybe the only proof that exists. Damn, how could
have been so gullible?"

"Shh. You weren't gullible." His arm came around her, an
Gaby gratefully leaned into the strong shelter of his body
"Back then you had no reason not to do as Adam asked."

"That doesn't undo the damage," she insisted. "It doesn'
get those files back."

"If they took them. They may have simply copied the infor
mation rather than erasing it."

She craned her neck to slant him a withering look. "You
don't really believe that if there was anything there worth see
ing, they would leave it?"

"No, but I was hoping you might believe it and feel better.'

"Thanks anyway."

"You're welcome." His hand stroked her arm. "There i
another possibility though."

"What is it?"

"How much do you know about computers?"

"Next to nothing."

"Me, too, but I remember Joel saying once that even if you erase something, it's not really gone until the computer writes over the space where that information was stored. Does that make sense?"

"No," she said, lifting her head, hope stirring inside her. "But I'm willing to believe it's true if you are."

Connor grinned. "Call me a believer. First thing in the morning I'll phone Lew—he's the detective heading up the investigation—and ask him to arrange to have it checked out. Can I give him permission to use your key to get into the house?"

"Yes, of course."

"I'll also have them contact Higgins, Biggins and—"

"Higgins, Blackwell and Clarke."

"Right, and see about checking out any computer he may have had access to there. Joel was nothing if not cautious. I'm betting he kept a backup of everything at the office."

"Do you think it would still be there? It's been almost two years."

"I think we'll have to wait and see. In the meantime," he said, squeezing her gently before letting her go, "let's see if there's anything else interesting here."

They finished going through the remaining pages of the final notebook, finding several more references to meetings with Adam, with accompanying comments that seemed to indicate a growing impatience on Joel's part. "Adam—no show" appeared on several occasions.

Several times they had to backtrack through the pages to double-check a date or clarify something they hadn't understood until a later reference provided clarification.

Fittingly the final entry was for his meeting with Connor and Adam at the Black Wolf on the day of the explosion. "Ten a.m.," it read, "Adam/Wolf. Show time."

"Ten a.m.," she murmured. "Before the restaurant opened for business. I always thought that was a blessing. Can you imagine if it had happened during the lunch hour? With the place packed...kids..." She shivered.

"Actually," Connor said, "we were supposed to meet later
Joel called me back and said that Adam had to do it early fo
some reason." His jaw hardened. "Adam."

"Joel told me you guys were getting together to discuss you
trip to New York to see some big basketball game."

"The Knicks and Bulls. I know that's what you said he tol
you, but I never understood it. That trip was all set. We had ou
tickets, Adam was going to drive. There was nothing to dis
cuss."

"And he never explained to you why he wanted to meet, jus
that it was important, right?" she asked, recalling what th
police had told her in the days afterward.

"Right. He just said he needed to talk to Adam and m
about something."

"Only Adam never showed up," she recalled, her eyebrow
lifting speculatively. "He said he had car trouble, but in all th
time I've been seeing him, Adam's never had car trouble. He'
too much of an autophile. Those cars of his are his babies, an
he treats them accordingly." She turned to him, her eyes swirl
ing with heat and horror. "Connor, the more I think about i
the more it all seems to make sense. And I . . ."

Her voice cracked and halted.

"Yeah, I know," he said, drawing her to him. "That's ho
it was for me, too. I went from suspicion to disbelief and the
to . . . I don't how to describe it. I'd think of Adam know
ing . . . of him letting us walk in there that day and . . . and I'
literally get sick to my stomach."

She nodded and kept her head pressed against the reassur
ingly solid wall of his chest.

"When I got back here from Mexico and found out that yo
were going to marry him in less than twenty-four hours, I los
it."

"I noticed."

"I knew it would be futile to ask you to hold off on the wed
ding until the investigation was finished."

"You could have at least tried asking."

"Not without running the risk of you spilling everything t
Adam. I couldn't take that risk . . . especially not when I knev

there was no way you'd ever listen to reason if it was coming from me. So I did the only thing I could think of."

"You kidnapped me."

"Borrowed," he corrected.

"Whatever." She lifted her face to smile at him. "Have I said thank you?"

"You don't need to thank me," he told her, his voice taut with leashed emotion. "Just help me to put an end to this."

"Do you think we can?" she asked. "I mean do you think what's in these notes is enough?"

"I'm hoping it will be enough to trip up Adam when he's brought in for questioning," Connor replied. "If you're asking if it will hold up as evidence in a trial..." He shrugged. "That's up to the D.A. It will depend on what they find on those computers and whose arms they can twist and—I hate to say it—but it might also depend on whom Adam's in bed with on this. The more I see, the more I'm convinced that whatever it is, it's too big for it to be him alone pulling the strings."

Before Gaby had finished mulling over that possibility, she felt him gently disengaging himself.

"Speaking of bed," he said, "I'm beat. I think we should turn in. You go on ahead, and I'll pack this stuff up so it won't be laying around when Toby gets up in the morning."

"Thanks. He's doesn't read well enough yet to make any sense out of anything he might see in there, but I'd rather him not ask a lot of questions...especially when I don't have all the answers."

"Yet."

"Yet," she agreed. "Anyway thanks for offering to pack up. I appreciate it." She stood and turned to face him, her palms ridiculously damp as she pressed them to the sides of her robe. "Connor, I know what you said this afternoon, about staying in our own rooms, but I—"

He cut in, his tone soft but emphatic. "I mean I'm really beat, Gaby. Let's just say good-night and I'll see you in the morning, okay?"

It was so not okay that she couldn't speak to say good-night to him. Feeling the flush of humiliation on her cheeks even be-

fore she turned away, she ran up the stairs and into the room
she shared with Toby.

Damn him, she thought, fighting back tears. As rejections
went, it might have been gentle, but it was still a rejec-
tion . . . the second one in a few days.

She'd endured the first, understanding that they came together with enough combined baggage to fill an ocean liner and
that things might never be simple between them. She could
understand uncertainty and the need to go slowly. She shared
that need with him. And though making love with Connor had
changed her forever, opening her eyes and her heart to the future in a way she hadn't thought possible for her ever again, she
still wasn't asking for promises from him.

But after yesterday, last night . . . this morning, for God's
sake, she also didn't expect to be shut out so totally and
abruptly with an excuse about needing to concentrate, an excuse so flimsy that she wouldn't try to slip it past Toby. Tossing an extra blanket on the bed, she slipped under the covers
and pulled them tightly around her, feeling as if someone had
tilted the ground beneath her feet just as she was finally beginning to regain her balance.

As tired as he was, Connor didn't go upstairs to bed. He
didn't trust himself to climb those stairs, to pass the closed door
to the room where Gaby was asleep, knowing that all it would
take was a soft knock, a few whispered words, the short walk
from that door to his bed for him to break the promise he'd
made to himself on the drive back from the city. This thing between Gaby and him had to end before it went any further, and
he had to be the one to do it. He couldn't expect Gaby, after all
she'd been through, to turn away from even a slight chance at
happiness. That's what he offered her at best, a slight chance.

The physical needs that had brought them together, as intense as they were, couldn't compensate for all the things he
wasn't. He wasn't serious and security minded. He wasn't father material. He wasn't Joel. He wasn't what she needed for
the long term.

So there could be no long term.

He packed up Joel's papers the way he had told her he would, covering the box and shoving it in a corner beneath a table, where Toby was unlikely to notice and ask about it. He took a walk outside, came back in and grabbed a can of beer from the refrigerator. Popping it open, he took one swig and poured the rest down the drain. There was no way he wanted to wake up tomorrow in the same condition he had the last time he tried to drink Gaby off his mind.

Besides, inebriation was no longer even a temporary solution. Before, Gaby had been only a temptation, a possibility, a craving. Now she was a part of his heart. Maybe the biggest part, he thought bleakly, returning to his chair in the living room. There wasn't enough beer in the world to make him forget that all he wanted and needed, the greatest chance for happiness he'd ever had, was in a room at the top of the stairs, just out of reach.

He fell asleep in the chair, his head at an awkward angle, and woke with what felt like a steel rod running through his neck and something hard and cold pressed to the center of his forehead.

He opened his eyes.

"Drop it, slime ball."

Toby.

Connor rolled his gaze upward to see what the kid had pressed to his forehead, and his heart lurched. A gun. His mind reeled before he remembered that his own was safely locked in the cabinet Charlie had built for exactly that purpose. As a precaution he'd removed it from the knapsack under his bed and locked it there before going to pick up Toby yesterday. Kids and guns didn't mix.

He refocused his still-blurry gaze on the small, fiercely grimacing face before him. "What did you say?" he asked.

"Drop it, slime ball."

Connor closed his eyes. "That's what I thought you said."

"Drop it," Toby repeated, plenty of grit in his high-pitched voice.

Connor cracked one eye. "What's 'it'?"

The little head tilted to one side. "Huh?"

"'It.' What's the 'it' I'm supposed to drop?"

"Oh." His mouth puckered into a pout as he thought it over. Just as his mother's did when she was perplexed, Connor thought, the loneliness that he had escaped with sleep surrounding him once again. "It," the boy announced at last. "Drop it."

"I have a better idea," Connor said, wincing as he shifted in the chair in an attempt to relieve the pressure on his neck. "Go bother your mother."

"She's sleeping."

"So was I."

"She doesn't like guns."

"What makes you think I do?"

Toby gave him a smile so much like Joel's it made Connor's chest hurt. "You do. You're a guy. Guys like guns."

"Yeah, well, that's nothing to smile about, kid. And it just so happens I don't like having them shoved in my face first thing in the morning. Got it?" he said, batting away the little hand holding the gun.

"Got it."

"Where did you find that, anyway? Did your mother pack it for you?"

Toby shook his head in that energetic way that sent his hair flying. "I found it."

"Whereabouts?"

"In the box."

Connor levered up. There hadn't been any toy gun in that box. Had there? Hell, if the kid had gone poring through that stuff after he told Gaby he'd make sure it was out of the way...

"What box?" he asked him.

"The one near the door, with the pails and sand stuff." He pointed, and Connor remembered seeing a box of beach toys near the door.

"I filled it, too," Toby added. "All by myself. See?"

Before Connor could duck or tell him not to, he squeezed the trigger and shot a stream of cold water at him, hitting him right between the eyes. Naturally. The water trickled down and dripped from his chin onto his shirt.

Toby's stared at him with widened eyes. "Oops."

"Oops doesn't cut it, kid." Connor reached for him. "Give me your arm."

Eyes growing wider still, Toby allowed himself to be jerked closer, his little arm stiff as a poker as Connor lifted it and used his sleeve to wipe the water from his face.

"Hey, you got my p'jamas wet," he exclaimed.

"You got me wet, too."

Toby eyed him suspiciously. "Those aren't p'jamas."

"I don't wear pajamas. You got my shirt wet."

"Not even to bed you don't wear them?"

"When else would I . . . no, not even to bed."

"What do you wear to bed?"

"Noth— None of your business." He glanced anxiously at the stairs. "Are you sure your mother isn't awake yet?"

"I'm sure. She doesn't wear p'jamas, either, you know."

I know, Connor thought, God, I know.

"Oh, really," he replied, trying to sound as if what his mother wore to bed was of no interest to him whatsoever.

"'Cause she's a girl," Toby explained. "Girls don't wear p'jamas."

"You know, for a five-year-old you've really got this girl-guy thing pretty squared away."

Toby nodded solemnly. "Jack told me. He knows a lot about girls. Do you?"

The question brought a sardonic slant to Connor's mouth. "No. Next to nothing, it seems lately." From the corner of his eye he saw the gun coming up. "Don't do it, kid."

Toby dropped his arm agreeably. "Okay. If you want to take off your wet shirt, you can, you know."

"I don't want to take it off."

"How come?"

"I just don't, okay?"

"Okay." That damn smile again. "I'm hungry."

"Yeah?"

His head bobbed up and down.

"What do you usually eat for breakfast?"

"Crunchies. But they're up too high for me to reach."

Connor stretched and got to his feet. He supposed it wouldn't kill him to pour the kid a bowl of cereal. He walked to the kitchen with Toby like a puppy at his heels, talking the whole time. Connor wasn't listening. He didn't want to know anything else about the kid. He didn't want to see him smile.

He stood with the cabinet door open, staring at the box of Crunchies cereal that Gaby had brought from her mother's and probably put out of reach intentionally.

If he poured the cereal, he told himself, he would have to pour the milk, too. He would have to put the bowl in front of Toby, after first helping him up onto the cushion Gaby had put on one of the kitchen chairs for him, the way he had watched her help him at dinner last night. He would be tempted to sit with him while he ate. Talk with him. Listen. He would learn things about him that would make him like the kid more than he already did.

He would have to confront the longing inside, the wish to provide Toby with all the things that were missing from his life . . . if only Connor could be certain they were his to give.

He slammed the door shut and turned to find Toby watching him expectantly, no doubt wondering how long it was going to take him to get down a box of cereal.

"Wait here," he told him more roughly than he intended. "I'll get your mother."

Chapter 11

She opened her eyes and saw him.

And thought it was a dream, the same dream she'd been having and waking from all night long. A dream about Connor and her, his mouth, his clever, reckless mouth all over her and his fingers on her skin, everywhere.

Then she blinked and he didn't go away and she knew. "It's not a dream," she murmured sleepily.

A sardonic smile creased his wide mouth. "More likely a nightmare, but it's not that, either."

She smiled and levered up on one elbow, a thousand questions racing around in her head, only one that really mattered. "You brought me coffee."

"Yeah." He put the steaming mug on the table by the bed. "It seemed the least I could do if I was going to wake you up this way."

"I'm glad you did," she told him, sliding up in the bed so she could sit with her back against the pillows and drink her coffee.

The sheet drifted to her waist, and she left it there, aware that one strap on her nightgown had slipped off her shoulder, exposing her left breast almost to her nipple and that Connor's gaze was riveted to that spot. She took a sip, slanted her most bewitching smile at him and added gently, "I knew you would come to your senses. I'm just glad it happened before we wasted any more time."

His head jerked. His lips, which had been relaxed and slightly parted as he stared at her breast, thinned to a rigid line.

"I haven't. Come to my senses, I mean..." The muscles at the side of his jaw tensed. "Nothing's changed since last night, Gabrielle. I just... Toby wants his breakfast."

Gaby, her cheeks flaming, automatically turned and patted the bed beside her, as if expecting to find Toby still tucked in there. "I... I'm sorry, I didn't realize he'd gotten up. I didn't even hear him. I hope he hasn't been bothering you."

Connor shook his head. "He hasn't. But I wasn't sure what he should eat, so..." He shrugged.

"Of course. Heaven knows, I don't expect you to feed him. I... I'll be right down."

"Right. I'll tell him that."

She held her breath until the door closed behind him, then released it in a rush of self-recrimination. God, she was an idiot. A complete idiot. She closed her eyes and shook her head and wished she could whisk herself and Toby out of there and back home without ever having to look Connor in the eye again. That would teach her to jump to conclusions, especially when she was still half-asleep.

She pulled her knees up and knocked her forehead against them, resting it there for several minutes before reluctantly swinging her legs off the bed and standing. No sense delaying the inevitable. Oh, well, she thought as she hurriedly pulled on her robe, at least she had the answer to her question and wouldn't have to endure the suspense of not knowing all day. Connor had laid it right on the line for her.

Nothing had changed.

As tempted as she was to take the easy way out and plunk Toby down with a bowl of Crunchies, she insisted on negotiating breakfast with him, and together they settled on one piece of French toast and a small bowl of his favorite cereal. Maybe she needed to prove to herself that she was still a good mother, even if she was obviously sorely lacking as a lover.

It was hard not to come to that humbling conclusion. No matter what else he might be feeling—remorse, guilt, trepidation—if the sex had been good enough, if she had been good enough, Connor wouldn't have been able to call a halt so quickly and easily.

Adding to her distress was the realization that she had no right to be so thrown by his sudden about-face. She had understood beforehand that Connor's main reason for wanting her just might be the fact that she had always been forbidden to him, and if that was the case, there was a good chance that he would quickly lose interest in her once the deed was done. She'd told herself she could handle it. And she could. It just wasn't turning out to be as simple as she'd foolishly let herself think it would be. Nowhere near as simple as falling in love with him had been.

She was even more thankful now that Toby had joined them. Entertaining him provided her with something to do as she and Connor went about their subtle dance of avoiding each other. If she and Toby were playing a game outside on the deck, he stayed inside. When they came inside to read, he found something he needed to attend to outdoors. There was no graceful way for him to avoid eating lunch with them, but he disappeared upstairs immediately after helping her clean up.

He came down a short while later and to Gaby's amazement, actually sought her out where she was reading in the living room while Toby played nearby.

"Can I talk with you for a minute?" he asked, nodding toward the kitchen to signal that he wanted to speak to her where Toby wouldn't hear.

"It's all set," he said as soon as they were out of earshot. "I spoke with Lew Marino earlier and told him what we'd found last night, and he said he would see about checking out the computer at your place and any others that might have been used by Joel at work. I just called Lew back, and he said it's all arranged. A detective from their own technical unit will be at your house this afternoon. The powers that be at Joel's old firm are willing to cooperate on their end, as well, but their in-house counsel wants to see a search warrant first just to cover their . . . just to keep it all nice and legal.''

"How long will that take?"

"Not long. A few hours maybe. According to Lew, the technical guy he checked with said the only hitch will be if the documents were already in fragments before they were erased.''

"That will mean we're out of luck?"

"No. But evidently it will make the whole process of recovering them a lot more time-consuming. That brings me to the bad news," he said.

Gaby bit her bottom lip, her arms folded in front of her. "What is it?"

"It looks like we may be stuck here longer than I thought. Until they get this done."

Her heart lifted, fell, twisted sideways in uncertainty. Part of her wanted to walk out the door right that second in hopes that the old adage, "Out of sight, out of mind," would prove true. Another part of her wanted to stay there with him forever.

"You promised me we could leave Friday," she reminded him. No need to let him in on her turmoil.

"I didn't know then that this was going to play out the way it has. Besides," he reminded her, "I only promised you that because you missed your son. That's no longer the case."

A short, harsh laugh burst from her. "No, now Toby's here with me, and I'm missing something else entirely. Care to hear what that something is, Connor?"

"No."

"Too bad, because you're going to hear it anyway."

"Gaby, don't."

"Don't what? Don't act as if there's more between us than any two strangers who happen to be sharing the same living quarters for a few days?"

His mouth twisted cruelly. "What makes you think there is?"

Gaby's breath hissed from her. She bared clenched teeth. "Damn you."

"Save your breath. I was damned a long time ago."

"Oh, knock it off," she cried, then remembered Toby playing in the other room and lowered her voice. "Everybody has hard times in their lives. I grant you yours have been rougher than most, but that doesn't give you the right to go around hurting other people for no good reason."

"You don't get it," he growled, stepping forward so that she instinctively moved back until she was up against the refrigerator. "I'm trying not to hurt you."

"Oh, I get it now, all right. You're trying to let me down gently. Is that it?"

He glared at her in silence.

"And I'm not cooperating, am I?" she continued in the same mocking tone.

"Not at all."

"That's because what happened between us—"

"What happened between us," he cut in, his tone as sharp and absolute as the crack of a whip across her heart, "was a mistake."

"A mistake?" Her voice collapsed under the weight of what she was feeling, forcing her to pause a second to regain a measure of composure. "Well, I have to hand it to you, DeWolfe, you're certainly blunt enough . . . if not especially bright."

"Meaning?"

"Why didn't you realize that it was a mistake after the first time out by the lake? Or the second? Or the fifth? For God's sake, Connor, you made love to me over and over again, all night, yesterday morning . . . I've never felt that way before, so wanted, so desperate." She sucked in a deep breath. "I couldn't get enough of you. You couldn't get enough of me. You said so. Were you lying?"

"No," he replied, staring at a spot somewhere between her left shoulder and the ceiling.

"Look at me when you tell me. Were you lying?"

"No," he said, jerking his gaze back to meet hers. "No, Gaby, I wasn't lying to you. I wanted you every bit as much as I told you . . . more. More than I knew how to tell you."

"Then why? Was I just another notch on whatever it is that men like you carve notches on these days? An easy lay to alleviate the boredom of being here? Then once you got your fill, you—"

He grabbed her roughly, hauling her against him. His mouth came down hard on hers, his tongue slashing like the sharp point of a knife along the seam of her tightly pressed lips, and Gabrielle was as powerless to resist as if it had been a knife. She couldn't have denied him entry if she'd wanted to, which she didn't.

His tongue filled her mouth, hot, insistent. His arms surrounded her, trying to pull her impossibly closer to him. Gaby wanted that, too. She pressed against him, muscle straining against muscle, her heart pounding against his. She felt his passion, rode it with a mixture of excitement and a heady, crazy relief. Desire, strong and urgent, erupted inside, tugging at her for a wild, gasping moment until the kiss ended as abruptly as it had begun.

"Did that feel to you like I've had my fill?" he demanded.

He was breathing hard, the restless movement of his hips drawing her gaze to the solid proof that she hadn't just imagined that he wanted her as fervently now as he had the first time they made love.

"And just for the record," he added, "you were anything but an easy lay. Hell, I have muscles that still ache."

"Good. You deserve it . . . and worse. Oh, Connor . . ."

She reached for him. He took a step backward, leaving her arms holding air.

"Damn it, Gaby," he said, "I swore I wouldn't let this happen. That I wouldn't let you do this to me again."

"Scared, Wolf?" she taunted, fully expecting that would goad him into proving to her that he wasn't.

Instead, he gave a curt nod, stunning her. "You bet I am. More scared than I've ever been."

"Of me?" she asked, incredulous.

He shrugged. "Maybe a little. Of what you do to me. Mostly, though, I'm afraid of what I could do to you. And to Toby."

"What are you talking about? Getting to know you would be so good for Toby. And you might even like him if you gave him half a chance."

"I already like him...too much. He's a great kid, Gaby. And you were right, he's a lot like Joel. It hits you when you're least expecting it. This morning he smiled at me and I...it just blew me away, that's all," he finished uneasily.

"Is that what you're frightened of?" she asked, her tone gentle. "Of being reminded of Joel?"

He gave an impatient shake of his head. "No. I think I've finally come to terms with that...as much as I ever will, anyway. I told you, it's not me I'm worried about, it's Toby."

"Why don't you let me worry about what's best for Toby?"

"And who the hell is going to worry about what's best for you?"

"Maybe I know what's best for me."

"You don't. Trust me. You were going to marry Adam," he reminded her.

Gaby waved that off with a frown. "For very specific reasons which had nothing at all to do with the way I feel about you...the way you make me feel when we're together."

Cynicism twisted his mouth. "Welcome to the world of no-holds-barred sex, Gabrielle."

"No. It's more than that and you know it. If it wasn't, you wouldn't be afraid."

"You're right, it's more than that. But it's still not enough. I'm not enough."

"Are you crazy? I never—"

"I'm not talking about sex. I'm talking about...everything else. I'm talking about that house you live in and the calendar you keep that has your life and Toby's scheduled down to the millisecond and fancy vases that can't be replaced."

Her laughter held a desperate edge of relief. "Is that what all this is about? That stupid vase?"

"It's not a stupid vase. If it was, you wouldn't have it where you can see it all the time, you wouldn't have been so upset when I almost knocked it over. That vase matters to you, Gaby.

That's not wrong," he added hurriedly before she could deny it. "It's just totally alien to me and everything I am."

"I know that our lives have been very different up till now, but, Connor, people can change."

"Maybe I don't want to change."

"Maybe I do."

He eyed her in frank surprise before shaking his head discouragingly. "You can't change that much. I wouldn't want you to. Gaby, you're looking at a man who's never lived with one woman long enough to unpack his clothes, who sees a walk-in dentist because he hates being tied down to an appointment six months ahead of time, who..."

"Who makes me laugh and makes me crazy and who may have saved my life. Don't sell yourself short," she pleaded. "Any man who can cook the way—"

"I cook when I get the urge to," he interrupted. "I can go months eating out of cans between urges and like it just fine. That's not your style. Face it, Gaby. I have. I walked into your house and looked around and I couldn't imagine what it would be like to wake up there every morning."

"I never said I wanted you to move in," she said softly.

"Don't you see? I want it. After only a few days I want to wake up with you every morning and I've never felt that way before, ever. I want to be there for you and do all the things you shouldn't have to worry about doing. I want to mow your lawn and take out your trash and teach Toby how to swing a bat.

"I just don't think I can," he went on. "Not for the long haul. I'm not the kind of man who deals well with schedules and routine. You said it yourself, dozens of times—I'm not responsible." His dark eyes were tortured. "I'm not Joel."

"No one ever could be. No one expects you to try. Just be you."

"That's the problem. You need a man who's housebroken, Gabrielle. And I'm not."

"I don't want to break you," she told him, holding a scream of frustration at the back of her throat as she moved close to him once more, this time refusing to be brushed aside. "I just want to change your mind about what kind of man I need. And I know I can, if you'll stop pulling away."

"I know you can, too," he conceded, closing his eyes as if the touch of her hands on his chest was hard to bear. "All too easily. That's why I spent last night down here, as far away from you and temptation as I could get. It's why I won't back down."

Gaby felt him withdrawing and looped her arms around his waist. "Want to bet? I dare you, you big jerk."

"Not this time," he said, removing her hands, kissing the palms lightly, lingeringly before finally letting her go.

"Connor, this is crazy. To turn your back on something that might be so good, because you're afraid it might not work out . . . it's worse than crazy, it's . . . unAmerican."

He shot her a puzzled look over his shoulder as he turned to go.

"All right, that's a stretch," she admitted, "but at least it got your attention. All I'm trying to say is that I understand the risks involved here and I'm willing to take them."

The puzzled look on his lean, whiskered face was edged out by one of regret.

"I'm not," he said softly.

Night fell in increments around the lake. First the sun dropped behind the tallest peaks of the pine trees ringing the water, changing the color of day from bright yellow to orange, as if there were a fire burning in the distant sky. It faded more as it moved lower, glowing through the crisscrossing branches with the look of burned orange lace. Gradually the orange mellowed and gave way to the purples and indigos of evening, the shades deepening, layer upon layer, until everything was black, the sky, the water, the trees, a vast expanse of shadows, waiting for the silver touch of the rising moon.

Connor didn't need to wait that long. At the first chirp of a cricket he was ready to call it a day, giving himself credit for making it through one more block of hours without weakening and doing what Gaby had dared him to do . . . what she continued to dare him to do a hundred times a day in a hundred different, wordless, soul-searing ways . . . what he wanted to do as much as he'd ever wanted anything. But going after what he wanted was to go back on his word that he would stay out of her life, something he was sworn to do because it was the best thing for her. And he was the worst thing for her.

Three days. It had been three days since they had stopped by her house and he had come to his senses. Three days of circling each other like bees around a honey pot too hot to touch. Three endless days.

The nights were worse. At least during the day Toby was around to act as a buffer. Even Connor knew enough to keep his hands off her in front of a five-year-old, a kid still too innocent to even wonder how this man who had once been a friend of his father's fit into his and his mother's lives now. It was a good thing he didn't wonder enough to ask, because Connor would have been hard-pressed to give him an answer.

The days he could manage. The nights were what got to him. Trying to sleep scrunched into that damn chair in the living room. He could have used the bed in his room, but since he was sleeping fitfully, up and down all night, he didn't want to disturb Gaby or give her an excuse to come checking on him, wearing that pale nightgown that clung and shimmered and made him want to slide his hands down her and feel her go all warm and fluid beneath the silk. That's how it would be. He knew it. He could close his eyes and feel it, feel her, smell her. Which is why he couldn't let her come looking for him in the night.

At first he figured that eventually he'd get tired enough to sleep through without waking. Instead, his restlessness was growing stronger. It was only partly due to the fact that he couldn't get his mind and body in synch where Gaby was concerned. The other part of it was something he was more comfortable with. He recognized it from his years on the force, a sort of sixth sense that was unlearned and unteachable, a hunch, a tightening at the back of his neck, an awareness that things were coming to a head.

These "things" changed from case to case. The feeling was always the same. And never wrong. This was a challenge he understood. He knew where this path led, all the bends and turns in the road, all the dark places where danger could be waiting. He was ready for it, even eager. He wished Lew Marino's hotshot computer whiz would get his act together so they would know exactly where they stood.

"Tomorrow," Lew told him every morning when he checked in by cellular phone. "He says he thinks he'll have something for us by tomorrow."

It turned out the files had been eradicated from the hard drive on the computer in Joel's office at home. Eradicated, as opposed to merely erased. According to Lew, who was in turn quoting the whiz, someone had gone in with a program designed for the express purpose of methodically and totally overwriting existing material so that it was rendered permanently irretrievable.

There was not, Lew explained, even the remotest chance that such a thing could be done accidentally. Which meant that either Joel or someone else had purposely wiped out the information so that no one would ever see it. There was still no proof who that might be, of course, but Connor knew whom he was betting on.

Fortunately the situation was slightly more encouraging at the accounting firm where Joel had worked. It turned out that the firm had updated its computer system within the past eighteen months. The computer from Joel's office had been one of those retained as a backup and had been rarely used, giving them a good shot at recovering anything Joel may have stored on it. The whiz found that files had been erased from it, as well, but not eradicated. Which meant they could be retrieved. The bad news was that it had to be done piece by piece, the file segments identified and strung together to form—hopefully—an understandable whole. The whiz, according to Lew, was doing his best. He'd told Lew that the job would be a lot simpler if Joel was around to help. Connor couldn't suppress a sardonic smile of agreement when he heard that. It seemed to him that everything would be a lot easier on everyone if Joel were still around.

Ironically one of the things that bothered him most during the long, hot days was also one that scared him the most. It was watching Gaby and Toby together, playing a game of checkers on the deck, or their heads bent over a growing pile of sand as they dug a tunnel to China, or simply sitting together in the evening, Toby's hair damp from his bath and his head tucked under his mother's arm as she read to him—all these affected him deeply.

Marvin K. Mooney. That was Toby's favorite story, requested several times a day, and already Connor knew entire passages of it by heart. He also knew that Toby's favorite dinosaur was Tyrannosaurus rex and that he liked worms and wasn't afraid of the dark unless it thundered.

He knew too much, more than was safe. Seeing the two of them together, it was impossible not to be moved by the bond between them, by the tight, perfectly meshed unit they had formed in spite of or maybe because of all that they had suffered.

It was so different from what had occurred in his own family after his mother's death, when each of them had seemed to drift in a separate direction, as if the others only reinforced the memory of what they had each lost. He had blamed his father for letting that happen until the day the old man died.

Now he wasn't so sure. Maybe his father hadn't known how to forge that kind of bond any more than Connor did. It pained Connor to think that maybe his father had felt as lonely and disconnected as he did now, watching Gaby and Toby together, longing for something he didn't understand.

Gaby tried to include him. So did Toby, for that matter. They invariably called him to eat with them, which he did, and invited him to join them for a walk or whatever else they had planned, which he politely declined with the excuse that he had something he had to do, usually work on the boat.

He had now taken apart practically the entire engine, cleaned it and put it back together—not an easy task for a man with only one good hand—and the damn thing was still sucking water under the cowling and stalling out after only a few minutes on the open water. It was frustrating, since ordinarily he was pretty good with engines and with his hands in general. The last thing he needed was a reminder of the bitter fact that some things were just beyond his expertise. In fact, he would have gladly thrown in the towel on the job days ago if his tinkering down at the dock didn't provide him with a ready excuse not to pick wildflowers or catch minnows in the shallow water by the shore.

Just yesterday Gaby had detoured by where he was working to ask if he wanted to take a break for a while.

"We're going swimming," she explained as he grunted and kept his eyes on the shift lever he was realigning. He pretended not to notice that a bathing suit, a sleek black one cut almost up to her waist on the sides, was among the essentials she had seen fit to bring back with her. "Why don't you come with us?"

He lifted his head and squinted, as if it was the sun blinding him and not the lure of her sweet, firm flesh. "Thanks, but I really ought to finish up here first."

"Maybe later?" Toby chirped hopefully from his spot by his mother's side.

Connor made a noncommittal gesture. "Maybe."

He bent over the engine again, waiting until they were well along the path before lifting his head and watching them walk away. He continued watching as Gaby took Toby by the hand and together they inched into the water, staying close to the shore as she patiently taught him to float on his stomach and kick his feet. She ought to get him accustomed to putting his face under, Connor thought as he stood watching. And his hands. He ought to be using his hands more along with his feet.

As the afternoon passed, he did more watching them than he did working, his concentration broken each time Toby laughed or shrieked with excitement. He might as well have taken the afternoon off for all he accomplished.

Not that fixing the engine was any longer the goal, he mused as he found himself back realigning the shift the next morning. At some point, born of his need to keep busy, the process had become the goal, the means to an end the end in and of itself. And why not? Everything else in his life had been turned upside down and inside out. Why should the way in which he whiled away his time be any different?

"Want some help?"

Connor straightened abruptly, peering over his shoulder to find Toby standing behind him wearing his mother's sunglasses, too big for his face, and holding a wrench he had no doubt found in the toolbox nearby.

"No. Thanks anyway." He wiped his forehead with the rolled-up sleeve of his faded denim shirt. "Does your mother know you have her glasses?"

"Nope."

"Do you think maybe you ought to bring them back to her before she finds out?"

"Nope."

"What if they get broken?"

"I won't break them."

"Not on purpose. What if you fall by accident, and they break?"

He thought that over and pulled off the glasses, holding them out to Connor. "You hold them."

"Why don't you just bring them back to the house?" *And stay there,* he refrained from adding.

"What if I fall by accident?"

Connor held out his hand. "All right, give them to me." He dropped them in his shirt pocket.

"Now can I help?" Toby asked for the second time.

It would not, Connor knew, be the last. That was something else he had learned about the kid. He was persistent. Make that downright stubborn. Only Gaby seemed to have the knack of short-circuiting his determination.

"I appreciate the offer, but this is sort of a one-man job."

"What's a one-man job?"

Evidently he had a lot more to learn about kids. "A job it takes only one man to do," he explained. Heading off what was certain to come next, he added, "And that man is me."

"Oh." Silence. A couple of days ago he would have assumed that put an end to the matter. Now he knew better. He was braced for Toby to regroup and try again.

"Are you really a wolf?" he asked instead.

Connor reached for a rag and wiped away a streak of grease from the boat's fiberglass hull. "A wolf? Who told you that?"

"My mommy. She said that's your nickname."

"She's right, it is."

"I don't have a nickname."

"No?"

"Nope. Just Toby. Can I call you Wolf?"

Connor smiled as he adjusted a wire leading to the starter. "Sure. Why not?"

A minute passed. "Wolf?"

"What is it?"

"Do you have a hero's chest?"

Connor froze, thinking he couldn't have heard that right, at the same time certain he had, and with no idea at all what the hell "a hero's chest" might be.

"Do I have a what?" he asked, turning so he could see Toby as he replied so he would be sure he got it straight this time.

"A hero's chest."

"What's a hero's chest?" he asked cautiously and against the urging of what passed for his better judgment.

"It's like this." Before Connor knew what he intended, Toby had lifted the Boston Celtics T-shirt he wore over his bathing suit and exposed his chest from waist to neck.

His skin was pale, his ribs tiny ripples beneath the surface, a pretty ordinary five-year-old's chest except for the three-by-seven-inch patch of wrinkled and raised, bright pink flesh bisecting it.

As scars went, Connor had seen much worse. Hell, he had much worse. It was the kid's courage that got to him. It was etched on his face as he stood there, exhibiting the single most massive imperfection on his young body to a virtual stranger named Wolf, of all things, a man who had been only curt, if not downright unfriendly to him since they got there. It was that stoic display of courage that sucked the air from Connor's lungs.

"See it?" Toby asked him finally, as if he might have somehow missed the scar that dominated the small chest.

"I see it, Toby."

He let his T-shirt drop. "That's a hero's chest," he said proudly.

"Who told you that?"

"My mommy."

"I see. Did she also tell you that I have a…" The words stuck in his throat. "A hero's chest?"

Toby shook his head. "Nope. I just knew all by myself."

Connor's gaze narrowed. "How?"

"'Cause you don't like to take your shirt off, not even if it gets wet or it's hot and 'cause you don't want to go swimming." His expression was so earnest Connor found it hard not to flinch from it as he added, "Sometimes I don't want to go swimming, too. Like when there's kids around who make fun of me and laugh."

"Does that happen a lot? Kids making fun of you because of the scar on your chest?"

"Sometimes," Toby replied, very matter-of-fact. "Sometimes they just look. Robby Peters wanted to touch it once."

"Did you let him?"

"For a quarter."

A smile flickered across Connor's lips. "I guess that makes you feel pretty bad when kids laugh."

"Sometimes. Not too much anymore, though. Not since Mommy told me about the hero's chest."

Connor put aside the pliers he was holding and moved to lean against the boat, close to where Toby was standing. "Do you think you could tell me about it?"

"Yes. A hero's chest makes you special, 'cause it means you did the job that had to get done and you didn't care who was going to laugh or make fun of you for it. I'm special because I let them fix my heart and didn't even cry. Not a lot, anyway. And Mommy said anyone brave enough to do that is a hero, and I shouldn't listen to anybody who laughs or makes fun of me. 'Cause I have a hero's chest."

"Your mother is a real smart lady."

"I know." Toby moved to lean on the boat beside him, stretching to prop his feet on the same rock as Connor's, folding his arms the way Connor's were folded. "So, do you? Have a hero's chest, I mean?"

"I wouldn't call it..." Connor paused. "That is, I never thought of it quite that way." Toby studied him in silence, as if still waiting for a straight answer. Connor sighed. "Yeah, I guess you could say I do."

"Did they have to fix your heart, too?"

"No. My heart was okay. I was burned."

"In a fire?"

"Sort of. There was an explosion and then there was a fire, and that's how my chest got burned."

"How did you get away from the fire?"

Connor could feel his muscles tensing, his spine becoming like a bowstring, pulling everything inside him too tight. "I crawled."

Toby waited.

"You see, the ceiling came crashing down," he said, not quite believing he was talking about it or why. "It landed so that I was on one side of the mess, near the door, and my friend was on the other side of it, trapped. I tried to get to him, to help him, but every time I moved, it just kept coming and coming, right down on top of us, until finally I couldn't see him anymore."

It was something he'd never told anyone about that day, the truth. Not the special federal investigators or the state cops or the reporters who badgered him for exclusive accounts of what had happened. Especially not the reporters. He'd known how they would crank it up to sell papers, calling him a hero for trying to save Joel when all that mattered was that he had failed.

"My daddy was in a 'splosion, too," Toby said and Connor's heart stopped beating for a second. "He died."

"I know he did, Toby."

"Was my daddy your friend? The one you tried to help?"

There was a long silence while Connor struggled to make the muscles in his throat work the way he wanted them to. Fortunately silence didn't seem to make Toby uneasy the way it did some folks.

"Yeah," he said at last. "Your daddy was my friend, Toby."

Connor kept his eyes on the water and didn't see it coming, so he was startled at the unfamiliar feel of a child's soft, small hand slipping inside of his.

"If you want to go swimming," Toby told him, "I'll go with you."

An unspoken message burned brightly in his eyes. *I won't let you be alone,* it seemed to say. *I won't laugh at you.* It broke Connor's heart and put it back together again in the few seconds it took him to find his voice. The kid could teach him a lot about guts and about facing up to your fears. Hell, thought Connor, he just did.

"You know, all of a sudden I do feel like a swim." Grinning, he yanked Toby away from the boat. "Let's do it, partner."

Chapter 12

From where she sat on the deck, Gaby watched in disbelief as Connor and Toby walked hand in hand toward the lake. Joel's son and his best friend.

It was a sight she had never thought she'd see. At first because she had no desire to have Toby spend time with Connor. Then, during these past few days, because Connor himself seemed to be going out of his way to keep a safe distance between the two of them.

She had been sitting there sketching while Toby played with his dinosaurs in the sand near the bottom of the deck steps. She had recently taken on a project that was going to give her an opportunity to restore a damaged stained-glass window and also create a new fanlight to be installed above it. The new window had to have the same feel as the old, and though she'd been toying with design possibilities for several weeks, she had yet to put anything on paper. This bizarre vacation seemed like the perfect time to get started.

She'd looked up from her sketching a while ago and had seen Toby wandering down toward the dock where Connor spent nearly every waking minute working on that damn boat. An avoidance technique, she was certain. She almost went running after him, but then decided to finish her sketch first.

It wouldn't kill Connor to pay a little attention to Toby, who was so obviously in awe of him. It might even be good for him. Perhaps it would also help influence him to change his mind about taking a chance on them. Heaven knew, she had no idea how to make that happen.

The next time she glanced up, the two of them were leaning against the boat, side by side. She grinned at the way Toby had mimicked Connor's stance. He even had the casual slant of the shoulders right. Oh, yeah, Connor definitely had himself a one-man fan club. Certain that by now Toby must be driving him crazy with questions, she started to go to his rescue. That's when she saw Toby reach out and take Connor's hand. She winced, waiting for Connor to brush him off. To her amazement, however, Connor let him. A minute later they started walking together toward the water, hand in hand.

"Well, will wonders never cease?" Gaby murmured out loud, feeling as if she was witnessing a minor miracle.

She settled back in her chair, holding her sketch pad as a decoy as she continued to observe them. She was half-afraid that if Connor looked up and saw her watching, the moment would be lost.

They stopped on the hard-packed sand at the water's edge and faced each other. Gaby caught her bottom lip between her teeth as she saw Connor unbuttoning his shirt, talking to Toby the whole time. He kicked off his sneakers, unzipped his jeans and dropped them to reveal his bathing suit underneath. The jeans were kicked aside, too. Then together the two of them pulled off their shirts, and Toby once more stuck out his hand and Connor reached and took it.

Her eyes filled and her lungs ached as the breath she'd been holding escaped in a giant rush of relief. She had been worried, she realized, aware as she was of all the subtle complications the action she'd witnessed held for both the man she loved and her son. Aware of all the ways they could each be hurt. Now, along with relief came a special kind of joy. Much greater than anything she could feel on her own behalf, it washed through her, giving her the sense that in just those few short moments the world had been washed clean. Her world, at least, the world she shared with Toby and longed to share with Connor, as well.

Her gaze followed their movements as they headed for deeper water. Deeper than where she would have allowed Toby to venture. She resisted the urge to call to them that they had gone out far enough. She trusted Connor with Toby, trusted him to look after her child as if he were his own. To her astonishment, she realized that she already trusted him around Toby even more than she had Adam. It was hard to define the difference. What she felt with Connor was the kind of trust that comes from someplace deep in the heart, the kind that can't be forced or coerced or faked. If she'd had any doubts that what she felt for him was real or that it was love, they were gone now.

She watched as they engaged in a wild splashing contest, something Toby loved because he didn't get to do it at the club pool where Adam was a member. He splashed hard for a little kid, and Gaby, his usual opponent, always let him win. Connor, she noted, did not. Another guy thing, she decided. Toby still ended up laughing, a sound so sweet and welcome it made her laugh, too, with sheer happiness.

After the splashing they got down to business, with Connor demonstrating to Toby how to put his face underwater while he swam, something he refused to even attempt with her coaching him. Naturally he didn't refuse Connor. In an amazingly short time he had mastered the feat and evidently felt comfortable enough to allow Connor to swing him in the air and toss him.

Gaby sprang from her chair before he hit the water and was leaning over the railing before he came up for air. Be careful. The warning was always at the tip of her tongue, instinctive and necessary in her opinion because of all Toby had been through. Be careful, she would warn whenever he rode his bike or played ball or wanted to go to his friend's house. Be careful of falling and getting out of breath and . . . of the wind in your face. She smiled ruefully and let the warning go unspoken. Just please be careful, she prayed.

The sound of a phone ringing reached her as she crossed the deck to her chair. She paused and listened. The commonplace sound struck her as decidedly out of place there, as startling as the nightly chorus of owls would be back home. She knew that Connor had brought along a high-powered police cellular phone that he used to check in several times a day, but this was the first it had rung to signal an incoming call.

She spun toward the lake to shout to Connor, then changed her mind. They were having too much fun to disturb. Instead, she ran inside and up the stairs toward Connor's room. If the call was urgent, she would get him. If not, she'd take a message.

The phone was in a case on the table by his bed. She grabbed the receiver. "Hello?" Static. She pulled up the antenna. "Hello?"

A pause. Then a deep voice asked, "Who is this, please?"

"This is Gabrielle Flanders."

"Mrs. Flanders, State Police Captain Marino here. Where's Wolf?"

"He's..." She glanced out the window to look at Connor, where he was once again working on Toby's swimming technique, then turned away. "He can't come to the phone right now. He told me to take a message for him."

Captain Marino seemed to hesitate. "All right," he said finally, "since this involves you I might as well fill you in on what's happening. The officer we've had working on the computer finished early this morning. Your late husband's secretary helped. Seems she used to type some nonfirm-related material for him on a fairly regular basis, but she didn't come forward at first out of loyalty. She didn't want anything to taint his memory."

Gaby smiled affectionately. Good old Lynn, she thought, still looking out for Joel even now.

"How was she able to help?" she asked.

"She was familiar with the documents as they originally existed. Once she realized no one was checking into anything improper your husband might have done, she spoke up and offered to help piece together whatever we came up with."

"What did you come up with?" Gaby asked, anxiously winding the phone cord around her finger.

"Enough to provide motive for the explosion that killed your husband."

"Are you saying it wasn't someone trying to get back at Connor, the way we first thought? That it had to do with the books Joel kept for the restaurant? That Adam was involved?"

Marino was silent for a few seconds even after she finished firing questions at him.

"Listen, Mrs. Flanders," he said finally, "I understand that you and Adam Ressler have plans to get married?"

"Not any longer," she replied. "My plans have changed."

"Yeah, that's what Wolf told me, too. All right, here's the thing. Wolf's hunch was right on the money. Ressler is using the Black Wolf to launder money for a big—I mean big and ugly—drug cartel out of some hole-in-the-wall country south of the border... I'm talking south of the Colombian border."

"Drugs," she whispered, sinking to sit on the edge of the bed as her knees turned to jelly. "I can't believe it."

Marino snorted on the other end of the line. "You will when you see the pile of facts and figures we're putting together here... most of it thanks to your late husband. He'd evidently been tracking this situation and documenting everything for quite a while before he made a move to confront Ressler about it and... well, you know the rest."

"Yes. I know."

She was still struggling to come to terms with everything that Adam's involvement in this meant, the betrayal and the lies to Joel and to her. He was actually going to marry her, she thought, feeling a wave of nausea she had to press her knuckles to her lips to squelch. All his kindness and concern over the past two years was suddenly thrown into a new light. Of course he'd hung around her. He had good reason to cover his tracks by appearing to be the loyal friend. He probably also needed to secure his control of the Black Wolf against any future threats of exposure, and marrying her was the surest way to do that. A small cry of anguish escaped her.

"Mrs. Flanders, are you all right?" Marino asked.

She nodded, then realized he couldn't see her. "Yes," she said. "I'm fine. Just a little bit . . . shaken up."

"Understandable," he said gruffly. "You just sit yourself down and take it easy. We're going to get these guys, Mrs. Flanders, you can count on it."

"These guys." She shuddered. "You mean Adam isn't the only . . . of course he isn't," she said before she'd even finished the question, never mind waiting for an answer. "There have to be others."

"There are. And we've got a good line on who those others are. I'll save the details for Wolf. Tell him to call me as soon as possible. Tell him we'll be bringing Ressler in this afternoon for questioning. Something tells me he won't be a hard nut to crack. Wolf might want to be here to see it."

"I'll tell him right away."

"Besides, I want you all back here, just to be on the safe side."

Her heart thudded in her chest. "You don't think—"

"Mrs. Flanders," he cut in, "I always think the worst. It's my job. I'll just feel better with you and your son back home instead of out there in the middle of nowhere. We can post a guard outside your place if we think it necessary."

"No," she said quickly. "I don't want my son to know about all this, at least not yet."

"Trust me, Mrs. Flanders. Discreet is my middle name. Tell Wolf to call. No, just tell him to get his butt back here. Better yet, tell him I'm going to see who I can shake loose to go up there and fetch you and your boy. That will speed things up by letting Wolf come straight here to headquarters."

"I'll tell him," she promised again.

"Good."

He hung up.

Gaby sat on the bed with the receiver gripped to her chest until it began emitting a high-pitched sound. She lowered the antenna, leaned forward and dumped it back into the case.

With her palms pressed together, she brought her hands up and held them in front of her face, wrestling with the aftershocks of the truth Marino had just dumped on her.

Outside, Toby squealed with delight.

Gaby's hands fell to her sides. Toby. She stood. She had to tell Connor what was going on. She had to get to Toby. She hurried to the door, reaching it just as someone rounded it from the hallway outside.

She gave a sharp cry of surprise, then went weak.

"Adam."

"Hello, Gabrielle."

Outside, Connor paused in the act of tossing Toby over his shoulder one more time. The kid was tireless.

"Did you hear that?" he asked.

"What?" Toby countered.

"A noise, like a shout. I thought it came from the house." He listened for a moment and heard nothing. Gaby had been sitting on the deck just a minute ago. She must have gone inside for something, he told himself. If she wasn't back in a while, he'd get out and check on her.

"I guess it was nothing," he told Toby, lifting him higher. "Or maybe just an owl."

"Why do owls hoot?"

Connor pretended not to hear.

"One, two," he counted, swinging Toby carefully. "Ready, set, three."

He let him go, and Toby gave his usual squeal of pleasure as he hit the water. Connor figured it would take him a few seconds to come up, then about thirty more to catch his breath and shake the water from his eyes. That meant he had less than a minute to come up with an answer to why owls hoot.

"Adam," Gaby said again, her dry mouth making it hard to breathe, much less speak. "How did . . . what are you doing here?"

He smiled, revealing perfect teeth.

Slick.

That's how her sister Lisa insisted on referring to him behind his back. Don't call him that, Gaby would admonish her, demanding to know why a man couldn't be well mannered and charming without being branded slick.

Slick.

Only now, too late, did she see how perfectly the name suited him.

"What am I doing here?" he repeated, his soft tone as incredulous as if she'd asked him his name. "Gabrielle, darling, I'm here for you."

"I see." Somehow she managed to flex her lips into a stiff smile. "It's just that I...I thought my mother would have told you why I—"

"Why you ran away from me on what was supposed to be our wedding day? The start of our new life together?" His smile was relaxed, but the look that came at her from deep within his eyes was cold and frightening.

"I'm so sorry about that," she told him. "It was unforgivable of me. I was all set to go through with it...."

She saw his mouth twitch at her choice of words and hesitated. "I mean I was looking forward to the ceremony, and then all of a sudden I...I don't know what happened, I just knew I had to get away, that I needed..."

"Time to think," he finished for her.

He smiled again. With his lean, aristocratic features and a physique honed at the most exclusive fitness center in the state he was undeniably a handsome man, but Gaby had never found anyone as repulsive as she found him at that instant.

"I understood all that," he said in a tone she'd once found so soothing. "Of course, I assumed at the time that you would be doing your thinking alone. I wasn't aware that my future bride would be sharing her hideaway with the man responsible for her late husband's death."

Gaby had to bite the insides of her cheeks to keep from blurting the truth, that he was the one responsible for Joel's death...for Joel's murder. Not Connor.

Connor.

Her breath shuddered from her as her stomach churned with sudden fear. Where was Connor? And Toby? Connor would never have let Adam be alone with her. How had Adam gotten in here without being seen?

The sound of water splashing, followed by a whoop from Toby eased the worst of her fears.

"So?" Adam prodded as she continued to stare at him in silence.

Gaby blinked.

He prompted her. "Wolf. You were about to explain how you ended up here together. I had no idea you two were so...close."

"We're not. At least we weren't. I needed a place to stay for a few days and..." She shrugged. "Did you get a chance to say hello to him on your way in?" She took a step to go around him. "I'm sure Connor—"

"Connor?" he repeated, moving to block her path. "Is it Connor now?"

Again she shrugged.

"He's crazy, you know." He watched her reaction closely. "Mad. I probably should have warned you. He's been badgering me for months to advance him his quarterly payments, ranting about selling his share of the business. He even threatened to go to you with some off-the-wall story about me doctoring the books." His lips thinned and turned up at the corners. "Crazy, right?"

Gaby nodded. "Right."

Liar, she thought, aghast at the realization that her reaction to these latest lies would have been dangerously different if he had told them to her a week ago.

"But to answer your question," he went on, "no, I didn't stop to say hello on my way in. You see, I wanted to surprise you first."

"Well, you did." A new thought narrowed her eyes. "I didn't even hear your car pull up. With that gravel drive you can usually hear people approaching a mile away."

"I know. That's why I parked down the road and hiked up the back way. To surprise you, remember?"

"Of course."

"Lucky for me I'd been here before and knew the way. It is a little off the beaten path."

"Yes. It is. Tell me, Adam, how did you know I was staying here?"

He smiled. "A friend told me they saw you leaving your mother's with Toby, heading this way."

"There's a lot of places I could have been staying between my mother's and here," she stated in as light a tone as she could muster.

"I got lucky."

Liar, she thought again, hiding her outrage behind a smile. Connor was right; Adam had had someone watching for her. Only he was even more clever than they realized. He'd been watching her mother's house, knowing she would show up there to see Toby sooner or later. And she had played right into his hands.

"I have to admit," he went on, "I was a little surprised myself when I got here. I mean, there's Wolf...excuse me, there's Connor," he corrected, giving the name an exaggeratedly formal accent, "frolicking in the water with Toby and I find my fiancée, who I fully expect to be deep in contemplation of whatever it was you needed time to think about, chatting away on the phone."

Gaby remained silent, fear coiling inside her.

"Who were you talking with, Gabrielle?"

"Who? Oh, you mean on the phone," she said, stupidly pointing to it.

"Yes, darling, on the phone."

"My mother."

"I see. I thought I heard you mention my name."

"Did I?" Her puzzled frown gave way to a brittle smile. "I was just telling her that I had given everything a great deal of thought this week and that I would be talking things over with you very soon...and that I was anxious to apologize to you for everything I put you through."

His teeth flashed inside a deadly smile. "And now you have your chance."

His arm snaked out and snagged her around her waist, pulling her against him.

Gaby stiffened, the self-preservation instinct kicking in hard and fast. The urge to shove him away, to scream and bite and do whatever she had to do to get free of him was held in check only by the slim hope that by playing along she could better protect Connor and Toby. She didn't care what Adam did to her. There was nothing she wasn't willing to face, no risk she wouldn't take to keep them safe.

"Skip the apology," he told her, his arm tightening even more, drawing her up until their faces were only inches apart. He smelled as he always did, of breath mints and expensive salon hair gel.

"I've been a most patient bridegroom, Gabrielle. I've waited and made excuses for your behavior to all our friends and guests, and given you time to...think. Now I want to hear you say that it's over, that you've come to your senses and you're ready to become my wife."

Gaby still hadn't come back out.

Connor had been checking every couple of minutes, telling himself there were plenty of things that could have detained her inside and that she had obviously seen Toby and him together and knew Toby was safe enough. Maybe she'd even gone inside to put on her suit and join them. Maybe. The thought alone was enticing. He would relish the opportunity to brush his legs against hers underwater. Maybe he would even get a chance to ask her the important question that had been on his mind ever since his little talk with Toby.

He glanced again at the deck and the empty chair where she'd been sitting. He could go on making up reasons why she could be taking so long, but he couldn't ignore that feeling at the back of his neck that told him something was wrong.

"Okay, partner," he said to Toby as he swung him in the air, "last toss of the day."

"Aw, Wolf."

"I think maybe your mother could use some help with lunch."

"Okay. But throw me real high this time."

"Real high? You've got it. See that tree?"

He pointed to the highest pine tree in sight.

"I see it," Toby said.

"Good. Don't bump your head on it on the way down."

Toby giggled wildly as Connor began the now-familiar count "One, two, ready, set, three."

As soon as he emerged, Connor was rushing him out of the water, hurriedly drying him off with his shirt.

"There," he said, "that ought to hold you until we can grab a towel on the deck. And don't let your teeth chatter like that when we get to the house, or else your mother will think I let you stay in too long. I can't afford to lose any brownie points."

"What are—?"

"I'll explain later," Connor said, cutting him off. "Now let's move it."

He yanked his jeans on over his wet suit and shoved his feet into his sneakers. Edgy without knowing exactly why, he ended up carrying Toby most of the way rather than having to wait for him to keep up. The instant he stepped over the threshold, the flesh at the back of his neck tightened like a hand was grabbing him there.

He stopped so abruptly Toby bumped into the back of his legs. A quick look around without moving from his position by the door told him that if Gaby was in there, she wasn't on the first floor. He considered calling to her and decided against it. No particular reason. Just instinct.

Turning, he took Toby by the shoulders and hustled him back onto the deck.

"Wait here," he told him, "and don't ask any questions." He looked around and grabbed a towel that had been drying in the sun. "Here. Wrap this around you to stay warm."

"But..."

"Later. And don't move off this deck until I come back for you. Okay?"

"Okay, Wolf."

Inside he went straight to the locked cabinet where he'd put his gun, loaded it and stuck it inside the waist of his jeans in back.

He'd brought the gun along as a precaution, not because he thought he would need it. There had been no reason to believe that Gaby or Toby was in any imminent danger from either Adam or whomever he was involved with. If not for the fact that she'd been about to marry Ressler and he had wanted to stop her from making what could prove to be a huge mistake, she wouldn't even be there now. The police investigation would simply have proceeded without Gaby even being aware of it until they showed up to arrest her new husband.

He told himself the odds were that he still wouldn't need the gun, that his uneasy feeling was just the result of the week's accumulated tensions. In fact, he thought, Gaby was probably going to be mad as hell at him for taking the gun from the cabinet and loading it with Toby around. He might even end up losing ground with her when he desperately needed to regain it.

He still liked the feel of having it tucked back there. He buttoned his shirt over it as he headed for the stairs and started up. Slowly. Keeping his weight on the balls of his feet and listening intently as he moved. Not that it did him much good. The interior walls of the cabin were also made of solid wood logs, and he didn't hear anything until he turned at the top of the stairs.

"...a real lying bitch, you know it?"

He froze in his tracks at the angry sound of a man's voice coming from his room.

Adam?

It had been a while and he hadn't heard enough to absolutely identify the voice as that of his supposed friend, but in his gut he knew it had to be. Damn it, how had Adam gotten in here without his seeing him? Had he been that engrossed in teaching Toby to swim?

Seething at his own ineptitude, he recalled the walk back to the house from the lake and the fact that he'd only passed one car in the driveway. Gaby's car. Which meant that whoever was in there with her had arrived on foot so his approach wouldn't be detected. Understanding how it happened didn't make him feel any better about it.

Something in the man's tone made him reach for his gun, moving as quickly as he dared along the hallway, staying close to the wall and taking pains not to make a sound. If he had his way, the next surprise was going to be his to deliver.

When he drew next to the open door of the bedroom, he brought the gun up so he was holding it in front of him with two hands, the safety off. He braced himself, then lunged forward and sideways onto his right foot, a stance he'd taken hundreds of time in his years on the force. This was the first time when what he saw as he rounded the corner made everything inside him go cold.

It was Adam, all right. He had Gaby cradled against him, twisted at an awkward angle so that her back was to him, her head wrenched back by his grip on her hair. In his other hand he held a small-caliber pistol with its barrel positioned just under her jawline.

Connor's sudden appearance caught Adam by surprise. For a few seconds, no more, all three of them remained absolutely motionless. And silent. It felt like forever. More than long enough for hundreds of disjointed images and impressions to streak through Connor's head.

He had a flash of a long-ago memory of Adam viciously kicking a dog that had done nothing but come begging for some of the sandwich he was eating. Then came the much more recent and crushing memory of how soft the skin on Gaby's throat was at that spot where he held the gun. Then he was hit by the alarming realization that the sense of disconnection that had always given him his reckless edge, allowing him to think with absolute clarity in situations like this one, wasn't with him now.

He felt the antithesis of disconnected. Or clearheaded. He felt more connected to the woman standing across the room— looking to him with her eyes full of fear—than he'd ever felt to anyone. He could feel her fear. Smell it. Taste it at the back of his throat. Or maybe that was his own fear he tasted, because this time, for the first time, he was the one who was afraid. He was the one who was desperate.

It took every ounce of training and self-control he possessed to force the fear back down and keep his hands from trembling as he held the gun pointed at Adam's head.

"Hello, Adam," he said, managing to sound as if they'd just bumped into each other on the street. "How've you been?"

"Just fine and dandy, Wolf," Adam replied. "You?"

"Never better. Now that the formalities are out of the way, why don't you let her go?"

Adam grinned at him, and a hundred reasons why Connor had never really liked the guy came back to him.

"Get real," he said. "That isn't going to happen. Now let me make a counter suggestion, one that at least falls within the realm of possibility. Drop the gun and kick it over here to me."

Connor glared at him without moving a muscle.

"Oh, that's good," Adam said, laughing. "You've still got that cop look down perfect. I'll bet a lot of sixteen-year-old punks have wet their pants when you give them that look, right, Wolf? Only I'm not sixteen anymore. Still, if you want to play, we'll play, and we'll just see who blinks first. Who really has the nerves of steel around here." He cocked his gun.

"Of course," he continued, his eyes on Connor, "I've always thought the key to picking the winner in any game of chicken was to ask yourself who's got the most to lose."

He yanked hard on Gaby's hair, forcing her head back even farther. Connor gritted his teeth against the small yelp of pain that the action wrung from her.

Adam's gaze never wavered, remaining as cool and steady as his tone. "Ask yourself that, Wolf," he suggested. "Ask yourself who's got the most to lose here?"

"Seems to me you do," Connor told him, willing to play any angle available to him. "After all, she's your fiancée."

"Not anymore, I'm afraid. Gabrielle just gave me the bad news. The wedding is off permanently."

"Is that what this is all about?"

"Is that what this is all about?" Adam mimicked, then laughed smoothly. "You mean, am I holding a gun to her head because she won't have me? Come on, Wolf, you're the crazy one here, not me.''

"Then what is it about?"

"I don't know. Exactly. I was trying to convince Gabrielle to tell me that very thing when you interrupted. All I know is my bride disappears from the steps of the church, and the next thing I know I've got state investigators crawling all over my life, checking into every move I've ever made...and every move Joel made, too, it seems. They're even tapping into the computers at that firm he worked for. Now I find all that is more than just a coincidence. I find it fascinating. Don't you, Wolf?"

He shrugged. "I guess I'm not as easily fascinated as you, Ressler."

"Don't sell yourself short. I guarantee you that before this is over I will have captured your complete and undivided attention."

The muscles in Connor's belly clenched at the panic that surged in Gaby's eyes. It was a struggle not to go to her in spite of Adam and his gun.

"Don't put yourself out on my account," he told Adam with a laconic smile.

"I won't. It's Gabrielle who's going to provide the entertainment. Isn't that right, darling?" He caressed her cheek with the tip of the gun, and Connor tasted blood. "She's going to start by telling us who she was on the phone with when I walked in and what the important message she promised to give you right away might be."

"Sounds good to me," Connor responded. "Why don't we all go downstairs and sit down and—"

"No," Adam said, cutting him off, his smile gone. "Right here. Right now."

"Tell him, Gaby," Connor urged softly. "Tell him whatever he wants to know."

Connor's sudden show of quiet cooperation drew a wary look from Adam.

"First the gun," he ordered. "Now, Connor. Kick it over here, or I really will shoot her and turn this quaint, rustic setting into a scene from a Schwarzenegger movie." He tilted his head close to Gaby's. "Tell me, Gabrielle, does Toby like action films?"

"No," she whimpered. "Please don't do this, Adam."

"I told you before. Don't beg. Talk. Tell me what I want to know . . . after I get the gun."

Connor's gaze shifted from Adam to the silent plea in Gaby's eyes. She nodded, a slight, pitiful gesture that was all she could manage with Adam's hand wrapped tightly in her hair. *Please,* she seemed to be saying, *please do as he says.*

Never give up your gun. The words rang in Connor's head. It was a creed he'd lived by and had always been prepared to die by, as well. Always before, he had been able to rationalize his inflexibility on that issue by telling himself that a hostage's fate was directly linked to his own, and that they both stood a better chance of surviving if he remained armed.

Even now he had a perfect bead on Adam's temple. He was an excellent marksman, utterly nerveless. And experienced, which Adam wasn't. The odds were greater than fifty-fifty that he could take the other man out before he got a shot off. There was at least a fifty percent chance that Gaby would walk away unharmed and a lesser one that Adam would fire as he fell and inflict no more than a flesh wound, or a more serious but still nonlife-threatening injury. Or the bullet could strike her carotid artery on an upward trajectory, and she would be dead before she hit the ground.

He slowly bent his knees and lowered the gun to the floor at his feet, then kicked it across the room. It landed close to Gaby.

"Perfect," Adam declared. "Now, Gabrielle, you and I are going to play a game of pick up the gun. We go down together, you pick it up and hand it back to me. Nicely, or else I see a trip to the orphanage in Toby's immediate future."

"Do exactly as he says, Gaby," Connor told her softly, torn apart inside by the sight of her trembling as she followed Adam's orders, bending her knees slowly, her fingers fumbling for the gun. When she finally got a grip on it, she slowly held it up for Adam to take.

Connor was encouraged by the indecision that caused Adam to frown as he tried to determine how to take possession of the second gun without putting down his own or relinquishing his hold on Gaby. He really was a novice, he thought contemptuously. Caught up in something way over his head. If not for Gaby and for Toby outside on the deck, Connor would tackle him right now. Years of instinct told him to do just that, that he could easily overpower Adam Ressler. It was something else, something brand-new and much more powerful that held him back, putting his concern for Gaby and Toby above all else, even his own pride.

"Don't hand it to me," he snapped at Gaby finally. "Reach around and put it in my pocket."

He thrust his right hip forward, indicating the pocket of the tan linen jacket he was wearing. Gaby hurriedly did as he directed, shoving the pistol into his pocket. Barrel first, Connor noted approvingly. It would be simple enough to grab if he could get close enough.

"Now we can go down," Adam announced. "I don't want Toby to feel left out."

"No, Adam, please," Gabrielle said, trying to turn to him and being brought in line by another hard jerk on her hair. "Ohhh. Please. Leave Toby out of this. He has no idea that any of this is going on or why Connor even brought us here. I'll tell you what you want to know, but please leave Toby alone."

"Where is he?" Adam demanded of Connor.

"He's still outside. On the deck. He's got some toys out there. The kid isn't going to cause you any trouble, Adam. Let him be."

Adam thought it over.

Another mistake a pro would never make, thought Connor. Then Adam shook his head, improving his score marginally. "No. I want everyone where I can see them. Now let's go.

You first, Wolf . . . or would you prefer that I call you Connor, too?'' he asked, giving the name a sarcastic emphasis.

"Suit yourself," Connor replied.

"Trust me, I intend to," said Adam. "Now move. Real slow. Downstairs."

Chapter 13

Connor led the way down the stairs, following Adam's instructions to go on to the living room and have a seat on the sofa. Adam pushed Gaby down on the opposite end and steppêd back so that he was standing midway in front of them, the gun still trained on Gaby.

"Now call Toby," he told her. "Tell him you want him in here right away."

She clasped her hands into a tight knot in her lap. "Adam, please . . ."

"Do it," he snapped. He lifted the gun, his eyes darting back and forth nervously between her and Connor. "Or I'll go get him myself."

Yeah, do that, thought Connor, ready to pounce if Adam made the slightest misstep. He groaned inside as Gaby caved in to the ridiculous threat.

"No, I'll call him." She swallowed hard and leaned forward on the sofa. "Toby," she called, her voice strained and weak. "Toby," she repeated, more loudly this time. "Come on in here, honey."

The back door cracked open. "But, Mommy, Wolf said..."

"It's all right, partner," Connor called to him. "Come on in."

He ran into the room, trailing the towel behind him, and stopped short at the sight of Adam. He took in the gun in his hand with an aplomb unique to five-year-olds.

"Hi, Uncle Adam. Can I hold that?"

"Just sit down with your mother," Adam told him. "And don't say a word."

"But..."

"Shh," Gaby said, gathering him to her and urging him down onto the sofa close beside her. "Do as he says, Toby, and everything will be fine."

"But..."

"Toby, please," she said, the desperation in her voice too obvious to be missed even by a child.

Toby scrunched himself deep into the seat and allowed his mother to wrap the towel around him.

"All right, let's hear it," Adam barked impatiently. "And don't try and con me again, Gabrielle. I know it wasn't your mother you were talking to and I'm losing patience."

Connor caught Gaby's quick glance in his direction and nodded. He had no idea what she was holding back. He wasn't even sure whom she had been talking to, whether she had made the call or simply answered a call for him. He only knew that he didn't want her taking any risks or trying to be a hero. They were going to play this straight until he had a chance to turn things around. The best way to buy time for him and get that chance was to keep Adam talking.

"You're right," she said to Adam. "It wasn't my mother on the phone."

"Nana?" Toby piped up. "Did Nana call?"

"Shut up," ordered Adam.

Toby's eyes widened to circles, but he didn't cry. In fact, he looked mad as hell, Connor noted, his estimation of the kid going even higher.

"Toby, please," Gaby said, "not another word." She looked back at Adam. "It was someone from the state police," she

told him. "He wanted to talk with Connor, and I told him he
was busy and couldn't come to the phone right then."

"What was his name?" Adam asked her.

"I don't remember."

He repositioned the gun on Toby. "Think."

"My God, Adam, have you lost your mind?" she cried,
hugging Toby against her.

Adam met her gaze and swung the gun back so it was aimed
at her. "The man's name."

"Marino," she revealed. "Captain Marino."

"And the message he gave you?"

She again looked at Connor.

"Forget him," Adam shouted. "He's nothing to you. He
can't get you out of this. He can't save your ass or your kid's,
Gabrielle. Only I can do that, so you damn well better start
looking at me and doing whatever the hell I tell you to do. Understand?"

"I understand," she said, her voice shaking. "Marino told
me that they found some information that suggests there might
be a problem with the books at the Black Wolf and that they
were planning to question you about it. He said he thought
Connor might want to come down to headquarters so he could
be there when they talked with you. Maybe they wanted to ask
him about it, too, I really don't know."

Adam looked very worried. "Where did they get this information? From the nosing around they did at Joel's old firm?"

"I don't know...."

"What did he tell you?" Adam demanded, shouting now.

Gaby nodded. "Yes, they found out about it at the firm."

"Of course," Adam muttered, evidently thinking out loud.
"They had to get it there. We wiped—" He halted, frowning.

"Tell me, Adam, how the hell did you know they were
checking out Joel's old records?" Connor infused the question with a note of grudging admiration that Adam snapped at.

He smiled smugly. "What's the matter, Wolf? Surprised to
learn that I'm good for something besides managing the Black
Wolf's wine cellar and glad-handing the regulars? It's about
time you gave me a little respect. About time you realize you're

not the only one with guts." His smile broadened into a grin. "About time you knew who's the real player here."

"But I don't," Connor countered. "Not really. I mean I still don't know how you got onto the investigation at Joel's firm. Did you have someone on the inside there? Was that it?"

Adam scoffed at that. "Didn't need to," he declared. "I have something better, someone inside the state police."

Connor made a show of looking stunned and trying to hide it. Adam's shoulders squared with delight.

"That's right," he said, "one of your own is in my hip pocket. Has been all along. That's how we knew exactly how to set it up so that the explosion looked like it was intended for you."

Gaby's soft gasp drew Adam's attention. "Oh, my God. Then it really is all true. I thought maybe there was some...oh, my God. How could you?" she demanded, her voice hardening. "Joel was your friend. He..."

Adam cut her off. "Joel was an idiot," he shouted. "He wouldn't listen to reason. I tried to talk to him, to explain how it is, that to make a buck in this business you have to have an edge, a connection. I had that connection and I wanted to bring him in with me, but he wouldn't listen. He kept after me and after me and then told me he was going to let Wolf in on it, too. I couldn't let that happen."

He glared at Gaby as tears flowed down her cheeks.

"You don't understand," he went on. "You can't know what it was like. It was too late to stop it like he wanted me to do. I tried to tell Joel that. I tried to make him understand that there was no way they would let me just walk away. What was I supposed to say? 'I'm sorry but my partner has decided this isn't a good idea?' " His laughter was short and ugly. "They don't play like that."

"Who's they?" Connor asked.

Adam looked at him and shrugged. "It doesn't matter."

"They're a drug cartel," Gaby explained. "From somewhere in South America. Adam has been using the restaurant to launder money from their drug operation."

Connor whistled through his teeth. "Oh, man, Adam, you really do have guts."

"What's that supposed to mean?" Adam demanded, his eyes glittering with suspicion.

"I mean you wouldn't catch me messing with those guys. South American drug runners?" He shook his head and whistled again. "No way. Not me. I can almost understand why you had to do Joel the way you did."

"I didn't do Joel," he insisted, darting a glance at Gaby. "I didn't have anything to do with that. I just told them we were supposed to meet and where and they said stay away."

From the other end of the sofa, he heard Gaby draw a shuddering breath. By now Toby was crying softly, too, though Connor doubted he understood half of what was happening. A blessing for sure.

"So you stayed away and saved your own skin."

"Like you didn't save yours?" Adam countered.

Connor leaned back and hitched one foot onto the opposite knee. "That must have been a major disappointment, huh? My getting out alive."

"Let's just say that your surviving wasn't the optimum result."

"Of course not. With both Joel and me out of the way, you and Gaby could have exercised your option to buy out my share of the business. Then you marry her, knowing a wife can't be forced to testify against her husband, and your control of things is all sewn up."

"Now, that result would have been optimum," Adam agreed. "But life is full of compromises. We decided we could live with things as they were."

"Sure, why not? I was as dumb as dirt about what was going on and then I helped out even more by leaving the country, giving you a free rein with the business."

Adam shook his head. "The question is, why the hell did you have to come back?"

Connor smiled at him. "You know me. I never did like taking the easy way out. So what now, Adam? Are you supposed to kill us, too?"

"I told you I didn't kill Joel," he snapped, sounding more and more tense. "I never bargained for any of this."

"That's too bad," Connor told him, "because you've bought it. I don't see any of your cutthroat pals standing there with a gun. I only see you. And from what I've seen of the evidence they've been stockpiling down at headquarters, that all points only to you, too."

"That's bull," Adam declared, his face flushed. "I'm just a damn middleman. The packages of money come in, and it goes right back out. I don't have anything to do with any drugs or with killing anyone. Nothing like that."

Connor held out his hand. "If that's true, Adam, why not just hand me the gun and we'll work something out?"

Adam's chin went up, and his eyes narrowed. "Oh, no. Forget it, Wolf. I guess what I should have said is that I don't want to kill any of you, no more than I wanted to see Joel get hurt. But I come first. Then and now."

"So what are you going to do?" Connor asked.

"Get away. I suggest you all do the same if you know what's good for you. But I go first." He darted a quick glance around the room. "I need some rope. Do you know where there is some?"

Connor shook his head. "I haven't seen any around," he said, suspecting what he wanted the rope for and knowing it would seriously interfere with any effort to wrestle the gun from him. There was no way he was going to submit to being tied up by Adam Ressler.

From her end of the sofa, Gaby watched Adam give another furtive look around the room. She glanced at the clock on a shelf behind him, wishing she knew exactly how long it had been since Captain Marino had called and how long it would take for the police car he was sending to get there. Until it arrived, all she could do was pray. And stall. Anything that would eat up some time was preferable to forcing Adam's hand.

"I know where there's some rope," she said.

She could feel the sharply disapproving look her remark drew from Connor. She didn't look at him, instead keeping her gaze focused on Adam.

He eyed her suspiciously. "Where is it?"

"Over there." She inclined her head toward the desk in the corner behind her. "Do you want me to get it?"

He thought for a few seconds before nodding. "Yeah. Go get it. And remember, one wrong move—"

"I know," she said, cutting short his threat before he scared Toby even more than he already was. "I'll just get the rope and hand it to you."

Adam followed her, stopping at the end of the sofa, keeping his eyes on Connor and the gun on her.

She took her time, dwelling on the comforting truth that every minute that passed brought them one minute closer to being rescued. She wished she could share the knowledge with Connor, knowing how hard this was for him. She could see that he was champing at the bit to lash out at Adam with everything that was in him, and she understood that it was concern for her and for Toby that held him back.

It was, she imagined, an entirely new twist on Connor's interpretation of self-sacrifice, and she loved him for it. She just hoped they made it through this so she could tell him so...and this time make him listen.

She'd seen the white, lightweight rope, the type used for clotheslines, when she returned the sewing kit to the desk drawer the other day. It was still there, tossed in a heap in the bottom, half-covered by the sewing basket. As she pulled the rope out, the basket tipped, spilling a pincushion and a few spools of thread. As she hurriedly tossed them back in, Gaby's gaze landed on the seam ripper that was also among the items in the basket.

Her grip on the rope tightened reflexively. The seam ripper was no more than three inches long, black plastic on the handle end and with a roughly U-shaped metal prong on the other that was used to rip out stitches. The prong, she knew from her limited sewing experience, was razor sharp.

Sharp enough to cut through rope if need be.

But why risk it? If Adam tied them up and left them, the police would soon be there to free them. There was no need for anyone to be a hero. Was there? What was the sense of courage merely for courage's sake? If she tried something and Adam saw her, anything could happen.

The thought brought her up short. Who was she kidding? Anything could happen anyway.

"What the hell is taking you so long?" Adam demanded, sounding a lot more anxious than he had only moments ago.

"It's all tangled up in here," she explained without turning around. "I think I've got it now." She pulled on the rope and unwound it from around a hole puncher also in the drawer and gathered it in her hand. Only at the very last instant did she pluck the seam ripper from the basket and tuck it inside the tangle of rope.

She stood and shut the drawer with her foot.

"I guess that will do," Adam said, frowning at the lightweight rope. "We need something to cut it, too. Scissors. Do you have scissors?"

"I'll look." She spotted a pair in the cup holder on top of the desk. "Here they are."

Holding the scissors in one hand and the rope in the other, she turned. Adam's eyes followed her as she walked back to him.

"Good. Now cut a piece. A piece long enough to tie a man's hands . . . and double it up so it's good and strong."

Gaby had no idea how much rope was needed to tie a man's hands. She cut a piece about five feet long, praying that the seam ripper wouldn't fall from where she had it pressed between her palm and the bunched rope.

"Down there," Adam ordered when she finished cutting and looked at him. He pointed with his chin to the end of the sofa where Connor was sitting and trailed along as she moved there. She noticed that he was frantically shifting his gaze from her to Connor to Toby, over and over again, and she prayed that he would be too distracted to pay much attention to the awkward way she was holding her hands in order to conceal the seam ripper.

"Lean forward," he told Connor, giving him a little shove from behind. "Put your hands behind your back."

Gaby saw Connor flinch and his shoulders tense and knew what it was costing him to be subjected to this without fighting back.

"Go ahead," Adam said to her when he had his hands behind him. "Tie them. Tight. I'm going to check, and if I have to waste time making you do it over, someone's going to pay."

He let his gaze slide to where Toby was cowering in the corner of the sofa, and her heart was suddenly in her throat. She never should have taken the seam ripper. If Adam caught her with it... Her hands were shaking so badly it took her two tries to get the rope looped around Connor's wrists and tie a simple knot.

And what if Adam tied her up himself? How would she hide it from him then? She concentrated on pulling the rope through without dropping it right in front of Adam. Ohmigod, ohmigod, ohmigod. She pulled hard on the rope to secure the knot and glanced up to find Connor looking at her over his shoulder, his smile as reassuring as a familiar landmark on a dark, lonely road.

Without thinking, she pressed the seam ripper into his palm. For a second he didn't react.

"Are you done?" Adam asked.

Her heart pounded. Then Connor's fingers curled up and around the seam ripper, and she let it go.

"Yes, I'm done," she said.

"Now tie his feet," Adam ordered.

Gaby obediently moved around and tied Connor's feet. She was so nervous that tears stung her eyes and she avoided looking up at him.

"Now Toby," Adam said when she was through. "Just tie his hands, though."

She didn't ask why, intent on smiling and winking at Toby as she tied his hands as loosely as she dared, hoping he might be lulled into thinking this was some sort of grown-up game. Not until Adam had ordered her to sit and had put the gun down long enough to tie her hands and feet did it occur to her why he might want Toby to have his feet free to walk.

"All right, Toby," he said when he was done, "come with me."

"Where are you going with him?" Gaby cried, tugging at the rope that was already chafing her wrists.

"Upstairs," Adam replied, shoving the scissors in his pocket.

Toby looked back at her with wide eyes. "Mommy..."

"It's all right, sweetie," she said, struggling to sound reassuring. "Adam won't hurt you...will you, Adam?"

He looked down at him. "I'd never want to hurt you, Toby, you know that, don't you?"

Toby nodded uncertainly.

"Good. Then let's go."

He pushed Toby ahead of him up the stairs.

"Oh, Connor," she said as soon as they were out of sight. "I'm so scared."

"Don't be. Adam isn't going to hurt a kid."

"I wish I could be sure of that."

"I'm sure. Trust me."

"Do you have the—?"

"Shh," he said. "Yes."

Toby preceded Adam down the stairs. Adam was carrying the cellular phone. "Sorry to leave you two incommunicado, but I'm counting on a little head start. I also took the liberty of borrowing the keys to your car, Gabrielle. I knew you wouldn't mind."

"Where are you headed?" Connor asked, sounding as offhand as if Adam were leaving on vacation. Gaby marveled at his poise.

Adam's smile was enigmatic. "Let's just say it's my turn to leave the country. But fortunately I have a rather nice little nest egg put aside and I won't be forced to spend my days in some pit of a town in Mexico."

"It doesn't matter where you go, you know," Connor told him. "If the feds don't find you, the cartel will."

"That's a chance I'll have to take. Say goodbye to Mommy, Toby."

"No," Gaby cried out, finally understanding why he wanted Toby free to walk. "No, Adam, please. Take me with you instead of him."

"Sorry, darling," he said as he dragged a sobbing Toby to the door. "You had your chance to fly away with me and you blew it. But don't worry. All you have to do is make sure I have four hours to get where I'm going, and I promise you I'll leave him somewhere where you can pick him up safe and sound. Remember, Gabrielle," he said, looking straight at her. "Four hours."

The door banged shut behind them.

"Four hours, my ass," muttered Connor, twisting his shoulders and wincing as if in pain. Watching him, frantic, Gaby suddenly recalled his injured hand. He would never be able to get free with his hand hurting him, she thought. She should have held on to the seam ripper herself.

"Connor, can I—"

"No. I..." He gave a hard jerk with his arms, and his hands came free. "There." He bent and worked frantically at the rope around his ankles.

From outside came the sound of the station wagon's engine, straining to turn over, the way it always did after it had sat unused for a few days.

The rope around his ankles gave and Connor lunged from the chair. "I'll be back for you," he said, rushing past her.

"But... Connor, wait...."

He was already out the door.

Gaby heard the engine roar and catch, and her heart raced like a runaway train. She pulled at the ropes, seething with frustration, when the glint of metal caught her eye. The seam ripper lay where Connor had dropped it, on the floor about five feet away.

She quickly worked her way to the edge of the sofa cushion and slipped off it so her back was to the seam ripper. Leaning back so far it hurt, she fumbled around for it with her fingers, finally managing to locate it, position it so she could grasp it and pick it up.

It took several tries for her to get it pointed in the right direction. Her hand cramped with the effort, and sweat beaded on her forehead and dripped into her eyes. She couldn't imagine how Connor had managed this with his sore hand. He must have been working on it the entire time that Toby and she were being tied up and while Adam went upstairs to get the phone.

The ripper would slice through a few strands of the coiled rope and then slip before she would have to maneuver it back into position all over again. She heard noises coming from outside, but she couldn't tell what was happening. Finally she could feel what remained of the rope slacken and she followed Connor's example and gave a mighty tug. It took her a second try, but finally the last strands of rope gave way.

It was much easier to cut through the rope on her ankles, where she could see what she was doing. A minute later she was free and racing for the door.

She ran across the deck and down the stairs to the driveway.

About twenty yards away she saw Connor and Adam on the ground, rolling in a patch of dirt and rocks by the edge of the woods. At first Connor was on top, then Adam reared up and sent him flying onto his back, coming down on top of him with his fist flying toward Connor's face.

Gaby grunted and saw the gun lying on the driveway and realized Toby was alone in the car with the engine running all in the same instant.

She ran to the open driver's door. Toby was on his knees on the passenger seat, whimpering.

"Get out," she said, reaching for him.

He shook his head. "Wolf said...Wolf said..." He was trying to talk around his tears. "...stay here."

"All right," she said, deciding Connor was right, that he was probably as safe there as anywhere. She reached to turn off the engine. "Stay there and I'll be right back for you."

She slammed the door shut and ran to pick up the gun. It felt heavy and awkward in her hand. She grasped it with both hands, the way she had seen Connor do, and walked toward where he and Adam were still locked in battle.

At the moment Connor was on top. His hand was covered with blood, and red streaks covered his face and neck and what was left of the shirt that had been almost ripped off him.

Adam was bloodied, too, but thoughts of Joel and Toby and the sight of Connor's blood-soaked fist and battered face stopped her from feeling anything for him but hatred, powerful enough to make her overcome the cautious ways of a lifetime, raw enough to make her do whatever she had to do to stop him.

She lowered the gun until it was aimed directly at Adam's head.

"Stop," she ordered. They kept fighting, oblivious to her. She stepped closer and shouted with steadily increasing fury, "Stop. Stop. Stop."

Both men froze. They turned to look up at her just as a police car pulled into her view across the lake, headed their way and sending the torrent of tears she'd been holding back streaming down Gaby's face.

The two young state police officers, who'd thought they were there on a simple escort assignment, were first surprised and then thrilled to discover that they were going to be the arresting officers in what they knew was a very big investigation.

Adam didn't resist and he didn't look at her as they handcuffed him, read him his rights and led him like a beaten dog to the back of the police car. She wished he had. She wanted him to see exactly how much she despised him. Not for her own sake or because of the heartless way he had tried to use her, but for the pain and suffering he had inflicted on those she loved, on Toby and Connor. And most of all, for Joel's sake.

The officers offered to call for another car to drive her and Toby back to the city, but Connor insisted he was capable of doing it himself and was damn well going to do it. He made it clear he wasn't letting them out of his sight until he was absolutely certain they weren't in any danger from anyone.

Besides, he said to her alone as he helped her into the car, he had something important he needed to ask her.

Gaby gratefully consented to letting him take them home. Bloodied and bruised as he was, there was no one she trusted more.

As for Adam, she thought as the police car with him locked inside pulled out ahead of them, there would be plenty of times ahead for her to make it plain to everyone how she felt about him . . . at the arraignment, the trial, the sentencing. And she would be there for all of it, no matter how grueling, no matter how long. If for no other reason, she would be there for Joel.

During the drive home she spent most of her time and attention reassuring Toby and answering his questions. His grasp on the details of what had happened was hazy, and Gaby decided that for now it was best to leave it that way. He was adamant about one thing, however, that Adam was a bad man. She decided to leave that alone, too.

Marino called on the cellular phone. Connor spoke to him briefly, saying he would fill in all the details later.

The phone was ringing as they walked in the door at her house. Captain Marino again. Shortly later he, along with several other officers, came to the house to take their statements, sparing them a trip to headquarters. Gaby thanked them graciously for going out of their way, but the truth was there was no way she would have left Toby or dragged him out again to go answer questions for anyone.

Marino also arranged for a medic to stop by and tend to Connor's hand, removing the stitches that had been broken during the fight with Adam and replacing them with fresh and considerably more professional ones.

When the police were done with them, she still had to call her mother to explain what had happened before she heard it on the news or read the morning headlines. Her mother had dozens of questions, about Toby, about her, about what was going to happen next. Gaby filled her in as best she could, promised to call her as soon as she learned anything more and reassured her over and over that they really were okay.

And they were. Thanks to Connor.

It was very late, after she'd answered all the questions and reassured everyone who needed reassuring and had rocked

Toby to sleep, that Gaby remembered Connor had said he had something important he wanted to ask her.

They were standing in the kitchen. She had just poured two glasses of wine. She turned, curious, and found him watching her with such blatant hunger she was rendered speechless. And breathless. And boneless, too, or so it seemed as, without thinking, she found herself floating into his arms, melting into him, going all heat and liquid under the quick, fiery possession of his mouth.

He kissed her long and hard and deep, the rough thrusts of his tongue foretelling a possession of the most fundamental sort.

Gaby's pulse skittered and raced in anticipation. Even through her clothes her skin felt singed everywhere that he touched her, her throat, her breasts, the backs of her thighs.

When he lifted his head, his eyes were bright with desire.

"Please," he murmured, kissing her face, the side of her neck. "Please."

"Oh, yes," Gaby gasped as his teeth found the tip of her earlobe.

"Now?" he asked.

"Yes, oh, yes."

He lifted his head again, smiling now, excited and impatient. "Where?"

Gaby took his hand and led him upstairs to her bedroom and inside. She locked the door behind him.

They tore at each other's clothes, leaving them scattered as they made their way across the room. When they were both naked, Connor lifted her, kissed her and placed her in the center of the big bed. The feel of the silk coverlet against her back was nowhere near as arousing to her senses as the feel of his skin against hers, his knee nudging hers apart, his tongue everywhere.

With his mouth and his teeth and the clever touch of his strong hands, he drove her steadily higher. She was racing, rising, falling, moving out of herself and into a realm where he was master and she was happy to be tamed.

There would be other times for them, many other times; she knew that now with a calming certainty. Slower, lazier times when she would be master and he would be tamed. There would be endless, sinuous nights when the passion between them would build stroke by stroke, layer by layer. But not tonight. Tonight she wanted only this, the fast, molten ride he was taking her on, his mouth streaking over her body, claiming her, sending her soaring.

He shifted her under him, gripping her hips, bringing her up off the mattress as he brought his body down and into hers. Hot, mindless pleasure jackknifed through her. Excitement hummed inside her everywhere.

His hips rocked against hers, ruthlessly, relentlessly, driving him deeper and deeper into her as he drove her higher and higher with pleasure.

Gaby welcomed him, urging him on with her hands and her soft cries until the tiny ripples began their dance deep inside her. They rushed through her as her mouth opened on a soft, silent scream, and she pulled him closer, impossibly closer, and felt him begin to shudder, too, felt everything that was happening inside her echoing inside him as they raced over the edge together.

Gaby closed her eyes. Opened them. Felt him still pulsing inside her, echoing the rhythm of her heart, which was beating in perfect time with his. She was home.

She smiled against his chest, pressing a kiss to his imperfect flesh and touching him there with her tongue, tasting salt and man. He sighed, a sound of satisfaction, of passions faced and desires met.

He lifted his head and took her face between his rough palms. "I love you," he said. "I love you, Gaby, and you have to believe me because I've never said those words to a woman before and I don't know how to convince you they're true."

"You don't have to convince me," she said, her hands moving over his damp back, coasting over scar and muscle and bone, glorying in all of it, in all of him. "I believe you. And I love you. And I need you, Connor."

"You're mine," he said, his rough tone full of wonder.

"Yes. Forever." She lifted her head to kiss his lips and added, "On two conditions."

Connor's eyes went black. "What conditions?"

"First that you never ever walk out and leave me tied up again."

His smile came slowly and was edged with relief. "I think I can agree to that. What's number two?"

"That you ask me the important question you wanted to ask me."

"Oh. That." His eyes crinkled at the corners, his smile sheepish. "It may be a bit anticlimactic under the present circumstances." He moved his hips against her provocatively.

Gaby reciprocated and made his breath catch low in his throat. "Try me."

"I wanted to ask you what a big jerk like me has to do to get a second chance with a woman like you?"

Gaby touched his cheek, her eyes filled with love for him. "You just did it," she told him softly.

Connor gave her a bewildered look that melted her heart all over again.

"You asked me," she explained, reaching for him. "That's all you ever had to do. Just ask."

Epilogue

It was a perfect day for a wedding.

The wind-driven rain had forced Gaby and her sister to wait inside the damp vestibule of the church for the start of the processional. Gaby considered it a blessing that it was rain and not snow, since this was being touted as the coldest November on record. In the shoes she was wearing, she'd rather dodge puddles than snowdrifts any day.

They had arrived at the church behind schedule after the limo driver took a wrong turn. Then, at the last minute Lisa realized she was still holding the rings and had to hurry down the side aisle to give them to the best man, leaving Gaby alone with her thoughts.

She was thinking that Toby better hold on tight to those rings until the moment came for him to hand them over to Connor. And that he better not fiddle so much with his bow tie that it came loose during the ceremony. He was taking his best-man responsibilities very seriously and was a little nervous.

The organ sounded the first dramatic introductory notes.

Hurry, Lisa, she thought, please hurry.

She ran her fingers through the front of her hair, worn loose beneath the short lace veil that matched her simple ivory wool suit and took a step forward to look for Lisa. She was on her way back down the aisle. She broke into a broad smile as she arrived, slightly breathless, in the church entry.

"Ready?" she asked Gaby.

"Absolutely," Gaby replied. She gave her sister a quick hug, followed by a wave of her arm. "After you."

Lisa preceded her into the church.

Gaby paused in the archway, as they had rehearsed, and saw the gathering of family and friends stand and turn to look at her. Her own gaze moved past them, drawn to the little boy and the man who stood side by side before the altar at the other end of that long row of flower-trimmed pews, both of them looking at her and smiling. Her son and the man she loved.

Her whole world was waiting for her.

She took a deep breath, her heart racing with excitement, feeling happier and surer and more eager than she ever hoped to feel again, feeling like exactly what she was . . . the luckiest woman in the world.

Outside, the wind howled and the lights overhead flickered, threatening the second power failure of the morning. It didn't matter. There would still be candles. And Connor.

Yes, Gaby thought as her eyes met his and she started down the aisle, a perfect day for a wedding.

*   *   *   *   *

The first book in the exciting new
Fortune's Children series is

HIRED HUSBAND

by *New York Times* bestselling writer
Rebecca Brandewyne

Beginning in July 1996
Only from Silhouette Books

Here's an exciting sneak preview....

Minneapolis, Minnesota

As Caroline Fortune wheeled her dark blue Volvo into the underground parking lot of the towering, glass-and-steel structure that housed the global headquarters of Fortune Cosmetics, she glanced anxiously at her gold Piaget wristwatch. An accident on the snowy freeway had caused rush-hour traffic to be a nightmare this morning. As a result, she was running late for her 9:00 a.m. meeting—and if there was one thing her grandmother, Kate Winfield Fortune, simply couldn't abide, it was slack, unprofessional behavior on the job. And lateness was the sign of a sloppy, disorganized schedule.

Involuntarily, Caroline shuddered at the thought of her grandmother's infamous wrath being unleashed upon her. The stern rebuke would be precise, apropos, scathing and delivered with coolly raised, condemnatory eyebrows and in icy tones of haughty grandeur that had in the past reduced many an executive—even the male ones—at Fortune Cosmetics not only to obsequious apologies, but even to tears. Caroline had seen it happen on more than one occasion, although, much to her gratitude and relief, she herself was seldom a target of her grandmother's anger. And she wouldn't be this morning, either, not if she could help it. That would be a disastrous way to start out the new year.

Grabbing her Louis Vuitton tote bag and her black leather portfolio from the front passenger seat, Caroline stepped gracefully from the Volvo and slammed the door. The heels of her Maud Frizon pumps clicked briskly on the concrete floor as she hurried toward the bank of elevators that would take her up into the skyscraper owned by her family. As the elevator doors slid open, she rushed down the long, plushly carpeted corridors of one of the hushed upper floors toward the conference room.

By now Caroline had her portfolio open and was leafing through it as she hastened along, reviewing her notes she had prepared for her presentation. So she didn't see Dr. Nicolai Valkov until she literally ran right into him. Like her, he had his head bent over his own portfolio, not watching where he was going. As the two of them collided, both their portfolios and the papers inside went flying. At the unexpected impact, Caroline lost her balance, stumbled, and would have fallen had not Nick's strong, sure hands abruptly shot out, grabbing hold of her and pulling her to him to steady her. She gasped, startled and stricken, as she came up hard against his broad chest, lean hips and corded thighs, her face just inches from his own—as though they were lovers about to kiss.

Caroline had never been so close to Nick Valkov before, and in that instant, she was acutely aware of him—not just as a fellow employee of Fortune Cosmetics but also as a man. Of how tall and ruggedly handsome he was, dressed in an elegant, pin-striped black suit cut in the European fashion, a crisp white shirt, a foulard tie and a pair of Cole Haan loafers. Of how dark his thick, glossy hair and his deep-set eyes framed by raven-wing brows were—so dark that they were almost black, despite the bright, fluorescent lights that blazed overhead. Of the whiteness of his straight teeth against his bronzed skin as a brazen, mocking grin slowly curved his wide, sensual mouth.

"Actually, I *was* hoping for a sweet roll this morning—but I daresay you would prove even tastier, Ms. Fortune," Nick drawled impertinently, his low, silky voice tinged with a faint accent born of the fact that Russian, not English, was his native language.

At his words, Caroline flushed painfully, embarrassed and annoyed. If there was one person she always attempted to avoid at Fortune Cosmetics, it was Nick Valkov. Following the breakup of the Soviet Union, he had emigrated to the United States, where her grandmother had hired him to direct the company's research and development department. Since that time, Nick had constantly demonstrated marked, traditional, Old World tendencies that had led Caroline to believe he not only had no use for equal rights but also would actually have been more than happy to turn back the clock several centuries where females were concerned. She thought his remark was typical of his attitude toward women: insolent, arrogant and domineering. Really, the man was simply insufferable!

Caroline couldn't imagine what had ever prompted her grandmother to hire him—and at a highly generous salary, too—except that Nick Valkov was considered one of the foremost chemists anywhere on the planet. Deep down inside Caroline knew that no matter how he behaved, Fortune Cosmetics was extremely lucky to have him. Still, that didn't give him the right to manhandle and insult her!

"I assure you that you would find me more bitter than a cup of the strongest black coffee, Dr. Valkov," she insisted, attempting without success to free her trembling body from his steely grip, while he continued to hold her so near that she could feel his heart beating steadily in his chest—and knew he must be equally able to feel the erratic hammering of her own.

"Oh, I'm willing to wager there's more sugar and cream to you than you let on, Ms. Fortune." To her utter mortification and outrage, she felt one of Nick's hands slide insidiously up her back and nape to her luxuriant mass of sable hair, done up in a stylish French twist.

"You know so much about fashion," he murmured, eyeing her assessingly, pointedly ignoring her indignation and efforts to escape from him. "So why do you always wear your hair like this... so tightly wrapped and severe? I've never seen it down. Still, that's the way it needs to be worn, you know...soft, loose, angled about your face. As it is, your hair fairly cries out for a man to take the pins from it, so he can see how long it is. Does it fall past your shoulders?" He quirked one eyebrow inquisitively, a mocking half-smile still twisting his lips, letting her know he was enjoying her obvious discomfiture. "You aren't going to tell me, are you? What a pity. Because my guess is that it does—and I'd like to know if I'm right. And these glasses."

He indicated the large, square, tortoiseshell frames perched on her slender, classic nose. "I think you use them to hide behind more than you do to see. I'll bet you don't actually even need them at all."

Caroline felt the blush that had yet to leave her cheek deepen, its heat seeming to spread throughout her entire quivering body. Damn the man! Why must he be so infuriatingly perceptive?

Because everything that Nick suspected was true.

* * * * *

To read more, don't miss
HIRED HUSBAND
by Rebecca Brandewyne,
Book One in the new
FORTUNE'S CHILDREN series,
beginning this month and available only from
Silhouette Books!

FORTUNE'S Children™

New York Times Bestselling Author
REBECCA BRANDEWYNE

Launches a new twelve-book series—FORTUNE'S CHILDREN
beginning in July 1996 with Book One

Hired Husband

Caroline Fortune knew her marriage to Nick Valkov was in
name only. She would help save the family business, Nick
would get a green card, and a paper marriage would suit both
of them. Until Caroline could no longer deny the feelings Nick
stirred in her and the practical union turned passionate.

MEET THE FORTUNES—a family whose legacy is greater than
riches. Because where there's a will…there's a wedding!

Look for Book Two, *The Millionaire and the Cowgirl*,
by Lisa Jackson. Available in August 1996 wherever Silhouette
books are sold.

MILLION DOLLAR SWEEPSTAKES

No purchase necessary. To enter, follow the directions published. For eligibility, entries must be received no later than March 31, 1998. No liability is assumed for printing errors, lost, late, nondelivered or misdirected entries. Odds of winning are determined by the number of eligible entries distributed and received.

Sweepstakes open to residents of the U.S. (except Puerto Rico), Canada and Europe who are 18 years of age or older. All applicable laws and regulations apply. Sweepstakes offer void wherever prohibited by law. This sweepstakes is presented by Torstar Corp., its subsidiaries and affiliates, in conjunction with book, merchandise and/or product offerings. For a copy of the Official Rules (WA residents need not affix return postage), send a self-addressed, stamped envelope to: Million Dollar Sweepstakes Rules, P.O. Box 4469, Blair, NE 68009-4469.

SWP-M96

Silhouette's recipe for a sizzling summer:

* Take the best-looking cowboy in South Dakota
* Mix in a brilliant bachelor
* Add a sexy, mysterious sheikh
* Combine their stories into one collection and you've got one sensational super-hot read!

Summer Sizzlers

MEN OF Summer

Three short stories by these favorite authors:

Kathleen Eagle
Joan Hohl
Barbara Faith

Available this July wherever
Silhouette books are sold.

Look us up on-line at: http://www.romance.net

🔻 *Silhouette*®

™

SS96

This exciting new cross-line continuity series unites
five of your favorite authors as they weave five
connected novels about love, marriage—and
Daddy's unexpected need for a baby carriage!

Get ready for

THE BABY NOTION by Dixie Browning (SD#1011, 7/96)
Single gal Priscilla Barrington would do anything for a
baby—even visit the local sperm bank. Until cowboy
Jake Spencer set out to convince her to have a family
the natural—and much more exciting—way!

And the romance in New Hope, Texas, continues with:

BABY IN A BASKET
by Helen R. Myers (SR#1169, 8/96)

MARRIED...WITH TWINS!
by Jennifer Mikels (SSE#1054, 9/96)

HOW TO HOOK A HUSBAND (AND A BABY)
by Carolyn Zane (YT#29, 10/96)

DISCOVERED: DADDY
by Marilyn Pappano (IM#746, 11/96)

DADDY KNOWS LAST arrives in July...only from

DKL-D

Listen to whispers of sweet romance with

Best of the Best™ Audio

Order now for your listening pleasure!

#15295 **FIRE AND ICE**
$11.99 U.S. ☐ $14.99 CAN. ☐
Written by Janet Dailey.
Read by Erin Gray.

#15292 **THE ARISTOCRAT**
$11.99 U.S. ☐ $14.99 CAN. ☐
Written by Catherine Coulter.
Read by Marcia Strassman.

#15293 **RAGGED RAINBOWS**
$11.99 U.S. ☐ $14.99 CAN. ☐
Written by Linda Lael Miller.
Read by Erin Gray.

#15294 **THE MAIN ATTRACTION**
$11.99 U.S. ☐ $14.99 CAN. ☐
Written by Jayne Ann Krentz.
Read by Marcia Strassman.

(limited quantities available on certain titles)

TOTAL AMOUNT	$	
POSTAGE & HANDLING	$	
($1.00 for one audio, 50¢ for each additional)		
APPLICABLE TAXES*	$	
TOTAL PAYABLE	$	_____
(check or money order— please do not send cash)		

To order, complete this form and send it, along with a check or money order for the total above, payable to Best of the Best Audio, to: **In the U.S.:** 3010 Walden Avenue, P.O. Box 9077, Buffalo, NY 14269-9077; **In Canada:** P.O. Box 636, Fort Erie, Ontario, L2A 5X3.

Name:_____

Address:_____ City:_____

State/Prov.:_____ Zip/Postal Code:_____

*New York residents remit applicable sales taxes. Canadian residents remit applicable GST and provincial taxes.

Available wherever audio books are sold. AUDB

The dynasty begins.

LINDA HOWARD
The Mackenzies

Now available for the first time, Mackenzie's Mountain and Mackenzie's Mission, together in one affordable, trade-size edition. Don't miss out on the two stories that started it all!

Mackenzie's Mountain: Wolf Mackenzie is a loner. All he cares about is his ranch and his son. Labeled a half-breed by the townspeople, he chooses to stay up on his mountain—that is, until the spunky new schoolteacher decides to pay the Mackenzies a visit. And that's when all hell breaks loose.

Mackenzie's Misson: Joe "Breed" Mackenzie is a colonel in the U.S. Air Force. All he cares about is flying. He is the best of the best and determined never to let down his country—even for love. But that was before he met a beautiful civilian engineer, who turns his life upside down.

Available this August, at your favorite retail outlet.

MIRA The brightest star in women's fiction

MLHTM

SILHOUETTE... Where Passion Lives

Add these Silhouette favorites to your collection today!
Now you can receive a discount by ordering two or more titles!

SD#05819	WILD MIDNIGHT by Ann Major	$2.99	☐
SD#05878	THE UNFORGIVING BRIDE	$2.99 U.S.	☐
	by Joan Johnston	$3.50 CAN.	☐
IM#07568	MIRANDA'S VIKING by Maggie Shayne	$3.50	☐
SSE#09896	SWEETBRIAR SUMMIT	$3.50 U.S.	☐
	by Christine Rimmer	$3.99 CAN.	☐
SSE#09944	A ROSE AND A WEDDING VOW	$3.75 U.S.	☐
	by Andrea Edwards	$4.25 CAN.	☐
SR#19002	A FATHER'S PROMISE	$2.75	☐
	by Helen R. Myers		

(limited quantities available on certain titles)

TOTAL AMOUNT	$_____
DEDUCT: 10% DISCOUNT FOR 2+ BOOKS	$_____
POSTAGE & HANDLING	$_____
($1.00 for one book, 50¢ for each additional)	
APPLICABLE TAXES**	$_____
TOTAL PAYABLE	$_____
(check or money order—please do not send cash)	

To order, send the completed form with your name, address, zip or postal code, along with a check or money order for the total above, payable to Silhouette Books, to: **in the U.S.:** 3010 Walden Avenue, P.O. Box 9077, Buffalo, NY 14269-9077; **in Canada:** P.O. Box 636, Fort Erie, Ontario, L2A 5X3.

Name:_____

Address: _____ City:_____

State/Prov.:_____ Zip/Postal Code:_____

**New York residents remit applicable sales taxes.
Canadian residents remit applicable GST and provincial taxes.

Silhouette®

SBACK-JA2

You're About to Become a *Privileged Woman*

Reap the rewards of fabulous free gifts and benefits with proofs-of-purchase from Silhouette and Harlequin books

Pages & Privileges™

It's our way of thanking you for buying our books at your favorite retail stores.

PROOF OF PURCHASE
SIM-PP155
Offer expires October 31, 1996

Harlequin and Silhouette—
the most privileged readers in the world!

For more information about Harlequin and Silhouette's PAGES & PRIVILEGES program call the Pages & Privileges Benefits Desk: 1-503-794-2499

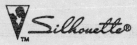

Silhouette®

SIM-PP155